The Gift of the Twin Houses

D1253795

The Gift of the Twin Houses

A Novel

V. & D. Povall

This is a work of fiction. Names, characters, organizations, places, events, and incidents are either products of the author's imagination or are used fictitiously.

Publisher: Dragonfly Media
ISBN (paperback): 9781642376920
eISBN: 9781642374667
Library of Congress Control Number: 2015912035
DragonflyMedia, Oceanside, CA.

Writing never happens in a vacuum.
Many are those who help in different ways.

Thanks:
To our daughter Chelsea for always being there to read, listen, advise,
and encourage, and for her unwavering love.

To Mike Sirota, who first guided our fledgling steps
and told us we were on the right path.

Special thanks are due to:
Dr. Judy LaBounty for lending her invaluable expertise, and
to her husband Dr. Hugh LaBounty for his undying support.
You both kept us smiling through it all.
You are the best friends anyone could ask for.
We love you.

Dedicated to:
Alvaro, Isabel, and Pauline

Contents

CHAPTER 1

The House

NOT SINCE THE age of six had I permitted this cursed psychic gift of mine to emerge. Now, fifty years later, it had erupted without warning and shoved me into an adventure I didn't want.

Dammit.

A sudden urge had propelled me out of my comfort zone. Unable to control it, I left my home in Pasadena at dawn and flew to Seattle. Upon arrival, I rented a Jeep at the airport. Uncharacteristic behavior on all counts for the "practical and levelheaded" Sarah Salas people knew me to be. Never before had I set out on a spontaneous journey without precise plans and reservations, let alone rented such an intrepid car. Yet, notwithstanding my aversion to this escapade, I now drove along a two-lane road through the Northwestern Cascades to an unknown destination. Something had called me to this part of the world, and I'd answered without question, without expectations, and obviously without reason.

I left the airport and drove north through Seattle without stopping. Whatever brought me to the Northwest intended for me to reach a destination other than the Emerald City.

Could it be someone in need? I've obviously opened a door to my soul that should've remained locked. I can't ignore it.

I traveled through Bellevue and Kirkland, and on instinct I veered east toward Monroe. Shortly after, I found myself driving along a marvelous two-lane road, twisting northeast through the Cascades in an emotional state that fluctuated between excitement and reluctance.

Damn this curse I was born with.

I'd been trained to bury it from the moment our dear neighbors and friends had dubbed me "spooky." That happened the day this *ability* of mine scandalized everyone at my best friend Lindsay's seventh birthday party, when I blurted out the horror she'd suffered at the hands of her uncle. I didn't know what it meant, but her rape, once confirmed, sealed my fate. "Sarah the witch" became my tag, and I lost all my friends. I'd just turned six.

As a child, I somehow saw and felt things no one else did, from the image of a house in flames the day before it burned down, to a neighbor in the arms of a woman not his wife, to the whereabouts of a lost puppy. Sometimes I knew things before they happened; other times I saw what a person had done or intended to do. Not always, and never intentionally.

The impressions just appeared in my mind, so naturally I chatted about them or simply retold them. After all, why not? Didn't everyone sense these things just as I did?

Not quite, as I learned on that fateful day. The fallout from my indiscretion pinpointed just how unusual I was. So, upon my demise as a "normal" child, my family escaped. We moved to a different neighborhood, closer to my father's office, in the heart of Boston, and there were stern admonitions from my parents that I learn to keep this antenna of mine well under wraps. Disavowed, not welcomed at all, I buried it. Without it I'd be safe from ridicule, my family wouldn't be detested, and no one would be hurt. In time, the practical and intellectual pursuits instilled by my parents replaced it. No allowances were made in the prohibition of this so-called gift of mine. Eventually, it simply went underground and vanished. I buried myself in my studies, my career, and of course, my devotion to my students. Teaching them to overcome their disabilities, regardless of the impairments they'd been born with or acquired later in life, simply absorbed me.

But now my own impairment had resurfaced, and *it* demanded attention.

"Why not?" I blurted out. "At this point in my life, what's the harm in allowing this irksome talent to pop up now and then? I'm retired, I'm alone, and I'm ready to enjoy the fruits of my labor. So there!" My voice pierced the silence in the car, startling me.

"Oh dear." I laughed. "How can my own voice scare me? That's just plain dumb, Sarah. Get a grip."

I opened the car windows, letting in some fresh air to clear my head. A hint of confidence settled in—just enough to allow me to give my full attention to the beauty that surrounded me.

Before I knew it, the Cascades worked their magic and brought about the sudden realization that I'd found the place where I belonged. I can't explain how I knew; I just did. Although this was my first visit to the Northwest, it seemed familiar somehow, soothing as a distant and peaceful memory.

A memory without an actual recollection...remarkable...there must be someone here that—

"Stop it, Sarah! Get ahold of yourself....But why? I like the sensation. It feels good...peaceful." Somehow voicing these thoughts allowed me to relax and welcome the sense of harmony that this new sensation brought with it.

Without a doubt, my antenna had resurfaced, and having taken full command, it was the reason I found myself on this two-lane road without any discernable purpose other than the internal certainty that I had to be here. No point in denying it any longer. And yet, these vibrations didn't feel the same as in my childhood...not at all as I remembered. These were different. They didn't appear to be tuned into the future or the recent past. They pointed elsewhere, as if picking up tonalities deep within that connected me to something—or someone—in this part of the world. Even though I didn't know a soul here, I felt at ease. Reassured.

The breathtaking splendor of bright-blue skies, the sharp intensity of the fall colors scattered amid the emerald evergreens, and the deep, sapphire and jade waters of the nearby rivers permeated my senses. With the worries and doubts that now rattled through my head, I could've gone right back to Pasadena, but the intoxicating power of the Cascades seduced me into continuing this journey.

After a short break for gas and essentials in Leavenworth, I drove straight through Chelan. The road now led me to a contrasting landscape of desert peaks and roadside lakes, apple orchards showered by refreshing misters, and grapevines encased in protective nets. The eastern Cascades also offered a striking mixture of desert plant life and occasional cultivated oases punctuated by a smattering of evergreens.

"Where am I going?" I wondered aloud.

I found no answer, but I felt an overwhelming sense that I was headed in the right direction.

"OK. Whatever or whomever you are, it is clear that I'm going in the right direction."

Moments later, I veered off onto Highway 153, and soon the waters of the Methow River that flanked the road appeased my spirit.

"I must be getting closer."

An hour later I arrived in the quaint western-style town of Winthrop, nestled amid the mountains, and stopped. I didn't know why I stopped there, either. I simply decided to do so. Obviously this was where I needed to be.

I found a nice little motel, checked into a cozy room, and had a quick bite to eat in a picturesque restaurant nearby. With my strength renewed, I strolled around the town and let the fresh air of an early fall invigorate me.

With newfound bravura and an unsolicited nudge from my untamed sixth sense, I decided to explore the surrounding area and got back in the car. I headed out of town as the afternoon shadows lengthened. My rented Jeep handled the narrow roads well, and the more I drove through the Cascades, the more daring I became.

All of a sudden, an irresistible force took hold of me, and I veered off onto a narrow dirt road.

"Oh God. This is it. Isn't it?"

No sooner had I crossed the line of trees that flanked the road than I realized I'd entered private property. Yet I didn't stop and turn back. I stayed the course. The dirt road crossed a beautiful valley, at the end of which sat a quaint two-story house framed by a stand of towering pine trees. The house looked as handsome as the photographs I had just seen in the airline magazine, in an article that described the Queen Anne styles of architecture typical of the nineteenth century. It was unlike any of the cabins and farmhouses I'd seen so far. This house, however, didn't appear to be lavishly decorated. Although imposing, it showed restraint in its embellishments. I wondered how such an exquisite structure came to be in the middle of a forest deep in the North Cascades.

The house enthralled me. Bewitched by its beauty and serenity, I stepped out of the Jeep and ambled toward it. It sat at the end of a valley that may have been used for pasture or cropland at one time, encircled by magnificent woodlands with panoramic views of the Cascades. It was perfectly maintained, proud in its old age, and superbly restored.

Overwhelmed with curiosity, and propelled by an uncontrollable need to be there, I climbed the steps to the porch. I needed to know more about this house, about its inhabitants, about its history, and about how it came to be in this valley. Pushed by this insatiable desire for answers and an attraction impossible to resist, I pressed forward and was about to ring the bell. It was then that I noticed a small handwritten note on the front door with a phone number. Without a moment's hesitation, I got my cell phone and dialed.

"Conrad Thompson," a man's voice answered.

"Hello, Mr. Thompson, sorry to disturb you on a Sunday. My name is Sarah Salas, and I'm standing on the porch of a fine-looking house in the middle of a lovely valley. The front door has a small for-sale note on the door with this phone number. Is it still available?"

"Sure. Want to see the inside?"

My heart jumped with joy at the possibility of going inside the house. "If it's not too much trouble, I would."

"No trouble at all. Be there in less than five minutes."

Perhaps it was my imagination, but I thought I heard a faint creak, as if the house felt as happy as I did.

Don't be ridiculous, Sarah.

I smiled and shook my head to stop these foolish impressions, then strolled along the porch that bordered the entire house. I made my way around it and peeked inside the windows here and there, but couldn't make out the interior. The perfection of the molding and how beautifully constructed the house appeared to be charmed me. My heart pounded, my ears rang, and a feeling of excitement crept through my veins.

"Hello, Sarah Salas."

Mr. Thompson stood by the front door as I came back around the corner. "Hello, Mr. Thompson."

Tall, with green eyes, and black hair with some distinguished gray on the sides, he didn't look like a typical real-estate agent at all. More like your friendly family doctor.

He shook my hand and smiled. "Call me Conrad, please."

He had rugged, warm hands, a nice smile, and appeared very much at ease.

Conrad produced a key from his pocket and opened the front door. "Come right in."

The moment I stepped in, I heard the house creak and crack with delight again. My heart leaped in rhythm—a silent greeting.

"Nice, isn't it?" Conrad said.

"Beautiful," I whispered.

Conrad turned toward me, and an unexpected warmth permeated my body. His eyes brightened and his cheeks reddened a bit before he led the way deeper into the house.

I followed, uncertain as to what had just transpired between us.

The house, though small, felt quite spacious, with well-appointed interior rooms, pine flooring, wood paneling, and lovely Queen Anne windows. All of a sudden, sunshine flooded the entry hall. I looked up, searching for the source of light, but all I saw were the wood beams of the high ceiling.

"The setting sun dropped under the clouds," Conrad explained. "I'm afraid that today it'll be a short appearance. It took its time showing up."

"But the house lit up."

"Indeed, it has a good location and enough windows to capture it all. Come, this is the living room."

I followed him into a lovely room with an inviting fireplace. A spacious bay window faced the valley and, along with the side windows, invited the sparkling sunshine to flood every corner. "It's like stepping into one of the rooms at Versailles," I said.

He chuckled. "Boy, Versailles. Tall order for such a small house."

"Sorry, I didn't mean to make it sound so grandiose. It's the use of light."

"Grandiose…that's a big word."

"I don't mean to sound so erudite…oh…sorry, here I go again." I must've blushed something awful, because he burst out laughing.

"No need to apologize. I like it. Fits your look—elegant but approachable, good looking yet not standoffish. Very nice all around."

I turned purple because he laughed again and changed the topic.

"I don't know if you noticed, but the porch lights are originals and quite unique."

"No, I'm afraid I didn't. I'll take a look when I go out," I managed to say, still in shock from the compliment he'd just paid me. Considering that I didn't think myself good-looking whatsoever, let alone elegant, his simple, kind words took me by surprise.

"Right through there is the dining room and the kitchen," he said. "Upstairs are three bedrooms and two full bathrooms. You go mosey around the house, and I'll wait for you out front. By the time you're done, it'll be dusk, so I'll turn the porch lights on and you'll get to see them in all their finery. Oh, by the way, the third floor has a landing and an attic."

"Thanks," I muttered. A sudden tightness in my throat and stomach had materialized with the word *attic,* and for the first time, a sense of foreboding came over me. "Attic," I whispered in spite of myself. "I'm here."

As soon as the front door closed, I willed my self-composure to return. I shook my head to banish the conflicting thoughts and emotions of fear and attraction that the attic had provoked, and resumed my exploration of the house.

Adjacent to the living room, the dining room displayed gorgeous wood paneling and windows. In the kitchen, I noticed that the owners had embraced the home's nineteenth-century architecture while also adding modern amenities. It was a true paradise for someone who enjoyed cooking.

The staircase and banisters were also made of beautifully carved wood in perfect condition. The three bedrooms on the second floor were small but ideally situated to make use of the natural light and capture breathtaking views of the Cascades. Whoever had built this place did it with great love for both the house and its surroundings.

The master bedroom was slightly bigger than the other two, and I walked over to the window to admire the sunset. I reached out to touch both edges of the window and heard myself sigh. A moment later I heard another sigh behind me. I turned toward the door expecting to see Conrad standing there, but I was alone.

Peculiar.

I came down the stairs, allowing my fingers to softly caress the banister, and I heard the curiously familiar creaks and cracks of the house again. I smiled.

I joined Conrad outside and noticed how the tint coming from the porch lights enhanced the orange hues of sundown. Unable to contain my admiration, I blurted out, "Wow...original Tiffany? How have they held up all these years?"

"Spectacular, aren't they? They're not as old as the house, and were probably installed many years after it was built. I venture to guess it was after electricity came this way. Originals, nonetheless."

"Mr. Thompson, this is a beautiful home. How come you don't have a bigger sign to attract people off the road?"

"No need for that. Calls attention to the fact that it's vacant."

"Oh, didn't think of that. You're right; it's pretty isolated."

"How did you find it?" he asked.

"I veered off the road. The dirt road looked appealing."

"The daring kind, are you?"

"No, just the opposite. Except for today."

"Well then, what do you think?"

Conrad Thompson was not the only one surprised by my answer. "I'd like to buy it."

CHAPTER 2

The Attic

I PURCHASED THE house without entering the attic, even though I knew it was the very reason I wanted this house. Well, truth be told, I didn't really "know." I sensed it. Aware of the attic's call, I refused to consciously accept its pull.

Unfamiliar emotions permeated my senses and propelled me into unknown territories—not only physical but spiritual, psychological, and even metaphysical. Unsettling all around.

Up until now I'd been in complete control of my life, every detail planned, with full knowledge of the ups and downs and an awareness of all the angles before decisions were made. I'd never experienced the sensation of giving in to a mere inclination. It had been forbidden. But now, given in to it I had, and any misgivings dissipated when the purchase of the house fell into place without any glitches.

"It makes perfect sense, Sarah. It's meant to be," I kept repeating to myself.

I'd already thought of using the gains from the investments of my inheritance and annuity by converting them into real property, in order to diminish any losses due to the decline in the economy. "This quaint house in the Cascades is the perfect investment," I rationalized.

What I didn't anticipate was my subsequent decision to get rid of my duplex in Pasadena so I could move to the new house and live amid the majesty of the Cascades. But when I put my condo on the market, and it sold yielding a small profit in spite of the declining home prices nationwide, I concluded once again that it was meant to be.

A few months earlier, I'd retired, having fulfilled my lifelong dream of being a teacher. I still remember my excitement as a little girl when I'd line up my stuffed animals and dolls to teach them everything I knew. To my delight, they learned it all to perfection. That same feeling of exhilaration, of knowing I could make a difference in someone's life through my teaching, motivated me through most of my career. But in the end, I'd become disillusioned after repeated rejections, or apathy, toward my ideas or my methods for new, innovative approaches to education. So I gave up trying and, like so many others, succumbed to the status quo. What a pity.

I don't remember at what point I lost my intellectual and professional innocence, let alone when the choice to conform stifled my life as a whole. But it became evident when I retired. Only then did I experience a real sense of freedom. No more pretending. I could be myself.

Just one problem—I didn't know who I was.

After so many years of pretending, I'd lost my true self. Hiding my oddity since early childhood had laid the groundwork for easy concealment. I'd become someone else at an early age, so as I grew up and had to go by the book, I followed the same pattern. Eventually, I turned myself into someone who wouldn't attract attention or appear on anybody's radar.

Now, a new beginning and a fresh opportunity awaited me in the Cascades, and the time had come to reclaim the real me.

"Only how or where do I begin?" I didn't have the answer, only the urge to proceed, so I did.

The events that followed the move to my new home occurred at a point in my life when the search for my true self took prominence; otherwise, the practical Sarah, the one who'd lived within the status quo, would never have accepted them. The impulse to buy an isolated house far from my trusted old home in Pasadena turned out to be a clear demonstration of my readiness to be bold. I'd stepped out of the norm and allowed uncharacteristic behavior to creep in. Somewhere deep inside, I sensed that this secluded house might show me the way. No doubt it was bizarre to give such credence to the effect a house could have on a person.

"So what? What do I have to lose anyway? Why not be adventurous and trust my instincts? What's the risk of letting my spiritual antenna fly free? No one will get hurt…well, no one but me. I certainly can handle that. What could possibly happen? That someone somewhere would think me abnormal? Sinister? OK, that's a frightening prospect, but isn't hiding from myself worse?"

So here I was, early November, all settled in, ready to embrace my new life in the middle of nowhere, unknown to everyone, lonelier than ever before, and talking to myself.

"Well, Sarah, is complete isolation what you want? What's in store for you? Why have you secluded yourself in this solitary house?"

And as usual, only the insistent call from the attic responded.

For a while I tried to ignore its summons, that sense of foreboding yanking me away. Years of practice at being someone other than myself and of containing my extrasensory capacities prevented me from giving into the sensation that the attic actually beckoned me.

But it refused to give up. It persisted.

In the end, my curiosity, coupled with the inescapable reappearance of this uninvited ability of mine, made it impossible to resist. After living in the house for little more than a week, I answered the attic's call and hesitantly entered.

At first glance it didn't impress me or frighten me.

"You're just a typical attic full of junk. Conrad should haul this stuff away."

A soulful draft of wind seeped in. The attic moaned.

"OK, OK...no hauling away."

With a creak and crack the attic called my attention to one corner of the room where I discovered the long-forgotten trunks with their small boxes, each one holding the photographs that needed me...

"Or is it *I* who needs *them*?"

I expected the attic to respond, but of course it didn't, and reality set in. "C'mon, Sarah, get a grip. Get on with it." So, during this first visit, I only peeked in, tiptoed through the room, whispered to myself so as not to disturb its contents, moved nothing, and just looked.

After I'd left, it became clear that such a visit wasn't enough. The attic continued to tempt me, invite me to partake in its stories, but I resisted.

Then, late one afternoon, I felt a difference. My stomach tightened, my heart beat a little too fast, and the clamminess in my hands spoke of fear.

"A premonition," I whispered, "The old abandoned photographs summon me."

It's hard to accept that a person can, in truth, hear inanimate objects "speak," especially for a trained skeptic like me. But they did.

"Sarah," my father's voice resonated in my mind, "discard all intuition. Always question everything that comes your way until you can prove its validity with known practical explanations or applications. We don't want you or others to get hurt again. We must try to control those things you feel. It's best for you not to trust those sensations. If they come up, reject them and question them until you find a logical explanation for what they're telling you. What would be best is for you to bury them and not feel them at all."

My mother's advice would of course follow. "Please, *cariño*, you must control your abilities. They're unique to you, and others won't understand. You need to keep them within and behave like all of us. It's best to always seek logical details for what you do or think, just as we do. Find something tangible, scientific, or demonstrable. Never give in to your instincts."

These mental playbacks invariably concluded with my Nana's gentle coaxing. "Your parents mean well, *ma chérie*. Skepticism will serve you well."

As I matured, these adopted character traits became second nature. Yet, the day I returned to the attic for my second visit, I made no effort to seek concrete justifications for its pull. Impulse had brought me here, and now it propelled me forward. Impulse…a peculiar emotion deep inside has tightened its grip. It pushes me to do something without the slightest regard of what could happen next. Out of character for sure, at least the character I'd crafted over the years.

So, despite my fear of the unknown and with full resolve to answer its summons, I climbed the stairs to the attic for the second time and presented myself.

The attic glowed with an orange hue. The light that filtered through the small round window seemed to change once it came inside, bathing the entire room and its contents in vibrant carroty and lemony tones. The room wasn't warm, but the light made it feel so. It enveloped me in a cocoon of comfort and security and invited me to be at ease and courageous.

The Gift of the Twin Houses

In addition to the trunks that cared for the photographs, the attic held an old floor lamp, a cluster of dated books, a couple of empty frames of what may have been cherished paintings, an abandoned mirror, a loved armchair, and a forgotten little table. Together, they rested in the comfort of familiarity.

I sat on the floor in the middle of the large loft surrounded by memories, looking into somebody's life…in fact, several lives from the look of it.

"Are they memories?" I thought so, hoped so, but wasn't sure.

Not knowing any of the people these old things belonged to made me feel like an intruder, someone who'd stepped into their private past hoping to persuade them to share their stories. How unusual this adventurous curiosity was for me, but it wouldn't be denied. Audacity steered my every move.

At first I was reluctant to touch anything for fear that it would disturb their peace. Yet, they welcomed me. Somehow it didn't bother them. I felt as if I fit in. I'd never fit in before, always a step or two out of the norm. So the attic's embrace and the sense of belonging felt delightful, and I allowed my curiosity to take over.

"Maybe the people in these photographs can help me find myself," I whispered aloud. "Why not?" And with that, I encouraged myself to proceed.

After opening the first trunk, I took out a box filled with old sepia photographs, many of them hard to see, fading images of times past, strangers staring back at me. They didn't ask me why I dared look into their lives and intrude. They didn't reject me. Quite the contrary, a sense of comfort and reassurance flowed through me, as if deep inside someone voiced gentle words of friendship and affection. Somehow they knew I was in search of myself and offered to help.

Of course the skeptic in me showed up, intimating, "You've lost your mind." I could feel an electric charge travel through my body, spreading fear, and encouraging me to bolt and escape from all these peculiar emotions and experiences. "These very thoughts, images, or impressions you're feeling are the culprits. They instilled fear and inflicted severe pain in your parents. They forced you to run away—"

"And caused me to disown a part of myself," I argued.

This time I didn't cower. The antenna didn't retract. Instead, I sensed that I'd found my true destiny—at least, I chose to see it in that light. One way or another, I wanted the photographs to help.

"The photographs' help? That's odd."

"I agree."

"Creepy?"

"Maybe."

"Frightening?"

"Without a doubt."

"Tottering between rational thought and madness?"

"Most certainly, but I'll risk it."

The sun had set, and the attic whispered good-night as it welcomed the shadows of the evening. With newfound courage, I closed the box of photographs and took it downstairs with me. The attic responded with a little *crick-crack*, and I felt that it allowed me not only to remove the box from its familiar surroundings but in fact suggested I bring it down with me.

As I shut the door to the attic, I caressed it.

"Caressing a door? That's peculiar…for sure a tilt toward madness."

I caressed it again. "There," I offered the doubter in me, "I stroked the attic's door in appreciation, and that's the only explanation you'll get." I couldn't come up with any other reason for these actions so out of the ordinary because, regardless of how bizarre my behavior had been of late, I couldn't stop. Something egged me on. I was traveling through undiscovered emotional terrain, bravely allowing all the unusual sensations to exist as I conquered my fears and insecurities, one at a time.

With my precious cargo, I went down to the living room and set the box on the coffee table. I stoked the fire, poured myself a glass of wine, sat on the sofa, and with great care removed the first photo from the box. It appeared to be one of the oldest—mid-nineteenth century, from the look of the garments of a woman who sat on the shore contemplating the ocean.

As I stared at the photo, I heard a voice, and I met Louise Whitman for the first time.

CHAPTER 3

Louise Whitman
1830

"You are here," I heard her say. She spoke with a cadence of yesteryears.

In the photograph Louise Whitman watched the waves break on the beach. It appeared to be sunset. She sat pensively, her hair dancing in the wind. Somehow I heard the sea and felt the wind, as if transported to her presence.

I was about to respond when a couple of feet appeared at her side.

She didn't need to look up. He sat next to her while she continued to stare at the horizon and placed his arm around her shoulders. She welcomed his companionship and dropped her head on his shoulder.

"Louise, you have to let go of your fear," he whispered, his speech bearing the same old-fashioned tone.

"It will not let go of me, Leonard. You know that."

They sat in silence for a long time.

"This cannot go on," Louise whispered. "It will destroy us."

"The alternative is even worse. You must accept it as I have. That is all there is to it." Leonard sounded so stern that Louise turned to look at him to make sure he was the one speaking.

Without a moment's hesitation, he kissed her. His lips pushed hers open, and before she could protest, his tongue searched for hers. She knew they shouldn't give into their desires, but she was tired. Tired of fighting, tired of being someone she didn't want to be.

"I want you," he whispered.

"Leonard, we cannot. Please, no." She protested but clung desperately to him.

He took off his shirt and gently opened her blouse. He helped her out of it and lost himself in her breasts.

His desire for her ran faster than he could catch it. It sped ahead; he could see it, feel it, as he reached urgently to capture it inside of her.

Louise, in starvation, devoured his intensity.

Their lovemaking had a desperate quality, as if they might never lie together again.

Their explosion jolted them.

Then, panting, they remained in a tight embrace.

"I want more," he said.

"I need more," she replied.

"Come what may?"

"Come what may."

The photograph went silent as Louise sat pensively, her hair dancing in the wind.

I felt as if I'd been there, experiencing the ecstasy of their forbidden sexual encounter and their love. Panting, I placed Louise's photograph on the coffee table.

I had no knowledge of love like this, let alone the passion Leonard and Louise had just shared with me. All the men in my life turned out to be temporary companions, mostly due to my apprehension of intimacy. After witnessing this scene, I wondered if at the core of my aloofness was the fact that I expected to feel this kind of ardor and hadn't.

I tried to make sense of the emotional impact the photograph had elicited when I noticed that Louise was alone. Leonard wasn't there.

"Where is he?" I asked her.

She didn't respond but remained watching the waves break upon the beach.

Somehow, even though he wasn't in the photograph, I knew what he looked like and what he experienced. *How strange.* Although Louise remained silent, I understood that in time I would meet Leonard.

After a warm shower, I rationalized that the images I'd experience were figments of my imagination.

"You're so pathetically lonely that not only are you talking to yourself but you're making up stories about these old photos. And what's wrong with that? Nothing. I imagine their lives and the images keep me company. It's fun to make up stories. It's like reading a book and visualizing the characters. Simply that, nothing more. It certainly isn't anything like when I had premonitions or saw things. This is just imagining what Louise was feeling or thinking when the picture was taken. That's all."

With that explanation, I turned out the lights and buried myself under my warm comforter.

I slept so soundly that night that when I woke up the next day, I felt young as a teenager. I worked on my yard, cleaned the house, and midmorning, allowed myself the pleasure of sifting through the box of photographs again. Hopefully Leonard would make himself known. I wanted to meet him in person, not his ethereal presence.

I went through the box a couple of times, but none of the photographs introduced themselves. They just stared back at me, wondering why I looked at them with such persistence.

"Maybe I'm trying too hard," I surmised, and went back to my chores.

Except, they didn't feel like chores. I loved my house and its surroundings. The mist of the late autumn, softly caressing the multicolored foliage and giving life to the evergreens, took my breath away every single day. I knew I'd made the right decision to start a new life here, away from my past, and with an unplanned future ahead.

To most folks my three-story house would look old and out of place. But she was much more than that. She had character, an internal knowledge that she was special, at ease in the valley, surrounded by the beauty of nature, offering a safe haven to her inhabitants.

I don't recall ever thinking, let alone feeling, that I "loved" a house. However, accepting for the very first time an emotion that tied me so completely to an inanimate object felt great. That fact alone represented a healthy sign. As a rule, I would've analyzed every single emotion, tried to make rational sense of each and every one, and in the end not give myself into any, particularly if I didn't understand them. So, I delighted in simply doting over my house and the sensation that I would live here, with her, till the end of my days.

That afternoon I went out for a long walk in the wilderness surrounding the little valley that cradled us. By the time I got back, I was soaked. It hadn't rained but drizzled that soft, gentle spray that becomes part of you without you even noticing it.

As I approached the house, a truck drove up. I saw Conrad step out, walk up to the porch, and ring the bell.

"Hi there!" I called out, and ran toward the house.

"The house isn't on fire. Slow down," he cried to me.

By the time I reached the porch, I was out of breath. "Didn't expect any visitors, just took a walk and—"

"Catch your breath. All is well. I thought I'd come by to see how you're getting along. Winter's on its way."

"We're fine."

"We?" He looked surprised.

"The house and I." The words blurted out. I could feel myself blushing.

"Glad to hear." He smiled.

He had a nice smile, and his eyes brightened up, offering a glimpse into his state of mind. I could feel my own eyes gazing, enjoying the serenity he held.

"I take it you have no regrets?" he asked.

"Regrets?"

"Buying this old house."

"Oh, no. I love it. Don't worry; I'm not going to ask you for the money back."

"Only making sure, you not being from these parts. Nice to hear you're staying."

He tilted his hat and stepped down from the porch.

As he walked toward his truck, he exuded a virility and self-assurance I hadn't perceived before, let alone how handsome he was. I guess I'd been too immersed in the paperwork during the sale of the house to take notice, and had only recalled how easygoing and friendly he'd been.

"Remember," he called out over his shoulder, "I'll be happy to return the lot if you change your mind. This house deserves the best."

"Thanks, but no need. I love the house."

"See you."

"Bye."

He got in his truck and, with a smile, waved at me one more time. I liked his smile.

I went into the house thinking about Conrad and the effect he had on me. The more I thought about him, the better I felt. Then I realized that from the first time I'd met him, there had been a pull between us. It wasn't physical attraction but a sense of comfort and trust. Throughout the entire transaction of the purchase of my house, he'd been honest and straightforward. He made it so easy.

As I entered my bedroom and caught my reflection in the mirror, I was horrified. *Holy crap.* My soaked hair was plastered onto my head, and I had no makeup. How embarrassing that he'd seen me looking this dreadful. To top it all off, I was also shivering. I ran a hot bath and shed my clothes. *I must've looked pitiful to him. No wonder he worried about my leaving.*

After a long bath, I fixed a plate of fruit, cheese, and crackers for dinner. Built a nice fire in the living room, and sat there contemplating it as I sipped my glass of wine and nibbled on my dinner. I'd only taken a couple of sips when I could've sworn I heard someone singing a lullaby, another whispering sweet words of love, and yet another softly welcoming me to the house and letting me know I'd been expected.

It wasn't my imagination or the effect of the wine. The voices were within me. Oddly, they didn't frighten me. Instead, I just allowed them to be and listened. I could hear their whispers floating in the air, reaching my soul and gently caressing it. The voices reassured me that I was in good hands, that all would be well, and that I should open myself to the experiences they were to bring forth. *No need to pull away and lower your antenna,* they coaxed, *free yourself instead.*

The skeptic in me didn't jump in to pull the sensitive me away. I don't know where that part of me had disappeared to this evening—away from my house and my valley for sure. All I know is that not a drop of skepticism or the fear of yesteryears remained within me at that moment, so I eased into the feelings the voices wished me to live through.

I took my box of photographs and pulled out a picture of three women sitting around a wooden kitchen table. Amy introduced herself.

CHAPTER 4

Three Sisters
1880

I FELT TRANSPORTED into the photograph as I watched from the kitchen door.

"I don't recall how it began," Amy told me. "One day we were all together again. Once more the kitchen smelled of freshly baked bread and pies."

"Is it the kitchen in this house?" I asked her.

Amy, a well-composed, attractive woman in her late thirties, looked around, smiled at me, and nodded.

"We sat around the wooden table," she went on, "drinking coffee and looking into each other's pasts. Laura actually sipped tea, and Cora hot chocolate with coffee. Maybe she had added a little something else when we weren't looking."

Amy talked, and I remained at the door, a willing spectator.

"We had drifted apart. They had removed themselves from home and gone as far away as they could. Mother's death called them back and dropped us in the middle of our turbulent past."

"Were you together after the funeral? Did you all live here in my house?"

Amy smiled at me and nodded again. "Cora's hands trembled with the lingering effects of alcohol. Her hair was in disarray as usual, and her eyes focused inward, searching for a quiet place in the recesses of her soul. I don't think she ever found it, but she kept on looking. She was so intent on finding this place deep inside her that she forgot to care for the parts that conversed with the outside world. Her hair was neglected, in a disheveled ponytail held by an old crumbling tie. I wondered why she held her hair in a ponytail if she did not keep it up."

"Maybe she did it to appease that part within us that whispers that as long as we seem all right on the outside, we must be just fine," I ventured.

"Obviously Cora failed to keep up with her external appearances."

"How about Laura?" I asked. "It's hard to tell from this photograph."

"Laura was different," Amy said. "In fact, all three of us were quite different from one another. We each inherited the emotional makeup that our parents lived through at the time of our births. Cora was troubled, Laura was absent, and I was forgiving."

"Why is that? How did you arrive at that conclusion?" I was so eager to find out, I was getting ahead of the story. But Amy didn't mind. She looked at me as she answered, a resigned gaze appearing in her distant eyes.

"Maybe it had to do with the order in which we were born. Five years apart from each other—all unwanted. We knew we were mistakes. Our mother reminded us time and time again, just in case we chose to forget. As a result, Cora cared deeply about her unwelcome status in life, and Laura chose not to think about it so she wouldn't have to feel. I, however, had come to terms with the fact that if we were all so unwanted, how come we were all alive and well?"

I chuckled with Amy's logic, and she smiled in recognition.

"Laura needed to look beautiful, a basic requirement for her. You can see her hair neatly pulled back, her face impeccable, her body nice and trim. Only her eyes betray her beautifully composed persona. Maybe you can't see her eyes as she sips her tea because they're lost in fairyland. As a child I was convinced that she had leaped from one of my storybooks and become real just to make me feel loved. I was certain she had turned herself into a fairy godmother just for me. Later on I realized that she lived in a world of fantasy and make-believe all the time."

"And you?" I asked.

"I thought of myself as grounded in reality, able to deal with the world as it was. I chose not to run away from it but to accept it, and maybe that's the reason I was different. All the years growing up, everyone always said, 'Amy is so different.' I thought of it as a badge of honor, but in the end it turned out to be a heavy burden, as if I had to be *different* all the time. No rest for the weary."

"Being different is difficult. I know what you mean," I tentatively offered.

"Laura looked at me," Amy went on, "just before this photograph was taken, as if all of a sudden she connected with my thoughts. She was so used to doing that. We smiled at each other, but I recognized the sudden pain in her gut. She knew I was withering. Nothing of the vibrant, energetic, happy little Amy was left. Where had it all gone? I guessed that she wondered how the last twenty years had robbed me of those attributes. At least that's what I thought she was reacting to."

"Was it?"

"No. In the end I would be proven wrong, but at that moment, that's what I believed. You see, on this particular day, we needed to go to the attic to put away the memories. Cora wanted to destroy them, but I couldn't allow that."

"The attic? My attic?" I blurted out.

Amy turned to me and nodded before she continued. "Laura wanted to take some of them with her, but Cora wouldn't have any of it. She believed that if they weren't destroyed, the house would be the safest place to hold on to them. They should not leave the place where they had been created. That was the intent of our parents, she insisted, and Laura would never act against Cora's will. That privilege was reserved for me, and only me."

Amy smiled at me. She could see I understood her meaning.

"That's why the house became mine, to be the keeper of the memories. After all, given that I was 'different,' I could handle it. At least that's what I said when Cora decreed that the house should be sealed until we sold it, and then we would burn the memories."

"So you are the one that placed all the items in the attic?" I asked, but Amy wasn't listening. She went on whispering in my mind.

"I could not agree with Cora's plan. I loved the house. The house had been good to me, and I cherished it. Funny, that a person could love a house like that. So I chose to keep the house and care for the memories myself. I demanded to be sole owner since they had rejected it. I didn't want any intervention from my sisters if they changed their minds in the future. If I cared for the house, it should be mine, and mine alone, along with its memories.

"The reaction of my sisters to my proposal went along the lines of their true personalities. Cora discounted it as absurd and ridiculous, while Laura fantasized that the memories would come back to haunt me. They simply couldn't understand why I wanted the house. But I did. So in the end, they transferred ownership of the house and its life history to me.

"In point of fact, the more we sat in silence around the kitchen table, the more I enjoyed the feeling that the house was now mine. A feeling that kept growing inside me, as if the house was so relieved and happy to be wanted that it embraced me and thanked me for wanting her. So the house and I took custody of the past and looked forward to a better future in the comfort and acceptance of our common destiny."

"Sarah...Sarah," Amy's voice whispered in my mind, coaxing me. "Wake up," she gently said, as I became aware of the coldness in the room.

I'd fallen asleep on the sofa, the fire was out, and at three in the morning, the house was cold and pitch black.

Too tired to build a fire, I turned on the heater. Needed to warm us both. *Both? Amy and me?* No, I was thinking of the house. She'd also become my companion, my friend.

Amy had loved the house as much as I did, and I remained with a desire to know more about both of them and those ominous memories she agreed to care for.

I went to the kitchen, where she'd been with her sisters, and warmed some milk on the stove. I poured some honey in a cup and dissolved it in the warm milk. I love the taste of sweet milk with its cradling effect.

Warm cup in hand, I went back to the sofa in the living room, covered myself with a blanket, and smiled at my house. I waited to see if Amy would speak to me, but she didn't.

"We'll be warm in a bit," I whispered to my house. "Sorry I didn't turn on the heater any sooner. I didn't think it could get so cold so fast. It won't happen again." I could have sworn I felt the house smile back.

Then a shiver of fear crept through me. "Here I am talking to a house and feeling it react, not to mention hearing the stories of the photographs. Am

I losing my mind? Are these the effects my parents feared? It certainly isn't normal, but it feels like it is. How could that be? Stop this, Sarah. You need to be careful; don't lose your grip on reality. But this is reality. It has to be. If not, what is it?"

The answers were lost in the silence that surrounded me, but I could sense that the house was hiding something. Or was it the attic? I could feel its need to be found, to be dealt with, but didn't know what it could possibly be.

Maybe the next morning I could search for these elusive answers when I would be more alert. I didn't wish to dwell on the negative. I just wanted to renew my visit with Amy. I pushed the fear away and concentrated.

Photograph in hand, I examined the three sisters. Aside from the fact that Amy didn't look withered, the description of her sisters was perfect. I could see every detail she'd portrayed, even Laura's eyes, distant and unfocused. They did look different from one another, sitting around the wooden table in the kitchen, unaware that a photograph was being taken. They weren't posing. Someone had captured this private moment in their lives without their knowledge. Who else was there with them? Who was the photographer? The more I looked, the more certain I became that in due time I'd learn all about this moment and these women. They'd lived in my house, and their memories would emerge.

I rummaged through the box of photographs, yet not a single one spoke to me. As before, every time I specifically looked for something, the memories remained silent.

It was clear that I needed to get out of the way to allow them to organize themselves and be revealed when they wished to. I'd wait and visit the attic later. Maybe there were more photographs of Amy and her sisters. Maybe that's where I would find Leonard.

I was nodding back to sleep when I heard Jeremy say hello.

CHAPTER 5

Jeremy
1891

"Hello." I heard a child's voice.

"Who are you?" I asked as I rummaged through the photographs seeking a face to put with the voice, but none stood out.

"Jeremy," he answered.

"Where are you?" I asked, hoping that insanity wouldn't be the answer. Here I was, finally getting used to voices that emanated from photos, and now this. "I can't see you," I added at last.

"That's OK. I'm used to being alone. I like it. I get up at four thirty like this every morning."

I felt my breath quicken and glanced around in case a hurried exit became necessary. I searched through the pictures again with the same result as before. "Why so early?" I heard myself ask.

"'Cause that's when the birds wake up. They start to sing real early. It's my favorite time."

"Because of the birds."

"Yeah. And because I can make up stories when the house is quiet like this."

"What kind of stories?"

"All kinds. Want to hear one?"

The answer eluded me for a moment. "How old are you?"

"Ten. Want to hear my story about the cowboy? It's a really nice story. At least, I think it is."

"Of course." It seemed to be my only choice. "Are all the stories about cowboys?"

"No, silly. They're stories about all kinds of people. They keep me company all day long. They like to show up early too. They just pop into my head. I call them my secret friends."

That concept didn't comfort me at all. "Really."

"Yeah, the cowboy helped me write a story for school last week."

"Oh, so this cowboy is a friend of yours."

"I guess. He just popped into my head and told me this story. Want to hear it, even if it's just make-believe?"

I must have considered my answer for some time, because I heard the impatience in his voice when he asked again.

"Well, yes or no?"

"Yes. Of course I want to hear it. Go ahead."

"I gotta tell it kinda fast. Pa'll be getting up, and Ma'll be making his coffee. Then they'll start waking everybody else up."

"OK."

"It's a Christmas story. And you're going to think it's about me and my folks, but it isn't. It happens on a farm like ours, but it's not ours. And my uncle's a cowboy, but he didn't tell me the story. It's about a girl named Elisa, and not about me. You got that?"

"I understand."

"OK, here goes. Elisa was a little girl who lived on a farm. Her family was very, very poor, so she never got any Christmas presents. My family's poor too."

"I see."

"OK. Her uncle was the cowboy, and he came to stay with her family when Elisa was seven years old. I'm ten, so you can see that the story can't be about me, right?"

"Yes. Absolutely."

"Her father's farm was in a little valley. I asked the cowboy if her farm was like mine. He said it was just the same as ours. Funny, huh?"

"Yes, that's quite a coincidence."

"The cowboy was herding cattle in Montana when he got injured. That's why he came to stay at Elisa's house. Her pa was the cowboy's brother. My uncle got hurt that way too once, but no one knows that at my school."

For some inexplicable reason, I nodded.

"The cowboy," he went on, "hurt the whole left side of his body and couldn't move. So Elisa was told to take care of him. My uncle hurt his left side too. Really bad. I had to take care of him when he stayed here. Isn't that something?"

"I guess."

"You sure you wanna hear the rest of the story? It's got a really fun part at the end."

"I'm really enjoying your story, Jeremy." That was the honest truth. Somehow, his little voice had reached into my soul and given me the comfort that I felt sure Jeremy, whoever he was, may never have felt.

"The cowboy knew that Elisa wanted to help with the farm and the animals, but her pa thought that farmwork was too hard for a girl, so she had to stay home and work with her ma. The cowboy asked her if he could send Elisa out to get him some things from the fields and the forests, and she said yes. What do you think the cowboy wanted?"

"I have no idea. Do you?"

He laughed like an angel might, with unrepressed joy. "Sure I do, silly. I wrote the story." He laughed and laughed until he could laugh no more. "You're funny," he said at last. "OK, so Elisa collected juniper berries and pine cones and all kinds of stuff. And she would come back and tell the cowboy where she had found what she brought back and where the biggest trees were and the best fishing and everything she could remember. The cowboy would smile and slip it all under his bed."

"One day her ma told the cowboy not to be wasting Elisa's time on account of she needed her to help with chores around the house. See, she was always outdoors getting stuff for the cowboy."

"Yes, I see how her ma might object to that."

"But do you know why?"

"Well—"

"I'll tell you why. 'Cause her ma's gonna have a baby, that's why. And she'd get really tired cleaning and cooking and all that. She wanted Elisa to help. See?"

"Yes, I see that. So, what happened next?"

"Oh, right. OK, the cowboy asked her to let Elisa do the errands until Christmas, which was just three days away. She smiled and said that would be OK. Elisa was glad to see her ma smile 'cause she didn't smile much. I like that part," Jeremy added.

"I like it too. Please, go on."

"Elisa was hoping that her ma's baby would be a baby girl. That way, she would be the youngest, and Elisa could help her brothers and her pa on the farm. Her pa wanted another boy, but a girl was OK too. Elisa's pa thought that girls couldn't work as hard as boys, and he needed more hands to make ends meet. But Elisa knew she could do it, 'cause she knew she could work harder and better than her brothers." He paused.

"Is something wrong?" I finally asked.

"No, just remembering something. Anyway, the story ends on Christmas day. You ready?"

"I sure am."

"All right. On Christmas morning Ma made all kinds of good things. The house smelled like coffee and muffins and eggs and bacon. It was snowing too, and everything was all white outside. Elisa and her brothers had the morning off, and her pa helped the cowboy to the kitchen table. The cowboy asked one of the boys to bring him an old bag that was under his bed, and he gave each and every one a Christmas present. This is the best part. You see, they didn't know what to do with the presents."

"What do you mean?"

"They never got presents before. Her pa didn't allow presents 'cause he didn't want them to be sad if sometimes they didn't get any."

"Oh, I see. How sad."

"It was OK. We didn't get any presents at my house either, and we got used to it. Then it all changed."

"How's that?"

"That's another story. Anyway, the cowboy didn't know that her pa didn't allow presents. That's why he made presents for everybody. Her pa forgot to tell his brother about no gifts."

"What did Pa do?"

"Wait, I have to tell you about the presents first."

"I'm sorry. Go on."

"Elisa got a pretty necklace made of juniper berry seeds, and when she put it on, she twirled and twirled and felt like the prettiest little girl in the world. Pretty nice, don't you think?"

"Yes, pretty nice. What did the others get?"

"The cowboy gave each one of the boys a piece of a map. When they put the four pieces together, it showed their little valley and where lots of treasures from nature could be found. Then he winked at Elisa, and she understood how the cowboy taught them that nature would always have gifts for them. This part I really like. My uncle taught me how to put a map together just like that, and we hung it on the wall in my room."

"I can just imagine. I'd like to do one myself."

"He gave Elisa's ma a juniper berry necklace too and told her he could teach her and Elisa how to make jewelry out of things around the farm. That was a good idea 'cause then they could go sell them in town at the market. What do you think?"

"I agree. I'm sure they could use the extra money."

"Oh, yeah. They sure could. My ma made jewelry like that too. She sold it at the market, and the girls and ladies wore it. You see, the cowboy had learned to make jewelry from a shaman he'd met in Canada. You know what a shaman is?"

"I think so, yes."

"My uncle knew a shaman too. He met him up in Canada. I am going to write a story about shamans one day."

"That's a wonderful idea, Jeremy. I hope I get to read it."

"Yeah, that would be nice. It's already in my head."

"You think about it early in the morning?"

"Yeah. Anyway, Elisa and her brothers didn't know what a shaman was, so the cowboy told them all about the people who had lived in our lands way before they'd even been born. He told them about their ancient customs and how they understood the spirits of the earth and nature and all that. That's really true. Bet you didn't know that."

"I didn't," I lied, "but I am always glad to learn new things. Thank you, Jeremy."

"You're welcome. Anyway, the cowboy gave his brother a picture to remind him how happy they'd been when they were kids and celebrated Christmas on the farm with their parents. Elisa's pa remembered, and a small tear just came down his cheek."

"That's beautiful."

"Yeah, I know. I still have the picture my uncle gave my pa. He gave it to me on account of my story. It's also on my wall. Now the best part. Ready?"

"As ready as I'll ever be. Read on."

He chuckled. "Read on. You sure talk funny. That Christmas day, Elisa's little sister Rachel was born, and the cowboy told his brother he had to fetch an elder from the Okanogan tribe to come to the house to bless the new baby and the family."

"Was that the custom?"

"Sort of. Her pa forgot that was the way. The cowboy reminded him, and since there were no presents for his brother, Elis'as pa thought that if this made him happy, he'd fetch the elder. When he got back, the elder gave Rachel and the whole family a real nice blessing." Jeremy went silent.

"Is something wrong, Jeremy?"

"I smell coffee. Everybody'll be up in a minute. Did you like my story?"

"I loved your story. I can never thank you enough for sharing it with me."

"I won first prize at school for that story. They gave me a red ribbon, and I hung it over my bed. They said it was the best Christmas story in the whole school."

"That's wonderful. Congratulations."

"You know what else?"

"What?"

"My little sister was born on Christmas day, and my ma and pa named her Rachel on account of my story. They also invited an elder to bless our new baby. The elder also blessed our entire family, the house, the farm, and the land, thanking the ancestors for their gifts to us." The pride in his voice was heartwarming. "The cowboy told me a good story, don't you think?"

"The best story ever."

I woke up before sunrise and immediately searched for a photograph of Jeremy, or the one of his pa and the cowboy, but they weren't there. I wondered how I'd heard Jeremy's story without a photograph.

"Was it just a dream?" I asked myself. "No, much more than that." Hearing my own voice was somewhat reassuring, even though I couldn't shake the fear of madness that lurked behind this forced façade of normalcy.

Hearing all about Jeremy without a photograph wasn't natural. *My descent into madness seems undeniable. Is that is what's happening to me?*

"I refuse to give into the dread of looming insanity. Maybe I'll find Jeremy's photograph in the attic. Perhaps I'll find Jeremy's story somewhere there as well. There has to be an explanation for the clarity of the vision other than my so-called gift."

Winter had descended on my little valley overnight, and I was very thankful for the distraction it brought with it. Snow blanketed the house and the Cascades, and the view from my living room window mirrored the idyllic winter landscapes captured in paintings and reproductions of well-wishing holiday cards. *What a treat.*

The Cascades, veiled in white, sparkled under the morning sun. The silence of the gentle snowflakes that embraced my house intoxicated my senses. I sat in the rocking chair on my small front porch all bundled up, sipping a nice hot cup of cocoa, listening. The silence was complete. Once in a while, I could hear the wind flow through the trees as it woke the fallen snow, rearranging the landscape. It's hard to imagine such peace and quiet. I knew that the sudden snowstorm would create havoc for those who needed to go to work or be somewhere, but for me, the snowstorm brought splendor and serenity.

The Gift of the Twin Houses

Enthralled with the majesty that surrounded me, I went about my household tasks choosing to look on the positive side of the memories my house had witnessed so many years ago. I now knew that Amy and her sisters, as well as Jeremy, had lived in my house some time back. I imagined Amy and Jeremy with their families and wondered how they'd spent their winters, how they'd kept warm and entertained themselves, what they spoke about, who slept where, how they'd furnished the house, and what they did at night after dinner.

With every passing moment, I confirmed that my impulse to move here had been right. I wondered how my life would have turned out had I not been asked to bury that part of me that tuned into these kinds of ethereal sensations and emotions. Hard to imagine after all these years, given the roadblocks I'd built.

By accepting my visions as normal and truthful, I had innocently provoked a reaction that had caused my family to change me, if only to protect me. Nevertheless, their actions splintered my personality. Now I found myself reassembling it piece by piece. The difficulty in doing so, however, rested on the panic instilled in me of these abnormal abilities and the resulting instinctive fear of the unknown.

If permitted to thrive, my extrasensory capacities might flourish. On the other hand, they might lead to my destruction.

CHAPTER 6

Conrad

I'D JUST FINISHED dressing when I heard the chimes of the front doorbell. As soon as I opened the door and saw Conrad, looking more handsome than ever flushed by the cold air, something within me stirred, and for a moment I lost myself inside the sensation.

He took off his hat and gloves, shook my hand, and exactly what happened after that is unclear. My brain zapped out of the present and disappeared to somewhere unknown. I lost track of everything around me—well, everything but Conrad. What I do remember is that we both stood there looking into each other's eyes, unwilling to say the next word for fear of breaking this invisible yet palpable bond between us.

Slowly, I felt Conrad's hand move in mine and saw him smile.

"I came by to see if you've got what you need for winter," he said.

"Think so," I clumsily managed to say as I slid my hand out of his.

"If you want, I can take a look to see what needs to be done with the house. It's been empty a long while."

"Sure, please come in."

Still in a daze, I remember following him through the house as he inspected kitchen, windows, attic, porch, and bedrooms. The intuitive Sarah was so attracted to him that the practical Sarah had trouble keeping a clear head. Somehow, I managed to ask all the essential questions every time he recommended something or made an assessment of needed upgrades or repairs. On automatic pilot, I went through the motions, concentrating more on the messenger than the message.

After a while my senses returned, and I recall following Conrad down the stairs toward the front foyer, and thinking that in a few moments he'd be gone.

"How about chains for your car?" he asked.

"I got those. I'll put them on later. I didn't expect it to snow this much so fast."

"I'll help you with them."

"You don't need to bother, really. I lived in Boston before moving to California. I've handled many a chain in my time." No sooner had I heard the sensible Sarah utter those words than I wanted to gag her.

"No bother, be happy to give you a hand," he said, and I thanked my lucky stars. "Do you have any more questions on what you need to ready yourself and the house for winter?"

I smiled and blushed. "Ran out of questions. I'd think you'd be sick of so many of them by now."

"No, not at all. I just wanted to make sure. Don't want you thinking it's my way to get you to spend money at my store."

"I hope you didn't think...I mean, I didn't—"

"Don't fret. Just checking. Better get it all sorted out up front."

"Your answers were straightforward and honest. I've never met anyone that owned a general store, so please forgive me if I sounded so incredulous. I'm a stickler for detail and tend to analyze—"

"*Incredulous.* Another fancy word," he said, and chuckled.

"Sorry, I've been a teacher a bit too long."

"No need for apologies. I already told you I like it."

I'm sure I must've turned red as a beet, because he laughed.

"Sorry for all the questions," I blurted out, turning away from him and quickly walking out onto the porch. I counted on the cold air to bring my emotions and composure back into check. "Thank you for your patience."

"I'll be happy to bring the stuff over. I'll help you with the house if you want. It's the least I can do."

"I don't want to impose and take you away from your wife and family."

He shook his head. "Widower. I live on my own, and I wouldn't ask if I didn't mean it. C'mon, let's start with the chains for your car, and then I'll show you how to walk to my house if you're snowed in and can't drive. I'm just across the valley."

After he put on the chains, we walked to the edge of the valley, and he pointed the way to his home just across a small clearing. I couldn't see the house itself, but the road seemed easy to follow either by car or on foot.

"Let's get you back to your house. This coat and city boots of yours won't cut it in these parts. You need some rugged winter boots and a waterproof coat."

We enjoyed a nice walk, but my wet socks and chattering teeth confirmed that he was right. In a matter of minutes, it became clear to me that thirty years of easy living in sunny southern California had melted away any and all winter know-how from my early years in Boston.

After we got back to the house, he smiled and tilted his hat. "See you tomorrow, late afternoon. I'll bring the stuff and get going on the house."

"You really don't have to—"

"Now Sarah, it's settled. Just smile and nod." I did as he asked, part of me delighted with the prospect, part of me worried and afraid.

So, for the next couple of weeks, our late afternoons were dedicated to readying my house, and me, for winter.

The mornings however were focused internally. Jeremy had helped me discover the wonders the early hours bring, even though I'd found no answers about how my encounter with him had been possible. Had it been a dream, or did his photograph lurk somewhere and I'd glanced at it but didn't remember? I didn't have the sensation that it had been a dream. The images of Jeremy and his family, of the cowboy, and of my house and my valley had been so vivid that they didn't fit into the realm of reveries. The clarity of his young voice and our easy give-and-take assured me that it hadn't been an illusion. I felt as if I'd been there engaged with Jeremy as he told me all about his family and the story he'd written. I knew for certain he'd lived here and formed part of the history of my new home, just as the three sisters, but how the encounter had taken place remained a mystery.

Every day I looked forward to the sunrise to witness the magic of the early rays of sun and the light peering through the foliage. How quiet were the birds at daybreak in the winter. I had to listen intently to even guess where they were or what they were doing to stay warm. I so loved my early mornings. As it had been for Jeremy, they offered a part of the day that belonged only to me. One morning as I sipped my coffee, I reflected on the last couple of weeks and how much I'd learned about myself.

It all had started with pondering over how unusual it was for me to identify with Jeremy and claim the early mornings as mine, a curious phenomenon indeed since no one but me lived in the house. There were no distractions, no obligations to others, not a single person to interrupt my day. Given the fact that I lived utterly alone, with no parents, no siblings, and no farm animals to tend to, how could the mornings belong to anyone but me?

I discovered that during the early mornings, the *new* Sarah, the impulsive Sarah, the trusting Sarah, who gave in to her intuition, heard stories from the photographs in her attic, conversed with Jeremy, and felt the emotions of her house, was in full residence. However, as the day went on, the Sarah of the past emerged, and of course she needed to be dealt with. That Sarah had been a worrier all her life, always analyzing this option or that one, and crafting plans to control whatever puzzled her. There hadn't been a single moment in her past life where she didn't feel in complete control of all of her actions and decisions. Proud of this character trait, she'd put it to good use.

So, with the recent appearance of the Sarah that experienced premonitions and trusted her instincts, the days had to be divided in such a way as to make room for both. Two Sarahs cohabitating.

"Have I lost my mind?"

That unsettling thought ran through me, but I also told myself that the awareness of these opposite personalities represented a healthy process of transformation and growth. After all, these alternate egos were reflections of what I searched for: the resurgence of my true self.

So when the Sarah of the past crept in and spun webs of despair, loneliness, and madness, the emerging Sarah asserted herself in spite of the fear and the unpredictability around her new life. A decent, if difficult, balance.

In the solitude of my early mornings, I saw and understood the change within me. I observed and felt the *old* Sarah, the worrier and planner, appear during the day and take control of things, but in the privacy of the early mornings, the *new* Sarah blossomed. Dawn belonged to her, and the dread about split personalities or going crazy could be set aside.

Only after the sun rose and the day awakened was the *old* Sarah allowed to be in charge. However, once the household tasks that needed her attention were completed, the *new* Sarah returned. A good compromise by all accounts.

With the arrival of winter, I knew that once I allowed all the worrisome what-ifs and the concerns about being stranded or snowed in, unable to heat the house, running out of food, and so on and so forth to assert themselves, they would take over in less than a second. So no sense fighting them. They needed to be dealt with. Once the *old* Sarah took over, the silence, the peace, and the ease of the early mornings abruptly ended, and the day filled with tasks. However, I knew that at the end of the day, the *new* Sarah would return and enjoy the fruits of the labor of her alter ego until sunrise.

To be honest, once I acknowledged and welcomed the rise of the *new* Sarah, life became easier and definitely more enjoyable. Particularly thanks to Conrad's appearance. Unbeknownst to him, his presence had quickly appeased the Sarah of the past and enabled the Sarah of today to emerge more often than just at sunrise.

My two Sarahs were learning to coexist.

When Conrad started working on the house, the skeptical Sarah got in the way, suspicious that all the things he brought were unnecessary, a ploy to make money off a stupid woman. But I intuitively trusted Conrad, and my new self conquered the old one.

I had no idea why I trusted him so quickly. No rational reasoning formed my opinion of Conrad. I guess the unquestioning Sarah took full hold of me and gave me the confidence to rely on my instinct and trust him. Unaccustomed to that type of assurance, it took a while to feel at ease with this new sensation. For someone like me, who never trusted anyone unless given full proof that the person deserved the lowering of my guard, it felt like treading in dangerous waters. Maybe the fact that I no longer fought my emerging spiritual antenna had something to do with it.

Whatever the case, my instincts were eventually rewarded, and the prudent Sarah was put at ease. Among the many benefits of doing business with Conrad was the fact that he owned the general store in town. He knew the merchants, the suppliers, and all the tradesmen in the area, which made the repairs and upgrades quicker and easier.

Maybe I trusted him because I found him so attractive. He seemed to be about my age, strong, and good looking. He emanated confidence, yet his demeanor was gentle and soothing. Somewhat taken aback by the magnetism he exuded, the vigilant Sarah immediately erected all known defenses. But his easygoing poise won the day.

Nevertheless, despite his looks and allure, I incessantly questioned the need for every household item he suggested, and every time the answers were simple and honest, all of which added to my sense of comfort and the attraction I felt.

"What do I need a generator for?" I asked early on.

"In case of an ice storm, or if the snow is too heavy and tree branches fall, breaking the power lines."

"You sure I need to store extra water? Whatever for?

"In case the pipes freeze and crack. You need water not only to drink, but to drain the toilets, for washing, and to stay healthy until they're repaired."

"Why this much canned food? I can't eat all of this."

"Enough to last a couple of weeks if the storm prevents you from leaving home. We're a bit far from town, so it's best to be prepared. You don't have to eat them all at once," he joked.

"Why do I need that?" I asked pointing to the object in his hand.

"OK, Sarah," he said patiently. "You know that I don't live far from here, so I'd be able to help you if the need should arise. But if for some reason you can't drive or walk to my place, here's a blow horn."

"What about just calling you on the phone?"

"It's for when there is no phone service." He chuckled and shook his head. He must've thought I needed brain surgery.

"But if I have a generator, why the extra blankets? I'm the only one here." I protested.

"You can't run the generator all the time; you need to conserve fuel. The blankets will help keep you warm along with the fire when you turn the generator off and the central heating shuts off."

After adding a thick, waterproof winter jacket and pants, water-resistant boots, warm heavy-duty gloves, and much more, I ended up well prepared for the winter. Both Sarahs felt safe and happy.

Conrad not only helped bring all the goodies from his store to the house but also oversaw all the upgrades and repairs and did many of them himself. A nice, uncomplicated man, he took the time to teach me how to prepare the house for winter in future years and how to maintain it.

He first showed me how to care for the pipes. "Just keep them warm," he explained as he insulated the first one. "This material is made with minerals and needs to be wrapped like a bandage around the pipes. I like to secure it with string instead of tape. It lasts longer. The pipes must be completely covered, with no gaps. Keep an eye on them through the winter to make sure they stay on. Now you do the rest." I insulated the rest of the pipes under his watchful eye and felt quite the handywoman.

The following days he showed me how to protect the roof and sides, but this time he did all the work while I watched.

Then we moved to the insulation of the windows and doors. He showed me how to fix one, and then I took over the remainder. I even learned how to chop wood, although in the end, he'd chopped enough wood to keep the fireplace going for at least three months. Watching him chop wood enthralled me, and I wished for winter to last forever.

We spent several late afternoons side by side, working on my house.

"How long have you lived here?" I finally asked one day.

"Most of my life. I joined the marines and traveled some of the world, but home's always been here. I can't get enough of the Cascades."

"I know what you mean. I'm quite taken by them myself."

"I felt pretty sure that was the case when you bought the house so quickly. Glad to hear I was right."

Come to think of it, maybe that's the main reason I lowered my defenses. I could appreciate his devotion for his birthplace since I'd fallen in love with this magical part of the world myself.

During these weeks, the attic was silent. The house, aware of our efforts to ready her to withstand the harshness of wintry weather, cracked and cricked in appreciation.

As we approached the completion of the upgrades, I brought up the matter of payment again. "Conrad, please hear me out. You've been working for a couple of weeks on my house and not tending to your own store. Are you sure I can't pay you?"

"Now Sarah, we've gone through this already. Tom's taking care of the store so there is no need—"

"Just because he's your son, it's not right for me to take advantage of his willingness to work without you."

"You sure are stubborn. We've already discussed this. Just pay me the direct costs on the receipts I gave you yesterday."

"Those are cosmetic and decorative, but what about—"

"All the repairs and upgrades we've made, I should pay for. Including the generator and all the stuff necessary for this house to weather the winter. It's my duty to sell you a house in perfect condition and to your liking. I only waited until you were settled in and felt sure you'd stay here to work on the needed maintenance of the house. No sense in doing anything till the new owner agreed with the work to be done. Winter just came up real quick this year. Anyway, it's the least I can do for my new neighbor."

And with that he refused to entertain any more discussion on the subject. Both Sarahs were at peace.

As I sat on my porch one early morning and looked out across my valley toward the Cascades, they filled me with joy and a deep sense of belonging, as if I were part of nature. No fear lingered on what winter might bring. Instead I'd become a part of winter. I attributed my sense of wellbeing to Conrad. A man who had been nothing but generous, offering his help and time with no expectations and no demands.

Although I looked forward to his visit later that afternoon, I dreaded the fact that it marked the last day I would spend time with him. His work around the house neared completion. Unacquainted with such feelings about a man I'd just met, a stranger really, I felt it necessary to question my emotions, but

I refused to worry. Today the *old* Sarah wouldn't be welcome, not even for a moment. The entire day belonged to the *new* Sarah.

For some bizarre reason, I wanted the house to smell of fresh-baked bread when he arrived. Only one problem: I'd never baked bread. As it happened, a few days earlier I'd retrieved my mother's old cookbook that had been neglected for years in a bookcase. My mother had created her own cookbook in a small three-ring binder where she had inserted many recipes, all of which had handwritten alterations or notes with her suggestions or my grandmother's. She had created an index in the front of the book and had included dividers separating the different types of dishes. I looked up the recipes for baking bread, chose the easiest one, and rushed out to purchase all the necessary ingredients and cooking utensils.

Thus armed, I bravely entered the kitchen. The recipe, the components, the appliances, and the baking gadgets were all ready. The real trick came down to my ability to bake the bread. Without hesitation I dove into it, gathered the ingredients, measured the exact amounts, combined each one, and then kneaded the dough with my hands. I had a grand time as I baked several loaves in search of the perfect look, flavor, and consistency. As I tinkered and toiled, I kept imagining Conrad's reaction to my homemade experiment, and each attempt that brought me closer to what I envisioned to be the perfect loaf filled me with excitement. To my surprise, I found that I enjoyed baking.

This type of endeavor had never been to my liking in the past. I thought it to be too time-consuming and impractical. Discovering that one can actually spend hours engaged in the practice of creating something just for the pleasure of it turned out to be a rewarding, fun experience.

I knew my plan had succeeded when the first thing Conrad said as I opened the front door was, "Boy, the house smells delicious."

"Been baking bread. Want to stay for dinner?" I blurted out the invitation without even thinking about it. I must've felt unduly courageous given that I'd just learned how to bake, yet I knew only too well that I didn't know how to cook.

"Sure thing, thanks," he simply answered.

My plan to have the house smell of fresh-baked bread had ended at the moment of his sensory experience. My plans did not include anything beyond that instant, and I most certainly didn't anticipate inviting him for dinner. A bold and dumb move on my part, considering that I had no clue how to fix anything tasty. I'd cooked only for myself for years, and my skills in the kitchen were limited to heating already prepared foods.

I did have one so-called specialty, spaghetti with meat sauce. While Conrad finished winterizing the house, I rushed to the kitchen and was relieved to find that I had all the necessary ingredients on hand. I hoped that my homemade garlic bread, a fresh vegetable chopped salad, and a nice bottle of wine would help conceal any flaws.

He finished his work by the time I had dinner under control. I offered him a glass of Chianti, and we sat in the living room watching the fire crackle.

"Thank you for all of your help."

"Not at all."

He was not a conversationalist, and I liked that.

"I think I'm ready to spend my first winter here in safety."

"I'd say so. But don't let your guard down. Nature has a way of surprising us all."

We felt no pressure to have an intelligent conversation and were comfortable to just sit in silence, watch the fire, and sip our wine. So we did just that.

After a while, we went into the dining room, and I served dinner.

"This sure is good spaghetti and meat sauce. The garlic bread is great. You're a good cook."

"This is it. I'm not a cook. This is all I really know how to prepare. Today was the first time I actually baked bread."

"Well, then I'm right. You're a good cook."

He paid me a sincere compliment, and it felt good—really, really good.

"I'm glad you bought this old house."

"Me too. Do you know who lived here before me?"

"She's been on her own for quite some time. I felt sorry for the old girl."

"Old girl?"

He smiled. He looked wonderful when he smiled. Something about his eyes changed.

"I think this house has cared for her residents the way a loving mother cares for her kids. Don't you get that feeling?" he asked.

"I do."

"Well, there you have it."

I wanted to tell him about the memories in the attic, ask him if he knew of the three sisters, or Jeremy, the cowboy, or maybe of Louise Whitman and Leonard, but I didn't want to share my secrets. I didn't want him to think me odd, or even worse, evil or a witch.

We finished our evening around ten o'clock, and as usual he tilted his hat and smiled as he left. The house and I smiled back.

I lay in bed later that night listening to the silence that cradled me in my new home, reliving my entire day. It had been splendid, filled with beauty, calm, and friendship. Our first dinner together had been simple, uncomplicated, and enjoyable.

I wondered when I would see Conrad again, given that the house had been tended to.

I realized I needed to be tended to as well.

CHAPTER 7

The Birthday

Now that the house had been cared for, my attention needed to return to the attic. I stood in the doorway, looked around the room, and absorbed its contents. It was midmorning, and the light was different. A combination of white and pale yellow suffused the room, inviting me in, intimating that it would be easier to see inside the trunks and find what I looked for.

The attic knew that I had a purpose, and hopefully it would respond this time. I wanted to find Jeremy and the photograph the cowboy had given to his pa. I also wanted to see if there were more pictures of Amy and her sisters and find out who had taken their photograph. Perhaps her sisters Laura or Cora might speak to me. Come to think of it, I also sought more information on Louise Whitman and Leonard. I thirsted for more stories.

The attic whispered that maybe wanting more details about my companions might not be a good idea. It reminded me that every time I'd looked for something specific, I failed to find it and suggested I open myself to whoever was willing to say hello.

Entering the attic this time seemed like coming home. It felt safe. I understood why the memories were safe here as well. It looked to be devoid of dirt, dust, spider webs, or any signs of abandonment. I didn't remember cleaning it, but I must have. It was perfectly inviting.

Being in the attic felt like tenderly rocking on my grandmother's cozy lap while she read a favorite story. I must have been dreaming of Nana when I'd cleaned the attic. I'd not thought of her in years, but lately I felt her presence most of the time. I loved losing myself in the memories that she evoked. Oh, how I'd wasted precious time not thinking of her. If only I'd known then how marvelous it was to visit with one's memories.

I made my way to the first trunk on the right side of the room and caught a glimpse of a short stack of books sitting in the corner. I picked up the books and brought them with me to the armchair, carefully placing them on my lap. I opened the first one, and a small photograph greeted me.

A young girl was blowing out the candles on her birthday cake. She didn't seem happy. I turned the photograph over to see if someone had dated it or written the girl's name when I realized that I already knew. Her name was Angela, and the year was 1919. I leaned back to listen to her story.

"I turn fourteen today," she told me. "I'd waited a long time for this birthday because on this day I was leaving home."

"Why?"

"I figured fourteen was the best time. I first thought about leaving when I was ten, but ten is too young. Eleven was barely out of ten and not grown up enough. Twelve was right before becoming a teenager, and I thought it best to wait till after that. Thirteen was the first year of the 'terrible teens,' as my pa would say, so I figured I needed to adjust to being terrible for at least a year. That's why fourteen is the perfect time to run away."

The day had come, her fourteenth birthday. On this fine morning, the summer sun seeped through the lace curtains into her bedroom. She could hear the birds, the crickets, the cows, the pigs, and of course, George the rooster. She could even hear the neighbor's barnyard stirring and wished she couldn't, particularly on this day, but she did. That was her lot in life.

"I'd never heard them that clear before," she told me. "That's because they knew what I was going to do. Maybe it was their way of saying good-bye to me."

She liked the animals. Actually she loved them. Riding Mollie was the best part of the day, and milking "the girls" was a great treat. They were so appreciative afterward. She didn't mind at all caring for the chickens and picking up the eggs. She hadn't been too crazy about feeding the pigs at first, but she'd opened her mind and heart to them and understood them. She would miss them. For sure she would miss all of them.

She'd packed all she could take in the little velvet bag that her grandmother Annie had given her, the same little bag that had been her wedding present when she'd married Grandpa Henry, and she wondered if it had been hard for Grandma to marry him.

"I wish I would've asked her. I somehow feel she was all right with it, but I'd like to have heard the spoken words."

It hadn't taken any time for Angela to pack. She'd been thinking about it for so long that she knew exactly what to take and how to pack it.

She made the bed, hid her grandmother's bag under it, and sat down. "It's a nice room," she said. She liked her room with all of her grandmother's memories. The curtains they'd stitched together, the quilt they'd hemmed, Grandma's armchair, and the doilies they'd had embroidered.

Angela liked old things, particularly Grandma's few possessions. They comforted her. They came from the woods of the Cascades, carefully crafted as furniture but bringing with them a part of the trees she loved so. Momma had wanted to get rid of them or put them all away in the attic since they were so old, but Angela had begged and begged, and Momma finally agreed to let her keep them.

"I'm sure going to miss you," she told her furniture. "I'll keep you in my thoughts and dreams. I'll never forget you," she promised them.

She looked at her guitar resting comfortably in the corner. She went to it and softly ran her fingers through the strings, listening to the soft hum they emitted. "I know, I know, but I can't take you. You'll be loved again. I don't know by whom just yet, but I know you'll be all right."

Her bookshelf was harder to deal with, and a couple of tears rolled down her cheeks. She'd packed two books to take with her, *Mother Goose* and *One Thousand and One Nights*. Now, she looked at her small library wondering if she shouldn't take something else. "Maybe I can fit the Jane Austen books." But she knew better; take one more and the others would want to come as well.

She shook her head and sat back on her bed. As soon as the old clock in the living room rang eight, Momma would come in, kiss her on the forehead, and wish her a happy birthday. She could already smell the coffee brewing and the biscuits baking.

Her parents always let her sleep in late on her birthday, even if for only a couple of hours. She knew that by the time breakfast was ready, her pa would have done her chores, milked the cows, and fed the hogs. All she would have to do would be to gather the eggs, but that could wait till after breakfast. Her pa was a good man, and the sadness of what the future held shook her. Silent tears streamed down her cheeks.

Then she thought of her Momma, who would see to it that on her daughter's birthday her chores around the house were forgiven. Angela would have the entire day to enjoy the woods, the birds, the flowers, and the streams. By dinnertime Momma would have baked a delicious cake and placed fourteen candles on it; they would sit down to a good dinner, laugh, and talk about their day. They would take her picture with her fourteen candles and give her a present. Then Pa would talk about...

She couldn't bring herself to even think about it, but it insisted. It would not be silenced. So she decided that thinking about it and saying it out loud would strengthen her resolve to leave home.

"Pa is going to talk about Richard." There, she said it. "He'll say that in just one more year, I'll marry Richard and our farms will join."

She stared into my eyes, and I felt her anguish and resolve.

"It's not that I don't want to marry, but I know it shouldn't be next year. There's something I need to do first, something I need to learn before I marry."

She stood by her window, looking toward the neighboring farm, caressing the curtains she crocheted with her grandmother.

"Richard knows I must leave. He doesn't like it, but he understands. He'll care for my parents."

She turned toward me.

"My parents...will suffer terrible pain. But I must answer the call that yanks me away from them, or I'll never be whole."

Her eyes overflowed with soundless tears, her grief palpable. I reached out for her with a hopeless desire to hold her in my arms and comfort her, but my phone rang, and Angela disappeared.

CHAPTER 8

Thanksgiving

"H...HELLO," MY VOICE cracked with the sorrow of Angela's story.

"Hi, Sarah, you OK?" Conrad asked. "Did I call at a bad time?"

"No. I'm OK. Just...reading something sad. I'm fine."

"Good. Have any plans for Thanksgiving?" he asked.

"Thanksgiving? Uh..."

"Be great if you could join me and my kids. Nothing fancy, just family."

I couldn't remember the last time I'd celebrated Thanksgiving. Over the years I learned to be content with the time off during the four-day weekend and simply enjoy long walks, window-shopping, or reading a good book. I'd deliberately forgotten what Thanksgiving was all about. If I didn't think about it then I wouldn't mind being all alone.

I'd moved away from home when I graduated from college, and as the years went by, it just became too difficult to get together with my family back in Boston for both Thanksgiving and Christmas. As a result, we agreed that Christmas should be the time to visit since I usually enjoyed a couple of weeks off from work and could make the best of a long stay to celebrate the holidays.

As I got older, I just didn't feel like joining others for Thanksgiving dinner. I felt like the perennial old maid and didn't care to be reminded of my social standing in life. The best antidote for that was to decline the invitations and ignore the reason for the time off from work altogether. So I did just that and put it out of my mind. I had lots of practice on how to do that to perfection.

"Hello? Are you there?" Conrad's voice shook me back.

"Yes, sorry. I have no plans, but...well, this is so sudden. Didn't expect an invitation."

"It'll be just like the old times when the folks that lived in our houses used to get together for the holidays. C'mon, you'll enjoy it. No sense in being all by yourself. "

"Well…OK, that'll be lovely. Thanks."

I accepted the invitation mostly because I wanted to see him again but also out of curiosity. When he said that my coming to his house would be like old times when the two households gathered for the holidays, I was hooked. I wanted to hear the stories of these gatherings, hoped to catch a glimpse of my secret companions in some photos of his, and maybe even find a photograph or two that told me more about the history of my house.

By the time Thanksgiving Day rolled around, I looked forward to whatever new discoveries were about to come my way. The first one appeared when I took a last look in the mirror. To my total amazement, my reflection in the mirror was quite nice. I actually looked pretty good. I hadn't liked myself for so long that this reflection shook me up a bit. If someone had asked me back then to describe myself, I would've answered, "Not noticeable." A simple woman, neither ugly nor pretty, not tall, not short, fat, or thin, mostly average, with shoulder-length brown hair now sprinkled with white. Neither loud nor quiet or particularly shy. Someone who, on first acquaintance, you might easily ignore or forget about. Even though my friends have told me on numerous occasions how pleasing and attractive I am, I never believed them.

On this Thanksgiving Day, everything about me looked different. Truth be told, I came across quite pretty. Nothing had changed. My hair was the same, my features the same, weight, complexion, all as usual. However, everything came together to create an image of a good-looking woman. I couldn't get used to it. I kept glancing in the mirror over and over. Every time I walked by my dresser, I'd take a peek.

Still looking fine, the mirror would confirm.

Maybe it was my house giving me courage to join Conrad and his family by telling me I was attractive and reassuring me that I wouldn't feel out of place. But the dresser and the mirror were from my old life, and they hadn't shown me as an attractive woman in the past.

A puzzling state of affairs, to say the least.

So with no logical explanation for the difference, I kept expecting the reflection to show the Sarah of yesteryears. But the unattractive Sarah never showed up. Whatever the reason, I looked nice, even attractive, as a matter of fact. I felt like a schoolgirl going out on her first date.

Thanksgiving dinner with Conrad was far from being on a date, but regardless, it felt like one. The fact that he'd called and asked me out made it feel like one. The location and the reason for our getting together weren't important. What mattered was that *he* wanted to see me.

"Enough, Sarah," I told myself. "You're behaving like a teenager. You're not going on a date. You're going to a family dinner."

With the sound of my words, anxiety crept up. I hadn't gone out with a man in so long that I didn't know how to behave. What was appropriate nowadays? What wasn't? But before I could get myself all worked up worrying about how to behave, the doorbell chimes beckoned. Conrad had arrived.

My heart leapt. I checked myself in the mirror one more time to see if I was still all right, and thank goodness, I was. I winked at myself as I left the room.

"What an odd thing to do," I thought out loud as I rushed down the stairs. "Why would you wink at yourself?" I shook my head and laughed. "Well, Sarah, you're full of yourself tonight."

I stopped before opening the front door, took a deep breath, and relaxed. A somewhat more serene Sarah opened the front door.

"Hi," I said, and was glad I'd forgotten to turn on the porch light because I'm sure I blushed when I saw him. He looked so handsome in his turtleneck and tweed jacket.

"Evening, Sarah. You ought to light your porch. It's pretty dark out here."

I did, and he helped me with my coat.

"It smells good in this house...bread and pies. Nice. Did you rehearse baking the pies as you did with the bread?"

"Four times." Before I could say anything more, he picked up the pies and bread I had laid out on the wooden bench of the coat rack by the front door.

"Should be good then. Can't wait to taste them. C'mon." He escorted me out, closing the door behind us.

"You look beautiful tonight," he said, and I blushed again, thankful that my back was turned to him as I walked down the porch.

He opened the door to the passenger side, and once I settled in, he carefully placed the pies and bread on my lap.

When he climbed into the truck, he was shivering.

"Conrad why aren't you wearing your winter jacket?"

"It's just a short way between our houses."

The ride to his house was indeed quite brief, and as we drove closer, I noticed that he'd placed a bunch of floodlights to illuminate his home. I looked at it and gasped.

"Yep," he said, "twins. Built the same year by the same folks, I guess. Thought I'd light it up so you could see it well."

"Why didn't you tell me? "

"And spoil the surprise?"

He helped me out of the truck, and as we went up the stairs and crossed the porch toward the front door, it felt as if we were entering my own home.

The inside of his house had the exact same layout as mine. With different furnishings, unique decorations, and personal touches here and there, his house had its own personality.

"A good old girl as well," Conrad said. "Been in my family for years."

The house welcomed me, offering warm friendship, and I felt immediately at ease. "Thank you," I whispered, and caressed the banister as we went into the kitchen.

"You know Tom, and this is Alyana. Their critters are Elan and Nina, and the one in the oven is still waiting for a name. Don't know if it's a boy or a girl just yet. Kids, this is Sarah. I'll be back in a bit. Got to collect the floodlights."

"Nice to see you, Sarah," Tom said as he shook my hand. "Wait up, Dad, and I'll help you." He rushed out.

"Hi, Sarah." Alyana shook my hand and smiled. "Surprised about the houses?"

"You bet. Twins?" I asked.

"For sure. Distinct personalities but twins nonetheless. Pretty unusual houses for these parts, don't you think?"

"Yes. You know how they came to be?"

"No. Just that they've been here for many a year. Your house, though, is more feminine than this one. Once you're in the houses, you can feel that this one grew up with a man in residence, and I don't mean Conrad, the other with a woman. Maybe whoever built them had that in mind."

"You can feel those things?"

"Oh, it's just a guess."

Conrad's loving, kind, and down-to-earth family welcomed me with open arms. In no time they made me feel as if I belonged and had been a friend of the family for years. There was no awkwardness between us, no pretension, nothing but the simplicity of being ourselves.

Through the evening however, Alyana's comment about the houses puzzled me. It seemed unusual for someone to openly share an impression so unique, unless you were like me—different.

After visiting for a while, Alyana left to finish fixing dinner, and I offered to help. Tom kept the little ones in the living room with their grandfather, leaving us "girls" to tend to the food. Under normal circumstances, or in my past life, I would've bristled if a man had referred to me as *girl*, but the term had been offered with no mal intent; instead, it carried with it the innocence of thinking of us as young and full of femininity.

"Thanks for baking the bread and the pies. It was a big help. Baking is what takes the most time," Alyana said.

"Just learned how to bake, so I hope you all like what I fixed."

"Papa says you're a good baker and cook, so they must be delicious."

"Don't know about being good, really. I just started all of that as well."

"He doesn't pay folks compliments unless he means it. I got the veggies and the turkey under control. How about giving me a hand with the salad?"

"Sure thing."

"Sarah, you seemed a bit taken aback when I made the comment about the houses."

"Nothing really, just an unusual impression, don't you think?"

"Unusual? No, not at all; things and places influence the people in them. Papa tells us you're very taken by the Cascades and your valley."

"I am."

"Same with these houses. One senses things about them."

"I guess."

Certainly she had no misgivings with this exchange, but the years of training to keep everything tight to my chest didn't allow me to share my own impressions of the twin houses.

In no time we fixed the salad and got the turkey ready to be served.

"Papa likes to carve the turkey at the table, and my little ones get a kick out of the electric knife. The turkey platter is in the upper cupboard."

I got the platter down and rinsed it. As I dried it, I noticed the intricate pattern. It was hand painted with delicate leaves and small flowers.

"Isn't it beautiful? It belonged to Papa's great-grandmother Annie. I don't know how they could've afforded such an elegant platter; they were all very simple folk. One of the many mysteries surrounding the twin houses, I guess."

"They lived here in this house?"

"I think so. If it's OK with you, I'd appreciate it if you'd transfer the turkey onto it. I don't want to lift it in my current condition. My mobility is somewhat limited. I've gotten way too big with this baby."

Thanksgiving dinner proved unforgettable. No pressure to perform, no expectations, not one single glance of reproach at my solitude, a happy and comfortable gathering with family. They accepted me without reservation, and it felt wonderful.

The bread and pies I baked were well received and quite good. I'd baked a pumpkin pie and a pecan pie from scratch. The first couple of pies I prepared were OK but not as good as these. I perfected the instructions by adding what my palate asked for, and I'd finally achieved what I thought to be perfection. They all claimed that my baking was exceptional, and Alyana even asked me for the recipe. I'd never been asked for a recipe in my entire life, an understandable fact given that I'd never baked or really cooked. I could hardly contain my sense of pride at having created something they liked and wished me to share.

"Sarah, I don't know if you'll be going to visit family for Christmas," Alyana said as they were leaving, "but if you're staying, we'd love to have you over to our place."

"I—" my voice caught in my throat as my eyes welled up. For a moment I could only stare at her. When I regained some composure, I managed to say, "I'd love to Alyana. I have no family to go to. I'm all that's left."

I sounded pitiful. How could I have just blurted out such personal grief?

"Well, then we're your family now," she said with such ease that it left no doubt that she meant it. "We start real early with the little ones opening their presents, and we just go through the morning and afternoon cooking, hiking, playing, and enjoying each other's company. Would that be OK with you?"

"Of course. Thank you so much. You're sure it's all right with the men? I don't want to intrude."

"They'd be delighted. We haven't seen Papa so happy in years. He's a caretaker, you know. That's just plainly who he is, and ever since he's been helping you, he feels useful again. Please say yes."

I couldn't repress more tears. They just insisted on showing up. Words refused to come out, so I nodded.

Alyana hugged me and kissed me on the cheek—such a simple gesture, yet so meaningful. At least it was for me.

"What's going on?" Conrad, with Elan in his arms, had just stepped into the foyer. Tom came right behind him carrying a slepping Nina.

"Girl stuff," Alyana chuckled. "She's agreed to come for Christmas, so Papa, pick her up bright and early."

After hugs and kisses for everyone, we watched them leave. "How lovely they are," I whispered.

"They're good kids. Want a cup of tea before going home?"

"Sure."

He went to the kitchen and put the kettle on the stove. As I followed, for the first time that evening, I noticed the photographs hanging in the hallway just outside the kitchen. I'd forgotten all about my original intent and hadn't asked a single question about the households or any photographs.

"Are these folks your family?"

"Yes, and of Dianne's, my late wife. She died over ten years ago. That's her," and he pointed to a picture of an elegant, stately woman in her midthirties. "She wasn't from these parts. Most of her folks are from back East."

"So were mine."

The kettle whistled, and he went back into the kitchen to prepare the tea. I strolled down the corridor and hoped that one of these photographs would talk to me. I expected these pictures to tell me a story, just as mine did. What a curious habit I'd picked up since moving into my house.

Then the photograph of a couple in front of a church the day of their wedding caught my eye. I stopped to look at it closely.

"Those are my grandparents Angela and Richard," Conrad said behind me, and handed me the cup of tea.

My heart skipped a beat. Could this be *my* Angela? She looked older, more mature. There appeared to be a resemblance, but with her wedding veil covering a portion of her face, it made it difficult to be certain.

"How old is she in this picture?"

"I think she was seventeen when she finally got married. She ran away from home when she was fourteen."

I think I gasped. Conrad turned to me and looked like he'd seen a ghost. "What's happened, Sarah? All color has drained from your face."

He took the cup of tea from my trembling hands and helped me to an armchair in the living room.

"What's wrong, Sarah? What can I do?"

At last I managed to speak. "Don't worry, please. I'll be all right. I just remembered something that I didn't expect. That's all. You know how it is when an old memory just grabs hold of you. Please don't fret. But if you don't mind, I would like to go home."

Too shaken by the sudden confirmation that I had spoken with his grandmother, I couldn't cope with Conrad's presence.

How could I tell him the truth? How to explain that I had met Angela, his dead grandmother, when she turned fourteen? How could I tell him she spoke to me and told me all about her plans to run away?

He'd think me crazy and a witch for talking to the dead. He'd shun me, and I didn't want to lose him.

CHAPTER 9

Momma and Pa

CONRAD HAD CALLED three times already checking on me. I don't remember a friend ever caring enough for me to fret so. My parents raised me to be independent and self-sufficient. Unless I told them I needed something, they just left me alone. It wasn't that they didn't love me; they just didn't wish to intrude. They'd given me all the tools to do well and trusted me to know what I needed or wanted. Unless I sought their help, they didn't worry. My grandmother was that way also. Learn the ropes, fend for yourself, don't depend on others, and you'll be fine.

I'd never gotten close enough to anyone to merit their worrying about me either, so Conrad's attention was both unsettling and enjoyable. A part of me wanted to run away to the privacy of my own world away from everyone, and another liked being looked after.

He was working with Tom at the store, a busy time the day after Thanksgiving, but nevertheless, he'd called to see how I felt and wanted to come over after they closed to make sure I was all right. I must've looked awful after I saw Angela's wedding picture because he sincerely worried about me.

I kept assuring him that I felt fine and that there was no need for him to come after a long workday. I insisted he take care of himself, go home, and relax after a long day of work and yet another the following day again.

We were engaged in a fun sort of dance with both of us learning the steps without trampling on each other's toes. To settle our give-and-take, I invited him to come over for Sunday brunch. He agreed to leave me on my own till then as long as he could call here and there to check on me. He called me every so often, and every time he called, I noticed that I enjoyed the feeling of being cared for more and more.

Conrad's attentiveness enchanted me, but I also needed time to sort out my thoughts. I needed to come to terms with what had happened, why my emotions were so raw, and how the real Angela had come to be in my conscious and subconscious.

I spent most of the morning glancing through Angela's books, the books that I'd brought down from the attic, the remnants of her little library. There were two books by Jane Austen, *Sense and Sensibility* and *Pride and Prejudice*. I also found Charlotte Bronte's *Jane Eyre* and Emily Bronte's *Wuthering Heights*. The other two books were by Alexander Dumas, *The Count of Monte Cristo* and *The Three Musketeers*.

What a lovely little girl she must have been, a true romantic. What a hard decision she had made to leave her family. I wanted to know more about her and her real life. Maybe Conrad wouldn't mind telling me her story. In the meantime I searched for that ethereal connection that had spoken to me through her photograph.

This antenna of mine seemed to be tuned into the past, into the history of my new home, particularly into the lives of the people in the photographs left behind in my attic. But why leave all these photos behind? Maybe after so many years in hiding, this ability of mine had been reshaped to this frequency, and whoever needed to be heard had found it. Whatever for? The key to these mysteries, I surmised, must be in the pictures themselves.

After lunch I went back to the attic, not sure this time of what I should do, and wandered through the room, glancing and hoping for something or someone to say hello.

And something did. In the very same spot where Angela's little stack of books had been, I spotted a small book. I must've left it behind when I picked up the rest. It was a collection of short stories by Mark Twain.

I sat in Angela's grandmother's armchair and opened the book. A letter fell on my lap. I unfolded the thin paper as if it were the wings of a wounded butterfly.

The Gift of the Twin Houses

Dear daughter:

I hope one day you'll come home, if only to pick up your books. I know how much you like them. I was cleaning your room today and found this book by Mark Twain with the short story entitled "Advice for Little Girls." After I read it, I understood why you left.

Pa died last year, and I've sold the house. I'm sure you've felt his absence by now. I'm writing to tell you that I'm leaving this place. Without you and Pa, it's not the same, and I can't bear being here. Something in my heart tells me you'll be back one day. You know how we both are about feeling these sorts of things. I hope you'll find all your loved belongings in good shape when you come back. You'll find in your old room or in the attic your grandma's armchair and mirror, your books, and guitar. The lady who bought the house said she would keep all as is, and I believe she will.

I hope you don't blame your pa for wanting you to marry Richard. It was not his fault. It really was mine. Your pa was set on having a big family, and after you were born, I could not have any more children. He never blamed me, never said a word, but I knew he was very disappointed. With only one girl in the family, the farm would be lost. So, when Mr. Thompson asked him if he'd like to join the farms by marriage, your pa agreed. It was just as important for him. With only one boy and three girls, they were in the same predicament. Although they were already sharing the chores between the two farms, they knew it could not stay in the family, so they were hoping that the two of you would give them boys and that the land would be saved. They shook on it, and that's how your future was planned.

Maybe I would've left too, if that had happened to me. Your pa didn't mean to chase you away. He just couldn't bear losing the farms. Doc said it was a heart attack. I was so distraught at the time that I lost my ability to sense what really was going on and couldn't be any help to him or you. I'm sure you'll understand.

I don't know where you are. You write to us, but you don't tell us where you are. That's why I couldn't tell you about Pa, but I think you already know. You could feel these sorts of things since you were little.

Anyway, I'm leaving some of your things and this letter behind so you will know for sure what happened.

Your pa had words with Richard, and he promised he'd keep looking for you. I've asked him to look after the farm animals once I'm gone until the new owners settle in.

I cannot tell you where I will end up because I do not know yet. Maybe I would rather not know. Sometimes it is better that way. First I will be staying with my cousin in Montana. So if you come by in the next few months, that is where you can find me.
With all my love forever,
Momma

I cried for a long time. When my tears dried, I read Mark Twain's story, and I also understood.

I wondered if Angela had ever come to the attic and read this letter. But if she'd come back to the house, why leave the letter and all her things behind?

I took the book and the letter downstairs, not sure what to do with them or what to think. I felt such deep sadness for Angela and her parents that I couldn't focus on anything but their grief. So I decided to take a walk, feel the cold air, and visit my little valley.

I put on my gloves and glanced at the box of photographs on the table in the living room. Maybe if I took one of the photographs for a walk with me, I'd have company. A peculiar thought, but nevertheless, I reached in the box and grabbed the very first one, and without looking at it, I slipped it into the side pocket of my jacket.

Less than ten steps into the valley, Pa stirred in my pocket.

"I suppose you think I'm some kind of coward for dying like that after Angela left," he said.

"No. I don't," I responded immediately. "I can understand how hurtful it must've been for you."

"It wasn't Angela's leaving that killed me. My ticker wasn't working right. I knew I would die soon. Doc told me I had no more than a couple of years."

"Why didn't you tell them?"

"Don't like folks fretting over me. You can understand that. I didn't want any pity, and I didn't want to worry them either. What's the use? I made a good arrangement. With the marriage, my girls would've been taken care of."

"Did you know how Angela felt about it?"

"I guessed. But a good future for both of them was more important, and eventually she'd come to understand. After she left I looked for her. Truly I did. Didn't tell Momma. No sense in worrying her more. I guess the strain of the search for my little girl while caring for the farm just wore me out sooner than I wished."

"Momma sold the house and left," I told him.

"Yes, she agreed in the end to do just that. I knew she'd get enough money to get by. At least I did that right for her."

"You did more than that. Angela came back and married Richard."

He remained silent for a long time, and I just let him be. We walked in silence listening to the snow crunch under my feet. I noticed it was getting dark and started to make our way back to the house. Just before we got back, I felt him smile.

"I asked that boy to keep looking for her. I'm glad he kept his promise."

"She was seventeen when they married, and she looked beautiful. Her grandson Conrad is my neighbor. Angela also has a great-grandson, Tom, who together with his wife, Alyana, gave her two beautiful great-great-grand-babies, a boy and a girl, and there's another on the way. They're a loving family. Conrad is a good man."

"That's why you trust him."

I'd reached the porch of the house and wanted to hear more from Pa. But he was at peace and didn't want to talk anymore.

Although Pa's story calmed me, I still felt unsure as to what was happening to me. Experiencing with such vivid detail the lives of the people who'd lived in my home brought with it exhilaration but also the panic of losing myself in those images and plunging into madness.

On the one hand, I wanted to continue down this path of discovery, and on the other, years of conditioning to avoid such experiences kept yanking me away. An internal tug-of-war had erupted, and indecision seemed to be the one feasible option. If I didn't do a thing and simply allowed all of these sensations to evolve of their own accord, maybe I wouldn't go crazy. Yet, I could never accept to be the victim of circumstances. If madness was in store for me, then I should be in full control of my decision to go insane.

I stepped into the house, and its warmth encircled me. A sense of comfort and security bathed me, and as if by magic, all fear disappeared.

Sanctuary.

Without warning, Angela whispered a challenge that entered my soul. *You need to finish this journey...the mystery must be revealed...be brave...be daring...the secrets of the twin houses must be unearthed.*

CHAPTER 10

The Grandparents

WITH A SENSE of renewed vigor, I spent most of Saturday cleaning the house. She needed attention, and it pleased me to provide it. I loved cleaning it, polishing the wood, tending to all of her needs. It didn't feel like housework or boring chores but more a labor of love. I'd heard that expression many times in the past and thought it to be corny, but now here I was living it.

After concentrating on the house, my curiosity as to who had built the twin houses increased, and I turned to my computer to do a bit of research. When I bought the house, Conrad told me he believed the house was built in the late 1800s, but since they didn't keep good records back then, it was hard to tell. The twin houses were certainly gems, with a unique combination of picturesque architecture and coziness. Both of them reflected the colors of the Cascades and the style of comfortable living for the housewives of times past, offering nice open rooms that helped moms keep an eye on the little ones while tending to their chores. I imagined that the porches wrapped around the houses were used to enjoy the outdoors even if it were drizzling.

The modern marvel of the Internet didn't help. It simply showed me the various architectural movements in America and the Queen Anne styles of both coasts but offered nothing specific to my house and her twin.

Turning to the attic for answers didn't work either. The attic was silent, offering little assistance. Even though I'd spent a good amount of time dusting and cleaning, nothing invited me to open any of the trunks or pick up any of their contents.

I left that endeavor and instead baked some bread and a lemon meringue pie for Sunday's brunch.

The joy of baking invigorated me. I couldn't believe that I derived such pleasure from a task that I'd not only misunderstood but also misjudged. I remember wondering why a person would spend time in a kitchen baking when there are bakeries that do it for you. Now I knew why. The simple act of making your own creation is special. It's about something pleasurable that you have shaped by mixing a collection of independent essentials into a unique design that ends up giving you and others great delight. I wondered if that was how artists felt when they sculpted or painted or when musicians wrote a song. I certainly felt like I'd created edible art. Well, maybe not quite art but my own pleasurable creation nonetheless.

Sunday arrived quickly. I made potato pancakes accompanied by an egg casserole of veggies and homemade turkey sausages for brunch, another first. Given my previous emotional state, I lacked the time to rehearse their taste and realized I'd reached the point where I trusted my newfound culinary skills.

As the morning passed, my mood improved. Although still unsettled about my conversations with ghostly spirits, I decided to make the best of my time with Conrad. The house not only smelled wonderful but also looked beautiful. Furthermore, I daresay I thought I looked beautiful as well. I felt so at ease with my physical self that it unnerved me. But once again, the mirror suggested I simply accept the pleasure of the feeling, and eventually I did.

When Conrad arrived, he looked even more handsome than usual all dressed up for Sunday brunch, holding a bottle of wine and a big gift box.

"Morning, Sarah. Boy, you sure look nice. I'm glad to see you're back to normal."

I know I reddened, because he laughed.

"You sure know how to make a woman blush," I said as I tried to look away while closing the door behind him.

"Not my doing. You blush easily."

"Didn't use to."

"I like it. Glad you do it. Mm…this house smells delicious. How much rehearsal this time?" he said as he placed the wine and gift box on the seat of the coatrack and took off his jacket.

"None, I had no time."

"Brave."

"You'll be the judge."

We immediately fell into a comfortable togetherness. He wouldn't let me open my "present" until after brunch, so while we got the meal ready, he told me all about the busy time they had at the store. It was so easy to be with him.

"Conrad, would you mind telling me about your grandparents?" I asked as we sat to eat.

"Nope, don't mind at all. I knew you'd ask. What do you want to know?"

"How did they meet?"

"They grew up together here, my grandmother in your house, my grandfather in mine. They were supposed to marry when my grandmother turned fifteen. My grandfather would've been seventeen. But she ran away from home."

"Do you know why?"

"My grandma was special. Exceptional, I'd say. She felt things, knew things even before they happened. Do you know what I mean?"

"Yes."

"I guessed as much. Well, you'll understand when I tell you that she left because she knew she had to," he said, and leaned back. "She knew that to become the woman she was destined to be, she needed to leave home. She never told me where she went or what she did. That part of her life was just her own. I don't know if she ever told my granddad."

"Did your grandfather find her?"

"He sure did. He'd promised her pa that he'd keep looking. One day he got this idea to place an advertisement in the newspapers in Tacoma and Seattle. The ad was really simple, just his picture with only one line under it reading, *Angela, I love you. Richard.* The following week she knocked on his door."

"Just like that?"

"Just like that. I've always thought that my grandma planted that seed in his head when they were kids 'cause my granddad was not the type to think of things like that. It had to be her. Like I told you, she was special. Anyway, they married a few weeks later, and the rest, as they say, is history."

"Were they happy together?"

"Sure thing. They were devoted to each other, to their kids, and especially to us grandkids."

We finished our meal, and as I cleared the dishes, Conrad stood up and, without missing a beat, helped me clear the table. We put the leftovers in the fridge and the dirty dishes in the sink.

"You wash; I'll dry," he announced.

"Only if you keep talking. Tell me about your granddad."

"He was an uncomplicated man. I think I take after him 'cause I'm nothing like my dad or my mom. My father, Aidan, was drawn to adventure, and my mother went along just to please him."

"You have brothers and sisters?"

"I did, not any more. They're all gone. My brother, James, was killed in Vietnam, and my sister, Denise, died of lung cancer a few years back."

"How about other family, like uncles and aunts?"

"My uncle Brady was in India working in their fisheries port till the day he died about six years ago. He was an engineer and oversaw things for them. I don't think he would have known what to do with himself if he didn't work or wasn't inventing something or another. Like my dad he inherited the yearning for adventure from my grandmother. He never married. My aunts…" Conrad stopped for a minute as if his mind had wandered to some distant place. "Well, that's a story for another day." He dried his hands and hung the towel. "C'mon, let's build a nice fire in the living room."

"Want some coffee or tea?"

"Not now. You're spoiling me with all this good food you make. I'm thinking about having another piece of pie later on."

"Sounds like a plan."

We strolled into the living room. I could sense that Conrad had purposely avoided the topic of his aunts and wondered what had prompted him to do so.

In no time, he got a nice fire going, and we sat to enjoy it, along with the view of the snowed-in valley that surrounded my house, now softly illuminated by the porch lights.

"Tell me more about your parents," I urged.

"Let's see. After his college stint in Seattle, my father married and came back home, but having lived in the big city, he was unable to settle 'in the middle of nowhere,' as he used to call our valley. My dad lived through the Great Depression and swore to never experience that kind of harshness again. He had a strong entrepreneurial spirit that, coupled with the impact of World War II, evolved into a rebellious streak and a calling for wild adventures—a dangerous combination. He was killed in the Korean War, and my mother passed on soon after of a broken heart."

"How did you end up here?"

"After my dad died, Mother brought us kids to live here with our grandparents. I think she knew she wouldn't last long without him. We were very young. My grandparents are the ones that actually raised us. Our folks were just two people we saw in old photographs and heard stories about."

"How sad."

"It wasn't for us. I think we were happier living here rather than with the ups and downs of my folks. They used to argue most of the time, Dad wanting more from life and Mother holding him back. Grandma told us that life in time of sorrow had to skip a generation to find its joy again. She said that we were the joy that life brought back. My brother and sister inherited a bit of the adventuresome streak, but I never did. I was content here, like my granddad. I love this place. I joined the marines 'cause it was my duty, but I always knew this was my home."

"I can see that in you. Tell me about your grandfather."

"There's not much to tell. His life was simple and happy. He was a man among men. What I mean is that he personified all the good qualities a man should have in life and didn't boast about it. He just *was*. When James and I joined the marines, we knew we'd been raised just right. We used to write to one another reminiscing about the good old times we had with Granddad, like the conversations with him while fishing or horseback riding or herding or working the farm and tending to the animals. We particularly enjoyed the memories of our times in the store."

"Your granddad opened the store?"

"My grandma's idea altogether. Granddad was a good man who worked hard, loved hard, and made the best of his life the lives of his wife, kids, and grandkids. Our town was weakening after the mines closed down and the Depression hit. It only survived by reinventing itself, and my grandmother was right there in the middle of its newfound identity. At times I think she was the catalyst."

"Conrad, I have something to show you. Please wait a minute." I went to my bedroom and brought back Angela's books, the letter from her mother, her father's photograph, and the picture of her fourteenth birthday.

Conrad held them with such care and tenderness that my heart burst open. An overflow of emotion came rushing out of my eyes, especially when I noticed that Conrad was also quietly crying. We sat in silence for a long time while he looked at his grandmother's belongings.

At length he turned to me and said, "You should open your present now. It's from my grandmother."

He must've sensed my shock, because he tapped my hand and smiled. "I told you she was someone special. Go ahead, open it."

Carefully I opened the gift box. It was filled with empty picture frames of all sizes.

"The day before I left to join the marine corps, my grandma gave me this box and told me that one day I'd meet a woman who would understand her house and its memories. She asked me to take care of it until then. I've never looked inside the box. I've just been changing the wrapping every so often to make it look nice. I think you're the woman she spoke of. Do you know why she'd give you these old frames?"

"I think so," I whispered. "To care for the memories."

"Memories?"

The moment that I so dreaded had finally come. Everything was on the line. If I took the next step and told him about my experiences in the attic, he might bolt. But if I didn't tell him, then I'd be keeping a secret that would forever stand between us. More importantly, I would revert to the Sarah that never took risks. After all, Angela was his grandmother, and maybe I was the conduit for something critical for him and his family. Did I have the right to keep that from him? The clear answer was no, so I asked him, "Did you know that Angela left a bunch of photographs in the attic?"

"I knew there were some old trunks and stuff left behind. I figured that if you wanted them out, you'd tell me."

"I've been going through the photographs. That's how I found these things that belonged to your grandmother Angela." My throat tightened, my hands shook, I licked my lips, and I dove right in. "As I pick up a photo, I seem to be able to hear the story of the people in it."

He didn't react like I was crazy, he didn't leave, and he didn't look shocked. Instead, he listened and smiled.

"Guess I was right. You're the woman my grandmother expected."

CHAPTER 11

Christopher
1881

CONRAD MEASURED ALL the frames and said he would order nonreflective glass for each one to protect the photos that would reside within.

I felt relieved that he didn't think of me as a witch, creepy, or insane. As a matter of fact, none of the reactions that had driven my family to build a fortress around me and disavow a significant part of my makeup materialized.

Instead, hearing all about Angela had been comforting. I'd felt reassured by Conrad's memories, and therefore able to tell him about the photographs and their stories. However, these new experiences were so uncharacteristic of me that I kept waiting for the other shoe to drop and for my newfound valor to come crashing down. Years of denial and fear had caused a sizeable fracture in my personality, and even though I continued to piece it together, I could feel its fragility.

I'd gone to bed early and slept soundly till around four in the morning. After waking up, I'd stayed in bed, just as young Jeremy used to do. But instead of writing stories, I was hearing them, sensing them. This particular morning, I lay in bed immersed in Conrad's recollections of his grandparents, my ability to enter into the lives of those who'd lived in my house, and wondering what it all meant. I felt torn. On the one hand, terror still had a firm grip, and I dreaded that I might end up in an asylum, talking to my imaginary friends. On the other hand, I didn't want the magic to end. Most of all, I didn't want my old self to come back and yank away the enjoyment of the stories or the excitement of their discovery.

As I weighed all these emotions, all of sudden something stirred within me, whispered *All is well*, and egged me on. I stopped and listened to my thoughts. No, not thoughts, but those inner vibrations that we all feel but rarely listen to—the sensations that travel through our souls but that we can only sense when we truly pay attention.

The pretender, the untrusting and controlling Sarah, watched in silence while the hopeful, sensitive Sarah emerged, nudging her alter ego aside. Nevertheless, the cautious one remained vigilant, too entrenched and still uncertain about the impact of these experiences. Although I perceived that no real danger lurked around the next corner, fear still permeated my senses.

"Angela," I heard myself whisper into the early morning, "what do you want from me?" But no response came from out of the darkness. "I'm afraid," I murmured. "Will I lose my mind? Is this evil? Is this unnatural? Dangerous?"

Silence again…then a deep sigh escaped my lips, and I felt enveloped by a warm embrace that little by little filled me with inner strength and confidence.

"Thank you," I muttered.

I don't know why I said that, or what I'd perceived. Never had I felt something so pleasing travel through my body. It felt like a silent exchange of emotions, a deep understanding, an awareness that flowed through me, consoling and reassuring, like a soothing, fresh breeze whispering tranquility. I imagined myself asleep in the clouds, tenderly rolling about, my hair blowing in the softness of the wind, embraced by the blue sky. Then the clear understanding that I needed to achieve something, that my presence in this house had a special meaning, came into view. I sensed that something had to be exposed and that I had been chosen for the task.

A few hours later, I woke up with newfound courage, made myself a sweet cup of cinnamon coffee with warm milk, and went through the frames Angela had left for me. Picking the frame for her birthday photograph turned out to be an easy task. The night before, I'd laid out the frames on the dining room table to give them a little time to get used to their new surroundings. I imagined how eager they were to welcome the memories they would hold dear and protect for years to come. A bit of airing might suit them quite well, the way daily brisk walks did for me.

Conrad had not wanted to take Angela's photograph with him. He knew his grandmother wanted it to be in her old house. I placed her picture in the frame, and I could've sworn she smiled. I also framed her pa's picture and then took them upstairs to my room and set them down on top of my dresser.

But Angela disagreed. She wanted to be in her old bedroom, but that room no longer resembled what I'd imagined when she told me the story on her fourteenth birthday. I hoped she would approve.

Angela's former room now held a bit of me, a bit of my grandmother, a bit of my parents, a bit of the modern world, and a nice collection of the books I enjoyed reading. It was what the old me liked to call an office, and my new self had renamed as sanctuary. *Curious how the same space has different meaning when a person changes perspective.*

I heard Angela agree when I placed her picture next to my nana's photograph. She also approved of the placement of her pa's picture next to the ones of my parents. I knew I would find a photograph of her momma somewhere in the house, and soon she could join the family.

I made my way down to the kitchen, poured myself another cup of coffee, and joined my box of photos in the living room. Too early to visit my attic, it was still dark outside, and the attic was at its best with natural light. I placed the box on my lap and took out a picture that rested next to the one of the three sisters. It was a photograph of a handsome man with graying hair, proudly posing with a young woman and her son in the early 1880s. *Oh, how I love these old photographs.* This particular one had not spoken to me in the past, and I was about to put it down when I heard a familiar voice.

"Christopher had come to pay his respects."

It was Amy, bringing me back to the kitchen as she sat with her sisters, some twenty years before the picture I held in my hands was taken.

"He brought his camera with him. When he took our picture at the kitchen table, it irritated my sisters to such a degree that they actually lost their composure and screamed at him."

"Hello, Amy. I'm so glad to hear from you again," I whispered, and leaned back to enjoy her company.

"When I saw the picture of the three of us in the kitchen," she went on, "I felt relieved to see that I didn't look as shriveled as I thought. To be honest with you, ever since I had entered this house, I'd felt wonderful.

"I was now the proud owner of the house, not because I had coveted it but because she wanted me and not my sisters. Cora and Laura were still holding on tight to a past that hurt and didn't want to have anything to do with the house that reminded them of the pain. I had never allowed their anguish to stake a claim in me, so in the end it all worked out."

"What made it different for you?"

"Maybe it had to do with being in love. My sisters never found love. They had slammed shut the doors to their hearts, and only their grief and despair resided within.

"After we got married, Christopher and I had to move to his folks' house. It was a tight squeeze, especially after Christopher's widowed sister-in-law, Madeline, moved in with her two boys. Her husband had died in one the many accidents in the mines.

"Come to think of it, I suspect that worrying about Christopher was what had turned down the lights inside of me."

"Is that why you felt shriveled?" I asked Amy.

"If it hadn't been for my daughters, Annie and Claudia, who kept the glow shining, I think I would've just shut down. Twin daughters had been a wonderful gift for us, even though Christopher's father kept pushing for me to have boys. We were happy with our girls. I think I didn't have any more kids just to spite the old man and his dismissal of my daughters.

"We had married for love, unusual for the times, but not unusual for my family. Our love never waned, and our youngsters sure could feel it. I could see it in their eyes, and that was all that mattered. The pressure for me to produce boys into the family lessened when Madeline moved in with her boys. The four kids took to each other right away, and life got a bit easier for a while with one more hand to help around the house and two boys to help the men around the farm."

"That sounds good. I'm glad you were relieved."

"But the ease of life did not last long. Three grown women under one roof proved to be difficult. We each had our own ideas and our own ways of thinking and doing things, so the pressure eventually mounted.

"Christopher could feel it, and it worried him. It was a pressure he surely didn't need on top of his work in the mines, around the house, and on the farm. Since his father had been injured in the mines not long after we married, the welfare of the entire family rested on my husband's shoulders. You'd think he would complain about it, but he never did. He just went about his daily business, working, helping, and loving us. Every morning he kissed 'his girls,' as he called all the women in the house, patted the boys' heads and his father's shoulder, and then left with a smile as he winked at me. He knew I'd worry about him all day, and this little ritual was his way of reassuring me. I certainly appreciated it. I loved him dearly."

"How special to have found such love. Christopher sure looks handsome in this picture."

"When I inherited the house, he was anxious about leaving his parents and moving away, but in the end he knew it was the right thing to do for his little family. Our daughters were growing up and needed their space and a bit of distance from their cousins. They were reaching that age when boys and girls need to be apart or watched all the time."

"I understand."

"You can well imagine how angry I became when my sisters yelled at my husband."

"You mean when he took the picture of the three of you in the kitchen?"

"Yes. I don't think they had ever seen me that angry. I didn't yell or lose my temper. It wasn't that kind of anger. It was the anger that comes from deep, deep inside and just glares, with no forgiveness. 'How dare you yell at my husband like that? Please leave my house.' That's all I said, and they knew they had crossed a barrier that would never be taken down again."

"You broke with them completely?"

"Don't get me wrong; I do care for my sisters, but I'm in love with my husband. They knew that. They knew how much Christopher meant to me and what a wonderful man he was. They knew and didn't care. They just let their irritation get the best of them, and they hurt him with despicable, demeaning words.

"He didn't mind that they yelled at him. He told me later that he shouldn't have taken the picture given their history, but he wanted to keep the memory of our getting together after so many years of being apart from one another.

"That shows you the quality of man I married. Always thinking of others, always attentive to our needs, whether we knew what we wanted or not."

Amy sighed, and I looked at the photograph in my hand. I could see Christopher's kind face smiling at the camera as he held a little baby in his arms, with a proud young woman at his side. I knew exactly who they were, and moments later Amy confirmed it.

"Jeremy was but a week old when I took this picture. That's my Annie, his mom. Doesn't Christopher look wonderful with his gray hair?"

She knew I agreed.

Amy's formal introduction of Jeremy as a baby presented another piece of the puzzle of experiences. I didn't understand the purpose Amy had in mind as she introduced me to her daughter, husband, and Jeremy, especially as a baby. I'd already met Jeremy as a young boy, knew about the kind of life he'd lived, about his father and mother, his newborn baby sister, the farm, and his house. I had no doubt that informing me that Amy was Jeremy's grandmother carried with it a hidden intention, but what that entailed, I had no clue.

It occurred to me that if I drew a relationship diagram of the residents of my house, the interconnectedness between my new companions might emerge. The idea gripped me, and I spent the next few hours drafting it, only to discover that I had more questions than answers.

V. & D. Povall

First Family Tree - Residents of the Twin Houses

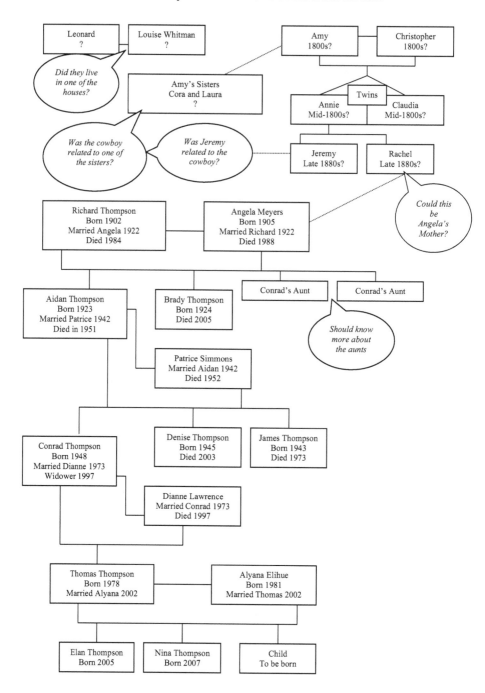

CHAPTER 12

Leonard
1850

AMY'S STORY GENERATED a myriad of questions I needed to ask Conrad when he came over for dinner. But my attic—or perhaps Angela—had other plans for me.

As soon as I opened the attic door, I heard mumbling from under a pile of old photographs. I'd looked through them several times before, and expectantly listened for their stories, but their age intercepted our exchange. The sepia in many of them had faded to such a degree that the people appeared to be vanishing, fostering the sensation that one could get lost in the ghostly images if one peered too deeply into their past.

Today was different, maybe because I'd changed. The memories Angela wanted me to hear touched me so deeply that my senses were raw, and hence, in harmony with the voices calling from the forgotten past. The images didn't appear ghostly anymore; instead they were appealing, somehow coming into focus as I observed them.

Careful not to blemish them, I went through each photograph until I found the one that called out to me. It seemed older than the rest and had lost most of its clarity. I could make out an elegant young woman standing on the porch, overlooking three little girls sitting on the steps, while an elderly lady sat on what appeared to be a rocking chair. They were all well appointed and tastefully dressed. The house resembled my house. I turned the photograph over and found a faded but still legible handwritten note: *1850 The Twin Houses.*

A deep, manly voice broke through. "Amy is different."

"Leonard, I do not see what the issue is. Whether she is yours or not is unimportant," responded the younger woman.

I gasped, coming into the realization that I was overhearing Louise and Leonard, the lovers in the first story I'd heard. The memory of the passion and desire they'd experienced was so vivid that it felt as if I were on the beach again, with Louise, the solitary woman whose hair danced in the wind, and with Leonard, whose likeness was yet to be revealed. I had not found Leonard's photograph in my past searches, nor did I have it now, yet his voice and presence permeated the attic.

"Cora and Laura are most definitely mine," Leonard insisted. "Their temperaments make that undeniable. Amy is different. You must tell me who her father is."

I took a deep breath, shocked at the discovery that Leonard and Louise were the parents of Amy and her sisters. A family lineage had just come into focus.

Still uneasy at hearing Leonard without seeing his image, I sensed his photograph awaited me. Careful not to startle Louise and her daughters, I placed their photo on my lap as I searched for Leonard through the remaining pictures. I knew he wanted to be heard and that his picture wanted to come out and join the one from Louise and the girls.

Delicately, I went through each photograph until I found his. It looked just as old, but I could make out that he was a handsome man with a thick mustache, proudly standing in front of the twin house, his hands clasping the lapel of his coat. Next to him was a little boy looking just as handsome, imitating his father's stance. I turned the photograph over and found the same handwritten note: *1850 The Twin Houses.*

"Well?" I heard Leonard ask Louise. "Will you answer my question?"

"There is no answer," Louise replied sharply. "You know perfectly well that I will never answer that question. As a matter of fact, it is impertinent of you to even ask it."

"Louise, you can be incredibly obstinate," Leonard uttered with restrained anger.

As I listened in, my heart pounded. I didn't like prying into this private moment between them, but they insisted on being heard. So I got out of the way, agreeing to listen and witness their exchange.

"Why here, Leonard? Why in this godforsaken wilderness?"

"God is in this 'wilderness,' as you call it," Leonard answered with determination. "It is here we will make our peace with God. We could not live together anywhere else in the world. You know that. At least here we are just two families in neighboring houses. You with our girls and Mother in one house, and me with my son in the other one."

"*Your* son. Not mine. You do not see me making a scene about him, do you? Leonard, you must understand that I cannot live so far from the city in this little house. Mother will drive me crazy, and the girls…well, the girls will be in the way."

"They are ours, at least two of them are. We must care for them. Mother will help; she will give them the love you refuse to give, and maybe one day, hopefully, you will care for them—and Ethan. None of us have any choice."

"You do. You will have solitude and peace when you are in your house across the valley—just you and your boy. We, of course, will cater to the two of you, freeing you of the pressures we females have to endure. On the other hand, I will be stuck in this hellhole with Mother and three demanding children."

Louise paused. I could hear her breathing, and Leonard's pacing, and suddenly I saw them face-to-face in their bedroom, replaying a scene they had performed many times already.

With renewed determination she faced Leonard and went on. "Why build the two houses exactly the same? Why taunt me so? Why put me through this?"

"Louise, you are getting on my nerves. Stop this nonsense. You know perfectly well that since Mother found out about us, her mind is weakening. Being away from all acquaintances will help us all."

"You say that, but I do not understand how," Louise snapped.

"Here we go again." Leonard responded with imposed patience. "The children are little, and they will not take in the details of our exchange. Both houses were built and furnished exactly the same. The perfect symmetry will permit us to exchange with less notice. As time goes by, the girls and Ethan will get used to it, and we will have more freedom to be with one another. We are far from town, and we will be able to live as we have chosen. I have told you this time and again. Mother has accepted—"

"Do not be fooled," Louise spat back. "Mother has chosen to ignore it. Her soul cracked with the pain of what we are. Do not be deceived. Her mind is not weakening. She has chosen to repair that crack by turning it toward the wall. Just as she did with the vase she had on the mantle. Remember how you dropped and chipped it? She simply turned the defect away from view. Problem solved."

"I do. That is why we are here, away from view. Use her example to help you do the same. Accept what is and look the other way. Be thankful for your mother. At least she loves the girls and Ethan. God knows they need the love you refuse to give."

I heard Louise take a deep and exasperated breath. She walked away from him, torn between the need to leave, and the desire to be with him.

"I must know, Louise. Who is Amy's father? I thought you were faithful to me."

Louise spun to face him. "Faithful? You, who married another? You, who insisted on taking me and gave me children? You, who—"

"Enough! Stop! You know our marriages were for appearances."

"Your 'appearances' produced a child. Your 'appearances' made me marry Anthony. Your 'appearances' brought on the death of your wife. Have you come to terms with that?"

"Her suicide is a burden I will carry to my grave."

"Then do not accuse me and demand faithfulness. You chose the husband I married."

"Is Anthony the father? You told me he refused to touch you after you foolishly told him on your wedding night that you were carrying my child."

"Did I?"

"Louise, do not toy with me."

"Leonard, you tore me apart when you made me yours. The leftover shreds of my soul are mine and only mine. I will not share any of them with you. I must have something of my own to keep me alive in this wasteland you have brought us to."

I sensed that Leonard's patience was exhausted. His breathing was rapid, his tension palpable.

"Louise, I have given up my past life as well. In our exile I have poured all my love into making these houses agreeable for the children and us. This is a beautiful place, and life amid the Cascades, in our twin houses, is far from being a wasteland."

Leonard took a deep breath, and his demeanor shifted. "In time," he said at length, "I am sure you will learn to love our houses and to love your daughters and even Ethan. You will learn to enjoy our new life in this beautiful valley. Please tell me you will at least try." His voice cracked.

"Do not look at me like that. You know I cannot bear to see you this way."

With Louise's last whisper, the attic fell silent. I waited for a long time to see if either of them would come back, but they didn't.

I was left dumbfounded, unable to grasp the true meaning of what they had revealed. Are Leonard and Louise related to one another? Cousins? Brother and sister? No, that can't be. Can it? Did he rape her? Is that what she implied? Yet, she seemed so willing when I first met her. She protested but she didn't refuse.

"Please come back, tell me more." I blurted out.

Silence was their answer.

Resigned, I went down to my kitchen to fix supper. Conrad had invited me out to dinner, but I liked cooking for him, and he enjoyed what I prepared, so in the end we'd agreed to eat at home.

While fixing our meal, I thought about the unusual birth of my house and its twin, and how it mirrored the births of Amy and her sisters. The girls and their stepbrother were just as unwanted and as alive as the houses. I imagined the difficult childhood of the four children and understood the resentment Amy's older sisters had developed. I marveled at Amy's forgiving spirit and wondered if Leonard might be right that Amy wasn't his daughter. Without doubt, she'd overcome her lot in life, and maybe her "difference" was simply that she wasn't Leonard's child. I wondered if Louise had treated her differently, and that was the reason she'd grown to be so strong.

When Conrad arrived, it didn't take long for him to notice that something had affected me. I was so emotionally brittle that I offered no resistance to his inquiries and showed him the photographs of Leonard with Ethan and of Louise with her mother and three daughters. I told him the story I'd witnessed.

He smiled and caressed my hand. This kind, simple gesture sent shivers through my body.

"I'll be darned! You have a bit of my grandmother in you." His smile filled my soul with pleasure and immense gratitude. At least he didn't think I was a nutcase making up stories from old photographs.

"Angela's great-grandmother," he went on, "was named Amy. I don't know much about their history, but it looks like you've tapped into it. Just as my grandma used to tap into things unknown to others."

This revelation offered so freely and without judgment disconcerted me. I didn't know what to make of it. In complete contrast from what I'd experienced as a child, Conrad not only didn't find me bizarre, but also he saw this antenna of mine as normal. In fact, my ability to tap into real moments in these people's lives didn't astonish him whatsoever. On the contrary, he reveled in the similarities between his grandmother and me. With him I had no need to be fearful, no need to run away, no need to pretend I couldn't feel and experience these moments. I fell silent, and Conrad understood my desire for self-reflection.

"Don't be frightened," Conrad said after a while, offering a comforting presence. "There are many things one notices in passing that for some reason don't become part of our conscience or thoughts. Then, when we least expect them, they pop up in our imaginations or our dreams or our thoughts. You may have seen her name somewhere, and it rang a bell. It could be just as simple as that."

"When you look at these pictures, do you recognize them? Is there any family resemblance?" My question was one of hope more than curiosity.

"No, but I must tell you that I like the stories you're tapping into. I think you're a good storyteller, mostly because you care about folks. You listen intently. I've seen you do that."

"You think me crazy because I hear stories coming out of these old photographs?"

I blurted out the one question I feared the most, not even hesitating for a second before asking it. Now, it hung between us in its naked truth, and I wished I could take it back. If he said yes, what would I do then?

"No, not at all." He offered a simple response in all of its proud honesty.

I stared at him, not knowing what else to say.

He smiled and reached for my hand again. "Don't forget that I was raised by Angela, a woman with special sensitivity. I don't know what to make of it, how it works, or why. I believe there are people like her in this world that can experience things that others can't. You are one of those people."

"People like that are thought to be crazy or witches or worse—evil, or something awful."

"Only by folks that don't have open minds. It certainly didn't affect my grandmother. She didn't hide her abilities, didn't flaunt them either. They just were there."

"But I've never allowed this to happen, quite the contrary. This is all new. Very new to me."

"Then, congratulations on having found whatever it is that makes you who you are now. Hope you enjoy it as much as my grandmother did."

I looked at him with sincere amazement, and he burst out laughing. "Don't fuss over it. Are you happy with this newfound gift?"

"I'm still frightened, but I don't seem to be able to stop."

"Then just enjoy it. Don't overanalyze it; don't dissect it. Just go with it as you have done so far."

"But at times it's frightening. Can you imagine what it's like to be engaged in conversations with people long gone? I don't know if I can keep on doing this. Where does it end? What's going to happen? I'm not used to being out of control. That's what scares me the most. Sometimes I even think that it is best to stop and just go back to the way things were. It's like being on a roller-coaster of emotions and experiences."

I must've frowned, because he reached and caressed my forehead. "Let's bring the Sarah I know back. Send this worrisome Sarah away." He grabbed my hands, pulled me toward the door, and added, "C'mon, you need a bit of airing."

Second Fmily Tree - Residents of the Twin Houses

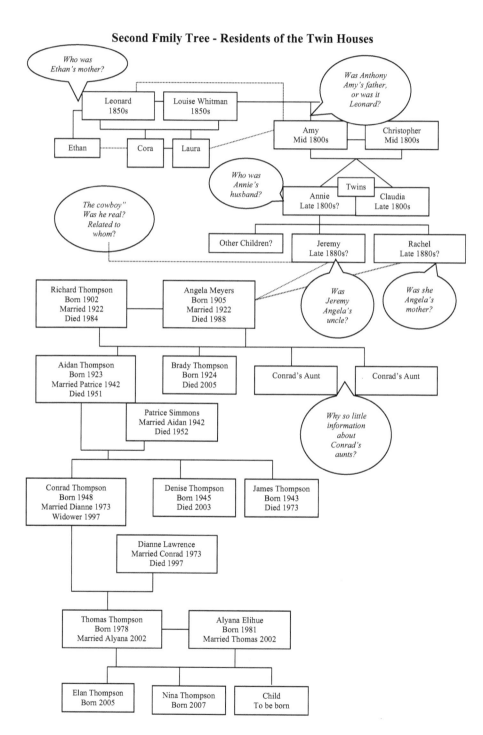

CHAPTER 13

Nana

WITHOUT A DOUBT, Angela had given me the exact number of frames for the pictures she wished me to care for. However, the photos far outnumbered the frames, so how to choose? Obviously the selected ones would have to make themselves known to me, but as I looked through them, they all remained silent. They were intimating that I needed to tend to something or someone else that wished to be heard. No idea what it could be, but I didn't let the unknown bother me. My newfound self trusted that whatever needed attention would come knocking in due time, and I'd be ready to open the door, the one to the attic, the one to the house, or the one to my soul.

So I turned to my mother's cookbook that had been a wonderful companion in the last few weeks, offering many recipes much to Conrad's delight, and as I looked for something new to bake for him, the man himself knocked on the door. It was midmorning, and his unexpected arrival jolted me. He certainly was not the one I expected to come knocking today, especially this early.

So the *old* insecure Sarah popped in, and at once I worried about my appearance, about what I was wearing, how my hair was combed. My stomach tightened up. I had no idea how I looked. I couldn't remember how I had combed my hair or if I wore any makeup. Busy tending to my photographs, I'd ignored my own care.

"So be it," I told myself and opened the door, hoping he'd look somewhere else except at me.

Unfortunately, I gasped so loudly, he had no choice but look at me as he laughed.

"Gosh, Sarah, it's just a Christmas tree, not a monster."

"Sorry, please come in. You surprised me."

"Well that's just what I was hoping for, but I didn't mean to scare you."

He came in and placed the tree in front of the bay window in the living room. It was a beautiful, fresh Christmas tree, and it looked majestic by the window. I heard the house creak a little as she sighed with pleasure.

"Looks good here, don't you think? The house needs its Christmas fixings." He winked. "She's been alone for too long."

"I haven't decorated for Christmas in years," I said, more to myself than to Conrad.

"How come?"

"I've been alone for some time, and it just didn't seem worth the trouble."

"No decorations?"

"I have a few boxes that I've kept from when I celebrated Christmas with my family. Haven't opened them in a long time."

"Well then, they need airing."

He walked to the front door, and before he opened it, he turned toward me and smiled.

"How about I come over tonight with a ham and we decorate the tree? I have some decorations from my family that might be happier here than at my place."

My heart leaped so high I was afraid it would hit the ceiling and shatter into little pieces. But it just stayed high, hovering over both of us, warmly held in the safety of my house.

"Sounds wonderful," I uttered.

"See you around six then."

He winked at me. He looked so charming and debonair when he winked.

"You look beautiful today. I like your hair done like that," he said as he closed the front door behind him.

I ran upstairs to look in the mirror of my dresser. I had left my hair loose, having simply pinned the sides just above my ears, and it did look nice. It made me appear a bit younger. I didn't have any makeup on, yet somehow it didn't matter. I looked just fine.

The Gift of the Twin Houses

Quite content with myself, I went to the empty bedroom where all the things that hadn't been unpacked were tucked away. In point of fact, these boxes hadn't been opened in many years. Some time ago I'd decided to have a bit more order in my life, so every year I put away anything that I hadn't touched or seen or used during that year. I'd packed several boxes that way, and they remained so. Peculiar behavior, but nonetheless, that's exactly what I'd done to declutter my life.

I'd inherited knickknacks and some decorative pieces from my family; items that had meaning to them but were of less importance to me. Or so I thought back then; now I looked forward to reacquainting myself with my very own memories. The new Sarah would certainly see them in quite a different light.

There weren't many boxes, maybe eight or nine. My family wasn't the kind that gathered things. They'd been a practical bunch, and I'd always been thankful for that, and the practical streak in the family had taken deep roots in the old Sarah.

I found two boxes labeled *Christmas,* took them downstairs, and placed them near the Christmas tree. As I started back up the stairs to look through the other boxes, I decided to wait. First, I wanted to bake something special for Conrad.

I went back to my mother's cookbook, and that's when my nana came knocking—the memory my house wanted me to listen to today.

In her light French accent, she suggested we bake a *Tarte de Mademoiselle Tatin.* The tart was her specialty, and she always baked it during the Christmas holidays, actually every day in December. When I arrived home from school, she would've baked a fresh tart, and we'd eat a slice accompanied by a glass of milk while we made our Christmas decorations for that year or gifts for friends and family.

Her recipe had been in her family for years, having changed from the original *Tarte de Mademoiselle Tatin,* which is an upside-down apple pie, to a stylized delicate apple tart. She made it with a thin, crisp layer of mille-feuille pastry, real cream, sugar, and thinly sliced apples. The slight crust and the delicate combination of the right amount of cream, sugar, and the slender apple slices gave the tart its subtle and unique flavor.

Today, ensconced in my new home and in the company of my nana, I baked a tart and reminisced. It turned out to be a magical day. Nana remembered how much she loved baking side by side with her own mother and grandmother and how difficult it had been for her to leave Marseille when she married my grandfather.

She'd married for love, a young Spanish attorney vacationing in her hometown. The daughter of a wealthy merchant, her family's requirements for a suitable husband were quite high, but as luck would have it, my grandfather also came from a wealthy family with outstanding credentials. As a result, there had been no opposition to their union. After the wedding they settled in Madrid at his family's residence.

Living the life of luxury on a large Spanish estate proved to be difficult for Nana, who was used to having much independence. Being the middle child among seven brothers and sisters, her parents, grandparents, and siblings left her to her own devices most of the time.

Spain, particularly Madrid, was different. They watched over her constantly, her entire day was planned to perfection by her mother-in-law, and her every move assisted by a myriad of servants and chaperones.

"Nana, how did you escape to America?" I asked, as I had many times before, but I feared that even today she wouldn't tell me. We'd never talked about her family or my grandfather's relatives. "They are dead to me," she would say. "You are my family." Today seemed no different, or so I thought.

After a moment, she sighed and said, "My parents disinherited and discarded me. They were ashamed of my audacity to leave my husband and take his child away. They couldn't forgive the disgrace I'd brought upon the family. My heart shattered into little pieces. I loved the home of my youth. The memories of those times supported me through the first years of living in Madrid. When they yanked that away from me, I knew it was up to me to create my own memories. I picked up the pieces and never looked back."

"What about my grandfather? Did he ever forgive you?"

I didn't expect her to answer. She never had before, but it wouldn't hurt to ask. After all, I'd changed; maybe she'd notice and be more open.

"Ah, *ma chérie*, I loved your grandfather when we married, and I am certain he loved me. But time apart from one another and the pressures of society got in the way. In the end, ideology broke the link between us. *C'est dommage.*"

"I guessed that's what had happened, but you never told me the story."

"Your mother Antonia was born ten months into the marriage, and the entire Spanish household focused on this child. My in-laws doted over their new granddaughter, but other than the child, they had little in common with me. My husband and his father traveled on business most of the time, leaving me with a mother-in-law who didn't understand my ways or agree with how I wished to raise my child."

I could imagine how the alienation of this young French bride increased year after year.

"During the Second Spanish Republic," she said, "your grandfather and his family became tightly associated with the leadership of the emerging socialist political party, the *Falange,* so one day I ran away. I left Fascist Europe with my daughter Antonia and came to America."

"Why not speak of it before?"

"We didn't speak of it, *ma petite,* because you had sensed it. You had 'guessed,' as you use to call it, what had taken place, so I decided to leave it at that. That spiritual antenna of yours is quite impressive, you know. Too bad we never spoke of it after you put it away. Anyway, the link between your grandfather and me just faded away."

Stunned by her willingness to speak about my grandfather, I held my breath when she paused, unwilling to startle her. I remained silent for what seemed to be an eternity. She didn't mind, lost in her own memories, so we focused on the tart and enjoyed each other's silent company as we prepared the mille-feuille pastry.

For most of my life, I hadn't known my grandfather's name. We simply never spoke of him. It wasn't till after my mother passed away and I found her birth certificate among her papers that I learned his name was Alfonso.

I didn't dare mention his name to Nana for fear she would recoil and leave me. But as I thought of him, she whispered, "Alfonso loved my tart," and like a young girl, she giggled.

"Did you bake for him often?"

"As you know we met during Christmas, and I baked it for him while he visited friends in Marseille. *C'était merveilleux*. Once we married and moved to Madrid, I tried to bake it for him, but they would not allow me to enter the kitchen. Not becoming to my social station in life, they told me, *vraiment absurde*."

She looked at me with a twinkle in her eye and said, "I am sure you are going to tell me how hypocritical it was for them to belong to a national socialist movement and yet stand on ceremony about my baking a tart for my husband in the kitchen."

I smiled, and she went on. "Now you're mature enough to understand why I could not live the lie they wished me to embrace in their hypocritical existence. Coming to America gave me back my honor and a new start in life with the freedom I craved."

"Why won't you tell me how you came all the way from Spain?" I dared to ask.

"There are things in life, *mon chou*, that must be set aside and forgotten. Not necessarily to run away from them, but because remembering them, and giving them life again through the telling of their stories, serves no purpose. If I thought something purposeful could come of my telling you the story, I would."

I wasn't pleased with her answer and still wished to know how she'd managed, but I didn't want to push too hard for fear she would leave.

"I know you want to know the details, but I think it is best if you don't remember me in that light. Don't try to discover them with those abilities of yours either. It's no good. You won't find them. That part of my life is gone. The memories of me that will last you forever are those of the woman I became in America. The nana you lived with is who I am. *Plus rien est important*."

"But you wouldn't have come to America had you not been the happy and independent little girl you were in Marseille, the beautiful young lady who fell in love with Alfonso, and the woman who refused to live in Madrid. All of that is what makes you."

"Yes, you're right, but those simple elements are all that is to be known. The rest is not important or significant. Arriving in America is what enabled me to become who I was destined to be, who I wanted to be. The details of the road I traveled to get there are not important."

We put the tart in the oven, and as I washed the utensils, she said, "Your arrival to this house has had the same effect for you."

"I'm scared, Nana."

"I know you are, *ma petite*. Do not be afraid of what this new life of yours will offer. Fear paralyzes. Look at what happened when your parents panicked and built a fortress around you."

"They didn't know what else to do. I can't blame them."

"Oh, *ma chérie*, this is not about blame. I joined in, remember? How could I blame anyone? *Non, non,* I became part of the means to protect you. Unfortunately, in the end, our efforts forced you to become someone you were not destined to be. We learned a difficult lesson about giving into fear."

"Hard not to, Nana."

"I know. Imagine how I felt when I left Europe."

She allowed me to reflect in silence. I saw her determination, and how she'd managed to create a new life without any reservations, without boasting about it, and with great courage.

"*Ma petite*, this is not about me, but about you. You have not opened your heart to a man since you were left at the altar many years ago and—"

"I brought that on myself. Fear of intimacy, didn't he say? But you know it wasn't that. I didn't want him to find out about my—"

"*Oh, non, non.* It no longer matters what the reasons were. The fact is that fear shut you down. Now it is time you open up. Trust your instincts, *mon chou*. Do not shut down again."

"Spiritual antenna up?"

"Let it fly in the wind."

I had my hands in the warm water, and I felt the gentle caress of my nana's hands intermingling with mine. "You're saying all of this because of Conrad."

"I am."

"What if he finds out I'm an old maid? A virgin at fifty-six. How shameful. He'll be horrified. He'll reject me. I couldn't bear the pain."

"Ah, the pain of rejection. Fear again."

"I can't help it. I'm too old for this."

"You do not believe that. I know you have feelings for this man, unlike any other man before. Am I right?"

"Yes."

"No fear about your uniqueness with him, am I right?"

"Yes. No fear of that anymore."

"And that is due to what, may I ask?"

"He understands all about it. Why are you asking me these things? You know all about it already."

"But you don't seem to. This man is different."

I sighed, unable to argue with her.

"If he has no difficulty with the one thing you were the most fearful of, why not trust him with the rest? Give it all a chance."

"But Nana, I'm a middle-aged virgin. It's pathetic."

"*Pas du tout, mon amour.* This new Sarah, as you call her, is the Sarah that should be," she added while clasping my hands under the warm water. "Allow her to evolve. No need to look back and regret what the old Sarah was or did. The past is just that—past, gone. No need for shame in your virginity. Think of it as an asset if you wish and—"

"An asset? You're joking."

"Not at all."

"Impossible."

"It will be up to you, but please don't shut yourself up. Why not take a risk?"

"But—"

"Hush. No more 'but' or anything other than courage. *Alors je m'en vais. Bon soir, ma chérie.* Look ahead to your new life and newfound freedom, just as I did."

I felt her kiss my cheek and release my hands, and I knew she would be forever present.

CHAPTER 14

The Christmas Tree

"The house smells delicious. What did you bake?" were the first words Conrad uttered when he entered the house.

"Tarte de Mademoiselle Tatin. My nana used to bake it throughout December in celebration of the Christmas holidays."

"She was French?"

"From Marseille, the southern part of France."

"Boy, what a treat, a French dessert. Here's the ham, but I'd like to skip dinner and just jump to dessert."

"C'mon. I'm sure you'll change your mind once we get the ham going. I also made some potatoes au gratin and some buttered veggies that I hope you'll like. By waiting for the tart, you'll like it even better when we get to it. Want to join me in the kitchen while I get the ham ready?"

He smiled, and as usual, we eased into each other's company as we sipped a glass of wine and I prepared the ham.

After we finished in the kitchen, we made our way to the living room and the Christmas tree.

"If you show me your Christmas decorations, I'll show you mine," he said with a wink.

*Mm...*I loved how he did that, a simple gesture, yet so evocative. As for me, I blushed—another habit I seemed to have picked up when he was around. *Do all young women feel like I do now?*

The silliness of some of my friends in high school always puzzled me. My youth had been absorbed by my mother's intellectual focus, and I just skipped the "ridiculous" period, as she used to call it. Now I dove right into it.

We each opened our boxes, and one by one we took out the ornaments.

"Did you make all these ornaments?" he asked.

"My nana did, with my mother at first and then with me. Every Christmas we made a different ornament for the tree, or to decorate our home, or to give away as a present."

"We did much the same with Grandma Angela. These were made by her, first with her kids and then with us grandkids."

"My nana also ran away from home."

"Did she, now?"

He could see that I wanted to talk about my nana, so he obliged me by asking about her, and I told him her story. Easy to do since I'd just relived it alongside her. I didn't stop to try to remember events, didn't hesitate, and didn't skip any detail. I enjoyed talking about my nana's newfound freedom in America. One thing I did keep to myself—her advice to the new Sarah. Not because I wanted to hide it from him, but because I needed to become more acquainted with it before I shared it.

By the end of Nana's story, the ham was ready, and we shifted into another effortless conversation during dinner. As we prepared for dessert, he spoke about his late wife, Dianne.

"I met her when I was stationed in Quantico, Virginia, and just as your nana moved to Spain to be with her husband's family, Dianne moved back here with me after we left the East Coast. She never got used to the Northwest style of living though. She just couldn't take to it."

"Was Angela alive?"

"Sure. Grandma knew how hard it was for Dianne and tried to help her adjust, but Dianne just couldn't do it. She gave it a good try, but the wilderness and the isolation from the big city proved too much for her to bear. Her heart longed for the life of her youth, surrounded by the many things city life offered. After a particularly cold winter, and given her state of mind, her lungs just gave up, so Doc suggested a change of air to help her recover faster. She went back East to stay with her parents and never returned. Grandma said her body would've given up, causing her to die young if she'd stayed here. Her lungs took her where her heart belonged, where she could be whole again."

"That's so sad. How did you cope? How did Tom cope? How old was he?" I was so taken by his story that I sat on the edge of my chair and must've looked overwhelmed, because he got up and kissed my cheek. I, of course, turned crimson as waves of electricity shot through my body.

"Thanks" was all he said and sat down again.

"Thanks for what?" I blurted out. "My God, Conrad, you're so together. I never would've guessed you'd lived with such grief, and Tom being so young."

"Don't fret. Remember that Tom and I had Angela and Richard at our side. He was six when his mother left. She'd already distanced herself while she lived here, so neither of us felt her true absence. We had Grandpa and Grandma, and they made it easy for us. To be honest with you, knowing Dianne was healthier with her folks and her old life was better than watching her shrivel up before of our very eyes."

"Why didn't you remarry?" The question just popped out. No sooner had I asked than I wanted to hide under the table and withdraw it.

But he didn't look bothered or offended. "She was my wife, absent, but my wife nonetheless. She didn't remarry either. We just respected our union and our need to be on opposite sides of the country. By the time she passed away, I'd gotten used to being on my own and just didn't think of marrying again."

When he finished answering my impolite, nosy question, I realized I'd painted myself into a corner, and panic set in. Now he would certainly ask me why I was a spinster. Maybe not in so many words, but the question would intimate the same concept. *I need to get away and change the conversation before he asks.*

"I think it's time for the tart. I'll bring it in. Just be a minute in the kitchen." I made a quick escape. By the time I reached the kitchen, my breathing came in spasms, and I was on the verge of hyperventilating. I didn't want him to even imagine my lonely and uneventful life. I didn't want to see myself that way, and the *old* Sarah wasn't someone I wished to introduce to him. I ran the warm water in the sink and placed my hands under it, hoping to feel my nana's warmth and reassurance.

"Can I help?" Conrad stood right behind me.

"Oh, you startled me. Please, go back and sit down. I can handle this bit. Just getting some water to warm the knife so that I can cut the tart," I managed to say, and surprised myself by how cleverly I'd gotten out of my juvenile panic attack.

"I'd rather be here with you. I'll hold it down while you cut," he said as he smiled.

So I warmed the knife, cut a piece of the tart, and put it on a plate.

Conrad, fork in hand, picked up the plate and took the long-anticipated first bite.

"Sorry, I just couldn't wait," he said with a mouthful.

I watched his face as he savored the tart. I hadn't tasted it and hoped it was as good as my nana's. Then I saw *him* blush.

"I've never tasted anything so delicious. Oh boy! It's...no words can describe it." He took another bite, then another, and another. "It's embarrassing the feelings it brings up," he said as he blushed with pleasure. "Aren't you going to have any?" he asked between bites.

"Yes. Sorry, I didn't mean to stare at you like this. It's just wonderful to see you enjoy it so much." I took a bite and felt myself redden as well. I closed my eyes and savored the memories that flashed through me.

Nana had invaded our senses.

When I recovered, I asked, "Would you like coffee, tea, or hot chocolate?"

"What did you drink when you ate the tart with your nana?"

"Milk."

"Then milk it is."

We took our milk along with the rest of the tart to the living room and settled in to enjoy our dessert and the memories the ornaments evoked.

We spent the rest of the evening slowly decorating our Christmas tree. He would pick up an ornament and share its story, and then I'd do the same.

We reminisced how our grandmothers had shared with us how to make little reindeer out of clothespins, Christmas characters out of small pieces of wood, wreaths of yarn or leaves and pinecones, silver bells out of cans, angels out of cotton, and many, many, more.

Our ornaments were not spectacular or exquisitely made. They were awkward, imperfect, and absolutely wonderful. They reflected the love and happiness each and every one experienced when they were created.

Conrad had placed a couple of strings of Christmas lights before we decorated the tree, and when we were done hanging all the ornaments, he suggested we step back to admire the tree before we turned the little lights on.

"Two completely different households made these ornaments, and they're compatible. Isn't that something?" And he reached for my hand.

My heart skipped. His hand was warm and soft. I felt my hand gently close on his, and enjoyed the hold he had on me.

"Yes," I whispered, "they're comfortable with one another."

"Like us."

He turned, tenderly drew me toward him, and kissed me.

A kiss of love, a kiss of tenderness, a kiss that lasts an eternity. I felt transported to heaven, suspended inside the sensation of unconditional love, enchantment, and eternal bliss.

When our lips separated, our eyes met and said all we needed to say to one another. We smiled in recognition of our silent exchange and turned to see our tree as he slid his arm around my waist and held me close to him.

"It's the most beautiful Christmas tree in the world." I rested my head on his shoulder.

"Certainly in our world. Ready for the lights?"

I nodded, and he turned on the lights. The house sighed with delight.

"Did you hear that?" I asked.

"Yep."

We snuggled on the sofa, his arm around my shoulders, and for a while, silently enjoyed our tree.

"I think our grandmothers would like our tree," I said.

"Would you make another tart for tomorrow and for every day until Christmas, just like your nana used to do?"

"Of course. But you'll have to come over every day to enjoy it."

"That's the point, isn't it?"

We finished our evening welcoming love into our hearts.

CHAPTER 15

Alyana

WHEN CONRAD LEFT that magical night, he offered to bring outdoor Christmas lights the next day to dress up the house. If he left work no later than two, there would be plenty of daylight remaining to hang them. Our good-bye kiss had been gentle and tender, sharing the knowledge of many more to come.

I slept the sleep of a child, unencumbered by the problems life sends our grownup way, unburdened by the insecurities of an adult mind, free of worries and apprehension, at peace with the world around me.

The next morning I woke up refreshed and full of energy. I had so much to look forward to. I turned on the Christmas-tree lights, sat there, sipped my coffee, and enjoyed the silence of the early winter morning. What a glorious time of day, when only my dreams lingered and I could hear the little noises of the house and its surroundings as they lazily woke up.

I enjoyed the sparkling Christmas tree in silence for at least an hour before the morning sun began to rise and caress the high branches of the trees, its rays bringing with them the gift of life and warmth. Sunrise in the Cascades is a masterpiece of colors and sounds that merge into a remarkable symphony that penetrates every pore in one's body. Sometimes it presents itself in gray tones with muted sounds, other times silently dancing in the whiteness of the snow, and at times bursting in so many colors that its rhapsody infiltrates the core of one's being. Today was such a morning, filled with colors, its shine caressing my house and my soul.

At fifty-six I was falling in love like a teenager and experiencing those emotions I'd only heard my friends talk about. I'd never actually fallen in love before—too frightened to open myself up to such risky feelings that just might unleash that antenna of mine. I'd tiptoed around them to fit in, even going as far as accepting a marriage proposal, only to pull away again. After that debacle, I'd only read about love, witnessed it in the eyes of newlyweds, saw it in the movies, or observed it in countless couples that walked by me hand in hand. Now, I'd given myself completely to the bliss and tenderness that genuine love offered.

Even so, the dread and insecurity of losing it were also present. The old Sarah would've given into this fear and run away to keep me safe and secure. These types of feelings are too dangerous. *They're uncontrollable*, she would've said and spent hours going over the millions of what-ifs destined to ruin any hint of happiness and love—all in the name of preserving the fortress around me that kept the antenna under wraps. The new Sarah, however, wouldn't run away. Instead, she fully embraced these emotions, comfortable with their contradictions, willing to travel the paths ahead, whatever might come.

I went about my day content and filled with anticipation. I played a CD from my Neil Diamond collection and did my chores singing along as I'd done many times before. However, this time something felt different, quite different actually. All of a sudden, I realized that as I sang along, I felt the lyrics. *How about that?* Before, I had intellectually heard the words, but today, I experienced them. *What a delight to be part of a love song and surrender to its soft embrace.*

I finished baking a couple of tarts, and as I was about to take one to the store for Alyana and Tom, the doorbell rang. Alyana stood there with her little ones.

"Hi, Sarah. Papa said to come by and see the Christmas tree. Is this a good time?"

"Of course, come right in. I was about to leave to go down to the store and give Tom a tart I baked for you. You saved me a trip. Hope you like it. My nana used to bake it every Christmas. "

The little ones ran into the house as we stood by the front door exchanging adult greetings. By the time I closed the door, they were already in front of the tree admiring it.

"Thanks. It sure smells nice, this tart of yours. Papa couldn't stop talking about it this morning. French, he said."

"It's almost time for lunch; could you all stay? I can fix some sandwiches, and then we can have a bite of tart with milk for dessert."

"We don't want to impose, Sarah. We just came by to take a quick peek at the tree. Papa's so proud of it. He hasn't put up a Christmas tree since Tom and I got married. We're both real happy that he's back into the swing of Christmas again."

After a bit of coaxing, she agreed to stay. Elan and Nina were literally spellbound as our Christmas ornaments worked their magic on them. I took a couple of ornaments from the tree and gave one to each. "This one I made when I was little with my grandmother, whom I called Nana. It looks like a Christmas present, doesn't it? Can you guess what's inside?" I asked Nina as I handed it to her. "This one, your papa made when he was little. It's a reindeer." Elan took it and smiled as I asked, "Can you guess what it's made of?"

"Yeah. Wood and berries for eyes. Right?"

"Be real careful with them," Alyana cautioned.

"It's all right Alyana; don't worry. They're pretty sturdy. You're right, Elan. Your papa made that one with your great-grandmother Angela."

"Wow, old."

While we fixed lunch, the children kept themselves entertained guessing how all the ornaments were made and which grandmother or great-grandmother had helped make them. We ate in the living room in front of the Christmas tree as I told them the story of each ornament.

"These angels my nana and I made with some pretty white satin cloth, and we sewed some beautiful white lace on top."

"Eyes closed. Why?" Nina ran her little fingers over their eyes.

"I was about eight when we made them and had just learned how to sew. You can see that their eyes are just a few stitches made with red thread."

"They're singing," Elan announced.

"Yes, how did you know?"

"Their mouths are like this." She puckered her lips.

Nina ran her finger over their mouths. "I can't hear them."

"If you imagine they're singing, then you can hear whatever song you wish, like the song that's now playing. Can you hear them singing it?"

Elan laughed. "That's silly, Sarah. They're not singing; it's the CD."

I turned the music off and asked again. "Now can you imagine them singing?"

Nina put the ornaments close to her ears. "Yeah."

Elan laughed and shook his head. "No you can't either, it's just—"

"It's about imagining," I interrupted before his sister jumped on him, "not actually hearing. Just as you do when you play with your toys."

"I guess."

"My nana and I used to listen to Christmas songs and sing along as we made the ornaments, so we just imagined our little angels were singing. If you let your imagination go, you can believe anything you wish. Right?"

He shrugged. "Maybe."

"Yes, you can," his sister insisted with both angels glued to her ears.

I took two reindeer ornaments from the tree. "This is the ornament I first gave you, and this other one was also made by your papa. Can you tell me the difference between them?"

"This one is made with clothespins, his eyes are buttons, and his clothes are glued, not painted." He paused as he examined the reindeer. "It's Rudolf! It has a soft red nose."

"You're great at seeing the difference. Now, imagine that Rudolf meets this other reindeer on the road and—"

"What's his name?" Nina joined in.

"I don't know. Papa didn't tell me, but we can make one up for now."

"Peter," Elan said.

"Good. What would Rudolf say to Peter if they met on the road?"

"He'd say hello."

"OK. Nina, you imagine Rudolf and Peter. What would they say to each other?"

"You be Peter, Sarah," Nina ordered.

"Nina, be quiet." Elan furrowed his forehead. "I'm imagining. You're hearing the angels. It's my turn to imagine." Elan placed both reindeer on the table facing each other. "Hello, Peter, guess where I'm going? Hi, Rudolf. You're going to help Santa. No, not right now. First I'm going to eat some tart. I'm going to Sarah's house. You want to come with me and get a bite? Yes, let's go!"

We burst out laughing. "Nicely done, Elan," his mother said. "But first let's finish lunch."

"Tell us more imagine." Nina crawled on my lap.

"Well, let's take a look at each ornament. We'll guess how they were made, and then we'll imagine them talking, dancing, singing, or doing something fun."

The little ones were delighted with the stories we made up, and when I finished, they wanted me to start all over again.

"You're a great storyteller, Sarah," Alyana said.

It felt wonderful. I liked remembering how each ornament had been created and hoped I'd done a good service in the telling of those that Conrad had made.

"Ready for a slice of apple tart with a glass of milk?" I asked.

Their little faces lit up with every bite. Alyana kept humming with every morsel. Of course the children wanted more, but they needed to wait until after dinner to share the remaining tart with their dad.

After lunch we played with a couple of ornaments, and I promised them we would make six ornaments together, one for everyone in our family. No sooner had I said "our family" than the old Sarah popped up to shame me. *How dare you count yourself among their lovely family?*

But her outburst didn't last long. Outnumbered, she retreated as quickly as she'd appeared. Neither Alyana nor the children reacted negatively. Truth be told, they didn't react at all. Six ornaments were just fine with them, and they considered me a part of the family as well.

"Sarah, would it be too much trouble if I put them down for a nap? If they don't take a quick snooze, they'll be impossible this evening when Tom gets home."

I couldn't have been happier to oblige as I helped the little ones onto my bed and covered them with my nana's favorite blanket. They didn't fuss or complain about taking a nap in a house different than theirs. They seemed quite at ease being in my house and sleeping on my bed.

I encouraged Alyana to relax on the sofa and put her feet up. She'd be giving birth in a few months and looked a bit tired. She started to protest with the typical grownup excuses, about not being ladylike to put your feet up, and other such foolish social norms. But I would have none of it, and finally she gave up and settled comfortably in.

"It's great to have you in the family, Sarah. I certainly welcome the company of another woman."

"Well, I'm not so sure about being part of your family quite yet, but I'm delighted to be with all of you."

The old Sarah had snuck by me and put up the barrier just in case the whole thing came crashing down. But Alyana wasn't worried about it. She just went on and welcomed me into her past.

"Oh, you've been embraced by this family as easily as I was when I married Tom. Papa saw to that. I'd been alone for a long time before I met Tom, and being received into their household with such unconditional affection was lovely. Papa may have told you that I'm adopted."

"No, he didn't."

"Not much to tell, really. My parents adopted me as a baby, and they were quite elderly, so I always knew I'd be alone in the end."

"I'm sorry."

"Oh, no, please don't get me wrong. It's not about being sad or any of that. I had a wonderful childhood. My parents showered me with love and gave me many good years. I've nothing to complain about. There are plenty of kids in the world who aren't as loved by their natural parents as I was by my adoptive parents. What I meant was that since they were in their late sixties when they adopted me, they prepared me for when they would be gone. And sure enough, they both passed on before I graduated from high school. I was pretty much on my own for several years until I met Tom."

"Do you know anything at all about your birth parents?"

"Only that my mother was sixteen and couldn't raise me. Nothing about my father."

"Do you want to know more? Are you curious?"

"No, not really. When I was younger I was more curious, but the older I got the less interested I became. I'd like to know about my genetic makeup, and what type of medical history my birth parents had, for my kids' sake. But in the end, I'm more content as I am than if I were to find out something I don't care to know. If there is anything I am destined to know, I will. My adoptive parents helped me see that. My presence gave them immense joy and happiness in their later years. They bathed me with love and support and offered great spiritual guidance. Their teachings made me the person I am today, and for that I'm eternally thankful to them. Losing them was hard. I loved them so."

"What did you do after they passed away?"

"I lived with my cousins. After I graduated from high school, I went away to college to become a nurse, the best career I could've picked. I love helping others, and coupled with the fact that in college I had to work really hard, I didn't have time to feel sorry for myself. My studies absorbed me. I did have a few friends and dated a couple of times, but I felt lonely nonetheless. I missed the company of my parents. In terms of love, none of the guys I dated made my heart stir."

"I know what you mean. Were you worried?"

"Not really. I just waited. Then Tom broke his leg skiing, and I happened to be on duty in the emergency room when he came in. I think you could say it was love at first sight. Papa says that he caught our eyes speaking to one another, and in that instant he witnessed us falling in love."

"I can just imagine it."

"I didn't know it at the time. I just trusted my instincts, not really knowing why I did what I did. I remember helping the doctor cast his leg, thinking how strong and good looking he was. Next thing I knew, I gave him my home phone number." She giggled, and her cheeks reddened a little.

"Soon after we began dating, I knew I'd fallen madly in love. We got engaged the next month and married five months later. The distance between our towns was difficult, and neither of us wanted to wait, so there was no point in carrying out a long engagement."

"Were you concerned that it was happening too quickly?"

"I knew, actually I trusted, that I was in good hands with Tom. Coming into his family is the best thing that's happened to me. I'm so blessed. You don't need to be afraid, Sarah, if you and Papa are—"

"Well…It's not that…It's…I'm not sure…I'm—"

"Sorry, you don't need to explain to me. I didn't mean to intrude. It's just that they're unique men. I'm sure you've noticed. Things are different with them. Papa's grandmother, Angela, had a lot to do with it. I'm sure he's told you about her."

"Yes, I know about Angela."

"I wish I'd met her when she was alive. She must've been quite special. Tom says that Papa lost a big part of himself when she died. Hard to believe, isn't it?"

"I'd say so. He's so together."

"Exactly. I've admired and loved Papa so much since I first met him that I could never imagine his lacking anything. But nowadays he's definitely a new man. I can see that he's found that part Tom said he'd lost. I gather he's back to his old self because I've never seen him so full of life and excitement. Tom's so relieved to have his Papa back, and it's all due to you, Sarah. Thanks."

"I'm glad to hear that, but I'm sure it has nothing to do with me."

The front-door chimes rang. Conrad had arrived with the Christmas lights, to "dress up the house."

In spite of our all-too-brief conversation, a bond had developed between Alyana and me. A beautiful woman with a shining spirit, she moved in this world with the assurance and radiance of inner peace. Her demeanor remained serene even when she reprimanded her children. Her long, soft black hair bounced around her shoulders with every step, happy to shine and frame her lovely face accentuated by deep green eyes. Her olive skin glowed with natural luster, and the softness of her touch only made it more appealing. Both her children had inherited her beauty and their father's captivating qualities.

The rest of the afternoon and evening, family bliss permeated the house. The children woke up from their naps to renewed storytelling by their grandfather of how he'd made the ornaments, and they volunteered their reenactments of the stories we had made up in the morning. Tom joined us after he closed the store, and we spent a fun-filled evening.

After everyone left, I stepped outside. The snowfall had ceased, the wind didn't blow, the Cascades slept serenely, and my house looked spectacular dressed in her Christmas colors lighting up the winter sky.

As I readied myself for bed, I reflected back on not only this day but also on the days preceding it and the many gifts my house had bestowed upon me. Louise, the first inhabitant of my precious home, hadn't welcomed her birth, yet in the end, Amy's love had given rise to how exceptional the house had become.

What a peculiar habit I've picked up, to relate to this house as if it's a person.

"Eccentric behavior, Sarah," I chuckled.

"Granted," I answered, "but my home is more than a just a house, it has personality, it communicates its emotions, it has *spirit*."

This *spirit* is what kept tugging at me when I least expected it. Just when I thought that all was peaceful and enjoyable, just as this day had been, I'd get the feeling it wasn't quite so. At such times, the house would egg me on, reminding me that there were secrets still to be unearthed, that the journey hadn't concluded, and that more was yet to come.

CHAPTER 16

The Courtship

CONRAD INFORMED ME that my formal introduction to the Cascades and its nearby environs, a must for the Thompson family, was to take place over several afternoons. He would pick me up early in the afternoon and take me to explore "my new neighborhood." The weather turned out perfect, which allowed us to travel easily, walk in the snow, explore the neighboring towns and their shops, and enjoy each other's company—a courtship in full swing.

Conrad, the perfect tour guide, showed me the beauty that surrounded the Cascades, all the while narrating the history and local traditions of the different towns we visited. He spoke of the time when the gold fever struck in the North American West during the late nineteenth century and how the Okanogan and the Methow valleys attracted many a prospector from California to Alaska. It all started in 1848 when an employee at Sutter's Mill in California found gold in the nearby American River and kindled the spark later known as the California Gold Rush.

"That's how California earned its name the Golden State," Conrad said as we drove down Highway 20. "The procession of gold seekers trudged north for more than ten years through the Okanogan and headed for rumored riches from the Sierra Nevadas all the way into Canada."

We visited Winthrop first, a wonderful old town that had been restored to look as it did in the late nineteenth century with a surprising number of original façades still standing along its main street. The town has been restored to the mood of yesteryears, and one can easily imagine how cowboys, farmers, cattle ranchers, and miners must've lived.

"Like most of Okanogan County towns in those days, mining was its lifeline," Conrad explained. "In the 1890s, Winthrop changed from a small transition town to a bustling distribution spot. When Colonel Tom Hart built a road thirty-four miles into the Slate Creek area, Winthrop's future was guaranteed."

"Is that when the twin houses were built? You think the owners were into mining? Is that why they're so exquisitely put together? A bunch of money must've gone into their construction."

"I'd say yes to all of those questions, but who really knows?"

"This town is so small; how has it survived all these years?"

"Smarts. By 1915, most of the mines had shut down. Winthrop was hard hit since it depended so much on the mines, and its population dropped. It struggled through the Depression years amid rumors that it was destined to become a ghost town. But Winthrop hung on, reinvented itself, and emerged as a tourist attraction."

"That's at the time your grandparents lived here."

"They got married, I think in 1922. So yes, they lived through all of this history."

I was so enamored with Winthrop and its resurrection from the ashes that we spent an entire afternoon visiting the small town, its shops, its museum, and its surroundings. I imagined Angela and Richard walking through the town, talking with neighbors, Jeremy going to school, and the three sisters gathering goods at the general store.

We were strolling down Main Street when Conrad reached for my hand. Of course, I immediately felt tears well up with the pleasure of being a couple. But I didn't embarrass him or myself; I simply enjoyed the feeling and allowed the tears to slowly wane.

"Your turn to tell me a bit about your folks," Conrad said.

"Let's see, where to begin? My parents were much in love and had, like I would imagine all couples have, quirks that made them unique. What my nana and I liked best about them was their little disagreements, which were just part of their playfulness, their private jokes, their secret ways of toying with each other."

"Sounds like they were fun to be with."

"They were. But where shall I start?"

"With your dad."

"OK. He was a corporate attorney for the Gillette Company. Have you heard of it?"

"Sure, they make razor blades and things of that sort."

"Their central offices were in Boston, and Global Gillette is where my dad worked. After he graduated from college, he was hired to work in their Mexico City offices, and when he rose up the corporate ladder, they transferred him to Boston. He'd been born to a wealthy family in Mexico and liked his independence. His folks had the same societal hypocrisies that my nana experienced in Spain with her in-laws."

"Rich *socialists*?"

"No, not socialists. It wasn't their political ideology that irked him. He thought them to be ostentatious and pretentious. My father, on the other hand, was a straightforward man and disliked their desire to impress others. When offered the transfer to the United States, he didn't hesitate. He wanted to create his own life and be his own man, away from his family's fortune and influence."

"That's how your folks met, working for Gillette?"

"No. My mother was a book editor, just like my nana had been, and worked for a publishing house. How they met is where their stories go their separate ways. My mother was finishing college with a major in literature, and she said they met attending a discussion on Margaret Mitchell's novel *Gone with the Wind*. The way she told it was that my father was well read and liked literature as much as she did, in spite of being a lawyer."

"She didn't like that he was a lawyer?"

"No, that wasn't it, but to recount the story of meeting her husband in a literary circle fit her need for class and elegance. She liked the fact that her husband could be thought of as being her intellectual equal. She was right on that score. My dad was an intellectual, but you wouldn't have known it."

"Why?"

"He never flaunted it. Mom didn't flaunt it either, but given her work circle, she was expected to show her bookish know-how. He was the oddity,

a corporate lawyer with impeccable artistic taste and knowled
loved literature and the arts. They were well suited for each oth

"Come, let me show you this shop. You'll get a kick out of i ... that,
he pulled me into what seemed to be an old saloon that had been converted
into an old-fashioned store with barrels filled with knickknacks, clothes, and
an assortment of oddities.

We had dinner at an old-west type restaurant that boasted of making the
best buffalo hamburgers in the region. We weren't disappointed.

As we left the restaurant and ambled down Main Street enjoying the crisp
air of a clear winter night, Conrad took my hand and placed it on his arm,
gently holding it in place with his other hand. In spite of wearing our gloves,
I could feel his warmth.

"Tell me your dad's version of how he met your mom."

"He insisted that they'd met when she grabbed his hand in a movie theater while watching *Gone with the Wind*. He said the combination of her
feminine fragility and forwardness swept him off his feet."

"I like his version," Conrad chuckled.

"My father—"

"Wait, say his name again. I like hearing your Spanish accent."

"Ernesto."

"Ah. And your mother's?"

"Antonia."

He smiled and placed his arm around my shoulder, bringing me closer to
him. "Go on. Finish your story."

"My father's tale of how he proposed marriage to my mother also differed
from hers. He insisted she proposed to him on the dance floor after kissing
him at a New Year's party. Her story went along the lines that in the middle
of a dance, he carried her in his arms to the balcony, and as the twelfth chime
rang, he dropped to his knees and proposed."

"I like her version. Which story do you believe?" he said as he opened the
driver's door to his truck.

I slid all the way in. "I think there might be a bit of truth in both."

"They never agreed on one story?"

"No. These are just a couple of the memories they disagreed on. Nana and I always enjoyed watching them argue about their different recollections. Nana said that it made it doubly good to have more than one story for each memory."

"Sounds like you were a happy kid," he said as we drove down Highway 2 on our way home.

"Yes. We were an easygoing type of family. When I was six, we moved to downtown Boston and fell into a routine."

"Where did you move from?"

Suddenly I realized I'd just given him a glimpse of the event that caused my family to run away from the home of my birth.

"Oh, nowhere special." I could hear my own voice quivering.

"What do you mean?"

"I don't mean anything. You're just making it sound like I do," I snapped.

"OK. Never mind."

"I didn't mean to—"

"It's OK."

He drove in silence, and I looked out the window, hoping to shut out a past that I didn't want to deal with.

The following days we visited Twisp, Carlton, Methow, and Pateros. Every sightseeing trip ended with a nice dinner at one of the local restaurants or coffee shops, a fun drive back to my home, and an evening of sitting in each other's arms in front of the fire chatting and kissing. Yet my inability to tell him the reason my family had escaped hung between us. Somehow, I needed to address it.

When we stopped for dinner after our visit to Lake Chelan, I blurted out, "We moved from the suburbs to downtown Boston."

"Listen, Sarah, you don't have to tell me—"

"You'd asked if I was a happy kid, and I was. I got jumpy for nothing. My family didn't have any major ups and downs. We were pretty boring really. My mother read all the time, focused on improving herself and of course me. My nana, ever vigilant, always protected my independence. My father watched over all of us and supported our endeavors as long as they didn't expose us to harm. The only rub for my dad was my paternal grandparents. He never interfered with my upbringing other than making sure that his parents didn't influence me. He was so much like my nana that the two of them could've been related. Ideologically they were in total unison, and neither wanted any inducement of hypocritical societal norms to be a part of me. So when my paternal grandparents traveled to Boston to visit, I was never left alone with them—always under my father's watchful eye or my mother's or grandmother's. When we traveled to Mexico, my nana never left my side. All my life my father kept me at a safe distance from his parents and his siblings."

"Boy. What was so wrong with his folks?"

"Nothing wrong, just snobs. They were the type that liked to flaunt their money and standing in life. They used money to gain respect and love instead of earning it. My dad didn't like that."

"Ah, I get it."

I knew he wasn't satisfied, but I hoped that I'd gained some time to summon my courage.

The lovely town of Leavenworth came next. "This town thrived with railway and timber industries," Conrad explained. "And when they were lost, it began a slow decline as well. Inspired by the effect of the Cascades and that the town looked like some Bavarian alpine villages in Germany, Leavenworth was turned into a Bavarian tourist attraction. As you can see, their efforts worked. Lots of tourists come by, and it's turned out great for the local economy. "

Like all the other towns, Leavenworth had been decorated for Christmas and also merited an entire afternoon meandering through its shops. By now I was accustomed to walking hand in hand with Conrad, and as we entered each shop, I noticed we had fallen into an easy routine of exchanging opinions and making jokes about all the knickknacks we looked at, like old married couples.

When we emerged from one of the stores, the sun had set, and the Christmas lights all over town were lit. We stood admiring the imposing Christmas tree that adorned the main square when Conrad held me in his arms and kissed me. How special it felt to be kissed in public. He held me in his arms for a while before we turned our attention back to the tree.

"Do you have any sisters or brothers?"

I sighed with relief. He was finally asking me about my family again. "No. My mother was just like Angela's mom. After me, she couldn't have any more children. It's a bit sad really. My side of the family ends with me."

"You have us now."

This time, I couldn't help but cry. What a wonderful image he had just offered me. His words created such elation that I had no choice but to allow the force of the emotion to release through my tears.

It didn't matter that we were in the middle of town, outdoors, and surrounded by many people. Just as a volcano erupts, so did I. I cried and cried while Conrad reassuringly held me in his arms. My tears washed away the old feelings of loneliness and isolation while welcoming the new sensation of companionship and togetherness. After my tears subsided, he kissed my cheeks and the tip of my nose.

"Better now?"

"Better. Sorry."

"No need to apologize. Christmas gets me too. Plus I liked holding you in my arms."

A couple of nights later, we were sitting in front of my fireplace after a fun afternoon of sightseeing when Conrad opened the door to my forbidden past.

"The other day, you mentioned that after you were six you fell into a routine with your folks. Why six? No routine before that?"

I broke our embrace and sat up. Obviously I hadn't been able to erase the impression I'd created. I wanted to bolt, to run away, and to avoid this conversation. Most importantly, I didn't want to remember.

Conrad gently placed his hand on my back and I jumped.

"Sorry," he said.

I stood frozen before the fire.

"What's wrong, Sarah?"

"I…well…It's just that—"

" I get it. This is something you don't want to speak about. It's OK. You don't have to tell me."

"I should. Really, I...well...It's just that I've kept this to myself for so long that...well...I don't...I'm not sure that—"

"Then don't tell me."

I turned to him, took a deep breath, and plunged into the truth.

"Listen, I know you've kissed me and you've held me in your arms, and I'm loving it, but if after I tell you about...well...after I tell you, if you'd prefer to stop seeing me, please understand I wouldn't hold it against you."

"What on earth are you talking about? Have you lost your mind? Why would I do such a thing?" Now he was angry.

"Well...this anger I see in you might get worse when I tell you."

"I'm angry that you would think me so stupid as to want to run away from you. What the hell is going on?" He stood right in front of me expecting an answer.

"OK, here it is. You've accepted the fact that I can sense things from the past. You've rationalized that it's because I'm just as perceptive as your grandmother. But it's much more than that."

"I'm listening."

"When I was little, I felt and knew things before they happened. Sometimes if I got close to someone—just a passerby, no one I knew—I'd see what he'd just done or what he was thinking of doing next. I didn't see it all the time or with everyone. I didn't choose to see it or sense it. It just happened. The visions just popped into my head. My grandmother thought this ability to be a gift, but my parents didn't agree, especially when our neighbors and friends thought me strange and were frightened of me."

"Frightened of you? Why?" He sat back down next to me.

"You have to admit that a little girl saying to someone, 'I'm sorry your grandfather died,' before he was gone is a bit strange."

"I can see that."

"What happened when I was six was horrible, the culminating moment when my so-called gift traumatized everyone at my best friend Lindsay's birthday party. All I did was tell her—unfortunately in front of everyone—how sorry I was that her cousin George had hurt her. Turns out Lindsay hadn't told a soul this middle-aged creep had played doctor with her. When George went to jail and Lindsay's mom killed herself, my family was ostracized, and everyone blamed me for the tragedy. From that moment on, everyone around us believed me to be possessed by the devil. They called me a witch."

"I see."

"My family escaped from that neighborhood and forced me to bury my abilities. Now, fifty years later, they've come back to life." I took a deep breath and closed my eyes, expecting him to get up, and then I'd hear his footsteps as he marched out the front door.

But he didn't. Instead he reached for me and embraced me. I tentatively uncrossed my arms and hugged him.

"I understand now," he whispered.

"Aren't you freaked out?"

"Sure I am. Who wouldn't be? I'm holding a witch in my arms. I don't suppose you can wiggle your nose and make things appear and disappear, 'cause I'd like a new truck."

We laughed so hard that tears kept running down our cheeks. We eased back onto the sofa and in silence watched the fire for a long while.

"Your fear and reluctance make sense to me now," he finally said. "It helps me understand how you can actually live through the photographs and even visit with your nana. It must be quite frightening to be in both worlds."

"At times it is."

"What's in store?"

"Don't know. I sense that my house has something to tell me."

"The house?"

"Maybe it's Angela. But at times it feels as if there are others that need to be heard."

CHAPTER 17

Ethan

THE NEXT MORNING I woke up with a powerful sense of gratitude for my house and the new life it had propelled me into. After breakfast and a shower, I went to visit with my attic. I needed to chat, share my happiness, and most important, offer my thanks for inviting me to come live here.

"It's been quite a ride these last few months," I told the attic. "You're to blame, you know? You're the culprit of all of my new adventures and discoveries. I don't quite understand it all, but thank you for the experiences you've given me. I can only imagine what is to come...Do you have more in store for me?"

But the attic offered no answers, only the familiar sensation of ease and comfort, with the invitation to relax.

"OK," I went on, "it's true that I'm still worried, not sure what's expected of me or why I'm tuned into the lives of these people, but I'm willing to go along with you."

I strolled about the room, running my fingers along the furniture, the trunks, and the boxes of photographs. I picked up one box and thumbed through the remaining pictures. They'd been silent the last few times I looked through them.

"Caroline was stunning," said an unexpected shy voice emanating from the box whose contents I'd obviously awakened.

I flipped through the photos searching for Caroline or the voice behind the picture. This box contained the old sepia photographs, and sometimes it took me a while to focus enough in order to bring the likenesses within them forward. I found a small photograph of an elegant family, a lovely woman, her hand resting on the arm of a strapping young man, and two little boys.

Is this Caroline?

As I studied their faces, I thought I recognized Leonard, but their garments didn't seem to be in the same style as the ones in the previous photographs. I turned it over to see if there was a date or any indication of who they were and found a barely legible inscription: *San Francisco, 1864.*

"She had been a widow for about one year when I met her. I fell in love the minute I laid eyes on her. Been in love ever since."

"Where did you meet?" But he didn't hear me. He spoke with someone other than me, so I quietly got out of the way and sat down to listen.

"I wrote to tell you I wanted to marry her, asking your permission to do so, and inviting you to join us for the ceremony. I wrote you several letters but never heard back from you, so I thought you were traveling again, and news of your whereabouts would reach me sooner or later. In the end we married without you. If you had met her, you would have approved. I know I have told you this story many a time, Father, but bear with me. I like remembering how it all began as I tell you how it is turning out."

He paused for a long time, and I feared he'd left, but then I heard him sigh.

"After the wedding we came back and found we had missed your funeral by a month. Wish Louise would have written to me, but you know how moody she was. Amy didn't know of your death until a couple of days before the funeral, and that was by accident. She ran into the preacher's sister, who extended her condolences. You can well imagine how Louise took your death. She was beside herself. Amy tried to give her some solace, but she would have none. Cora and Laura didn't come to the funeral after Amy wrote to them, nor did they write. They were off tending to their anger as usual. I felt sorry for them all these years, never married, never getting close to anyone, always distant and angry. Poor souls."

Suddenly, I saw Ethan kneeling on the ground before Leonard's grave. He was not the young handsome man of the photograph but a man in his late seventies or early eighties.

"Caroline's been the joy of my life. Her two sons, Henry and Stuart, were a handful but great to have around and watch them grow along with Amy's twins. You remember I've told you that our twin boys are but a few years older than Annie and Claudia, Amy's girls. I have told you before, right? Watching them grow so well, and their mother so at ease and happy to live in our house, has been good for me. Nothing like it was with Aunt Louise and you. I have been a lucky man to find such a loving wife.

"I can only imagine how hard it must have been for my Caroline's late husband. You know, Hugo Thompson. I've mentioned him to you. Anyway, when his body gave up and he knew he would leave her with three-year-old twins, the pain he must have gone through is hard to imagine. I don't think I could have endured it. The thought of losing Caroline even by my own death terrifies me. Thank goodness I've not had to deal with that in my lifetime. My admiration for Hugo has never waned. And the effort he made to do right by her and the boys is commendable.

"I learned well from you, Father, and have put the money from her trust fund to good use. I honored him by insisting that his boys keep his name in spite of Caroline's request that I give them mine. Time confirmed I made the right decision. Every year on the day of Hugo's death, we remember him and honor his memory and legacy. It's been a good lesson for the boys not to forget their birth father and to have no guilt or shame for their love for me. The boys and I are endeared to one another just as much as you and I were.

"As I have told you before, we have had some bad years, but with the profit from the trust fund and the little we got out of the mines before they closed down, we have been able to make ends meet. Along with Christopher and Amy, we have kept the twin houses and the land alive and well cared for. Granted that both are a bit different than when you and Aunt Louise were alive. Christopher and I have had to adjust to farming and cattle ranching. Caroline and Amy are truly taken by the houses, and they tend to them as if they were precious jewels. We tease the women something awful, but they like it. Christopher's been a good husband to Amy and a dear friend to me. He was at your funeral along with Amy, their twins Annie, and Claudia. Aunt Louise didn't even notice; she was so broken up. I'm glad you had some of your family around to bid you farewell."

He paused again, and a few tears dropped on my lap. The loneliness of Leonard's death weighed heavily on my heart.

"I gave Amy some of the old photographs to keep in that attic of hers. Neither one of us bear any resentment. We actually wish to keep the memories of times past that we all enjoyed and even the pain we endured. It is part of who we are. Having found love ourselves, we can recognize its influence. At best, the two of us accept what was and aren't bitter about it. We both loved you, and have chosen to remember all the good things you did for us and even some of the good times we experienced with Louise when she was in high spirits."

He paused again, and I thumbed through the photographs searching for the memories he'd just mentioned. All of a sudden every ghostly sepia photograph came into focus. There were photographs of Ethan with his father, of Amy with both of them, of Louise and Leonard with the three girls, and of Louise with her mother.

As I held each photograph, I perceived the moment and the emotion captured within it. I'd been transported to the instant when each was taken.

The photographs of Ethan and Leonard clearly showed that they were close and shared trust and friendship. Although there were no more than six pictures of the two of them when Ethan was young, an obvious silent connection emanated from each photo that communicated a strong bond between father and son, between allies. Ethan looked handsome and composed, filled with happiness and assurance, sometimes mischievous, sometimes pensive, but always connected with Leonard by a resilient bond.

However, in the photographs where Louise was present, Ethan seemed to cower, to shy away, to become less expressive, to move into the background as if wishing to disappear from the moment. The happy, secure, and strong Ethan returned when photographed with Amy but would retreat somewhat when photographed with his cousins Cora or Laura when Amy was absent.

The photographs of Louise and Leonard alone always showed deep emotion, a silent exchange between them, sharing the certainty that they were destined for one another yet exuding a palpable desire to communicate detachment. Their love for each other was as evident as was their apprehension of it.

The three photographs of Louise alone or with her mother spoke of resentment and denial. Neither woman looked at the camera, they didn't gaze at each another, and their eyes focused internally, away from the moment.

"I still cannot understand why you went to the mine. You had no business there. You owned the place. Why put yourself in such danger? What possessed you to go in and try to save them?"

I heard rustling as if something or someone were stirring. I looked around the attic but found only stillness.

"Father, don't be angry. You know I always ask this of you when I visit your grave. Please understand that I want to know…I need to know. Amy is convinced your actions are a reflection of who you were as man. Apart from the bond between you and Aunt Louise, you were a man of honor. I know that as well. I can understand you wanting to show your support for your men. But you could have done it from a distance. Amy tells me you went because you needed to feel you were a good person, given that you kept chastising yourself for what you and Louise had done. But I know you better; there must have been another reason for you to want to die with them."

Then silence surrounded me. I couldn't hear anything, not even the slightest whisper. I waited.

Quietly, I thumbed through the remaining photographs, finding a handful of pictures of Ethan with Caroline in front of their house, tending to the farm, and working with the animals.

"Caroline and I never conceived our own brew." Ethan continued with no reference to what his father might have answered or if he'd answered his plea at all.

"Good thing," Ethan went on, "given our family's history. Her boys turned out to be much better for all of us than if they had been mine. They have no resentments, no skeletons in the closet. They are hardworking kids, and life has been good for all of us. Henry has taken to farming and Stuart to cattle ranching, a true cowboy."

I found a few photographs of Henry and Stuart as they grew up, Henry always tending to the farm animals while Stuart rode or cared for the horses. There were also several photographs of Annie, Claudia, Henry, and Stuart in moments of play or as they celebrated birthdays and holidays.

"Thank goodness for Christopher's notion of picture taking. He's been real good with his camera at preserving the memories. Amy keeps the photographs in the boxes she makes for safekeeping and then hides them in that attic of hers. She brings the boxes out at Christmas and we all reminisce about years gone by. Who would have thought we could have such fun remembering what was?"

Unexpectedly, I realized the photograph that the cowboy had given to Jeremy's pa was in my hands, and I bolted up. Was it possible that this was the photograph I'd been looking for? Was it possible that Stuart was the cowboy in Jeremy's story? It certainly felt like it, no doubt about it. Yet, with the same force that carried that certainty, a myriad of questions invaded in my mind.

My instantaneous realization caused Ethan's retreat.

"Ethan, you can't just leave. I need answers," I pleaded. "If Stuart was the cowboy in Jeremy's story, was Henry his father? Who was his mother? Come back, please," I begged, but to no avail. Ethan had left.

Actually, he'd never been there.

Remembering that this entire exchange had occurred with Ethan kneeling before his father's grave offered a possible path to follow where I could find some answers. I rushed out of the attic and headed for my computer to search for the cemeteries in the area. If I could find Leonard's grave, maybe I could find all of the other graves and piece the stories from the photographs together.

My online search resulted in finding several potential cemeteries, but none showed Leonard Whitman, let alone someone called Louise connected to him. Neither appeared on the lists posted by those who surveyed the graveyards.

Maybe if I went to the cemeteries within driving distance, I could find a clue or something. First I drove to Sullivan Cemetery, east of Winthrop, but although it had some old gravestones, I found no trace of the Whitman legacy. My visits to Beaver Creek, Methow, Melson, and Okanogan cemeteries yielded little information as well.

By the time I made my way back home, it was dinnertime, and Conrad was scheduled to arrive in less than half an hour. I quickly whipped up garlic and olive oil pasta, tossed with sautéed shrimp, and a nice salad. With no time for freshly baked bread, a swift warming up of the leftover loaf did the trick.

As usual, Conrad arrived right on time, and our evening began with a warm embrace and tender kisses. Immediately, I relaxed and related Ethan's appearance along with my visits to the cemeteries. As we ate dinner, Conrad listened to my story and calmly looked through the old photographs.

After dessert we made our way to the living room, and Conrad took another look at the pictures. We sat in front of our Christmas tree, and multicolored lights danced on the old sepia photographs, bringing them to life. I hoped they would ring a bell and prompt him to tell me more about them.

"I can't say I know any of these folks, sorry," he said with a smile. "And I'm not surprised you didn't find any tombstones or genealogy records either. So much has changed in these parts through the years, even though I imagine we've changed less than other states in the union. My family, though, has preferred not to have stone or any other manmade markers, just natural burials whereby they can become part of the earth, the Cascades, one with nature. That way we can remember them throughout all of our surroundings, free as the wind or the water of the rivers, the rain, or the snow instead of locked up in one place. It'll be difficult to find tombstones for my clan."

"Do you think Stuart is the cowboy in Jeremy's story? Because if he is, then his sister Rachel is Angela's mother."

"Could be. From my granddad's side of the family, we're named Thompson. That fits with what Ethan said about last names. My granddad's father, Ernest Thompson, married Elisabeth, my great-grandmother. I think his father was named Stuart. But these names are pretty common names."

"How about on Angela's side?"

"Her father's name was John Meyers, and her mother's was Rachel, as you know. Her grandmother was named Annie, and I believe her husband was Henry Thompson. You already know Angela's great-grandmother was named

Amy, so it seems you're ahead of the game. All these names could make one's head spin, and to be honest, I haven't paid much attention to these things in the past. Sorry I'm not much help."

"You're right. I do know these things. Amy's twin girls married Ethan's twin boys!" I sat on the edge of the sofa, my forehead furrowed, my lips puckered.

Conrad leaned over and kissed me. "You are so kissable when you get worried," he uttered between kisses.

"Don't stop," I muttered, "but when you have time, it'll be great if we knew about Jeremy. You think he was Angela's uncle? Were there any other children?"

He laughed and laughed and then nodded and said, "OK, one-track Sarah, I'll look into it. I believe that Stuart married a Linda, although I remember a Claudia in the mix. Like I said, haven't paid much attention really, and Granddad didn't speak of his folks as much as Grandma Angela did. I'll take a look. What will you do with the information if it turns out you're right?"

"I don't know. It's all garbled in my head. To begin with, there are only questions and so far no answers. For instance, why do I hear these stories? Why am I experiencing true stories from years past? Some stories are told to me, some I witness, in some I'm a participant, and others I live as if I were there, even though I know I'm not."

"I can't help you there. I'm just as baffled. Guess we'll just have to wait and see. It looks as if every time you see a photo that was silent before and decides to speak or does whatever it is these pictures do, you learn something new. Just give them time."

"But you'll find out about Jeremy, won't you?"

He laughed again, "Yes, I will; don't worry. Now let's go outside, take a stroll, and enjoy the outdoor lights and the crisp winter night. How about it?"

"I'd love to."

Hand in hand we headed deep into the valley till we lost sight of the lights. As we strolled back, the Christmas lights twinkled through the trees, a beacon welcoming us home. Conrad held me in his arms to say good night, and we kissed, giving into the sensation of our lips gliding, exploring, taking pleasure in each other.

As I slid into bed, I reflected on the unusual emergence of the sepia photographs. The love expressed by Ethan, the happiness he'd found growing old in our valley, and how, along with his wife, Caroline, and Amy and Christopher, they'd cared for the twin houses. How ironic, that in the end, the unwanted birth of the houses hadn't destroyed them but instead given pleasure to the heirs of their builder.

Yet Ethan's story was incomplete. Leonard's death troubled him. Why insist on retelling his life story to his father? Maybe it had been for my benefit, to tell me the story. The remaining question, after all these years, was why Ethan didn't know how his father had died. And what about Louise? How did she die?

Each story presented a piece of a puzzle; some had fallen into place, but many more remained beyond my reach.

V. & D. Povall

Third Family Tree - Residents of the Twin Houses

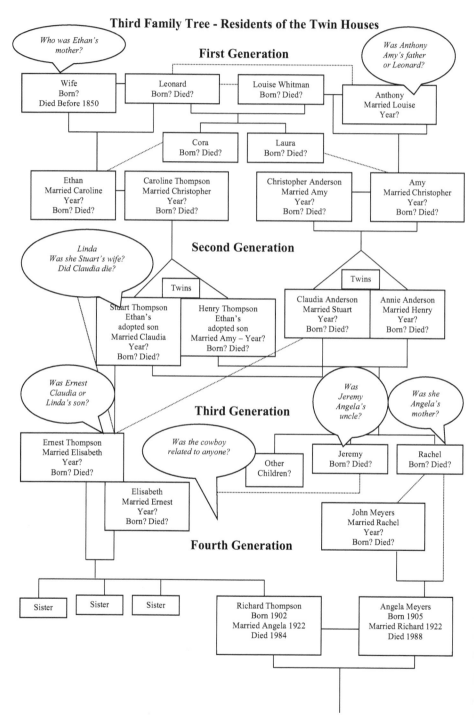

First Generation

Who was Ethan's mother?

Was Anthony Amy's father or Leonard?

Wife
Born?
Died Before 1850

Leonard
Born? Died?

Louise Whitman
Born? Died?

Anthony
Married Louise
Year?

Cora
Born? Died?

Laura
Born? Died?

Ethan
Married Caroline
Year?
Born? Died?

Caroline Thompson
Married Christopher
Year?
Born? Died?

Christopher Anderson
Married Amy
Year?
Born? Died?

Amy
Married Christopher
Year?
Born? Died?

Second Generation

*Linda
Was she Stuart's wife?
Did Claudia die?*

Twins

Twins

Stuart Thompson
Ethan's
adopted son
Married Claudia
Year?
Born? Died?

Henry Thompson
Ethan's
adopted son
Married Amy – Year?
Born? Died?

Claudia Anderson
Married Stuart
Year?
Born? Died?

Annie Anderson
Married Henry
Year?
Born? Died?

Was Ernest Claudia or Linda's son?

Third Generation

Was Jeremy Angela's uncle?

Was she Angela's mother?

Ernest Thompson
Married Elisabeth
Year?
Born? Died?

Was the cowboy related to anyone?

Other
Children?

Jeremy
Born? Died?

Rachel
Born? Died?

Elisabeth
Married Ernest
Year?
Born? Died?

John Meyers
Married Rachel
Year?
Born? Died?

Fourth Generation

Sister

Sister

Sister

Richard Thompson
Born 1902
Married Angela 1922
Died 1984

Angela Meyers
Born 1905
Married Richard 1922
Died 1988

126

The Gift of the Twin Houses

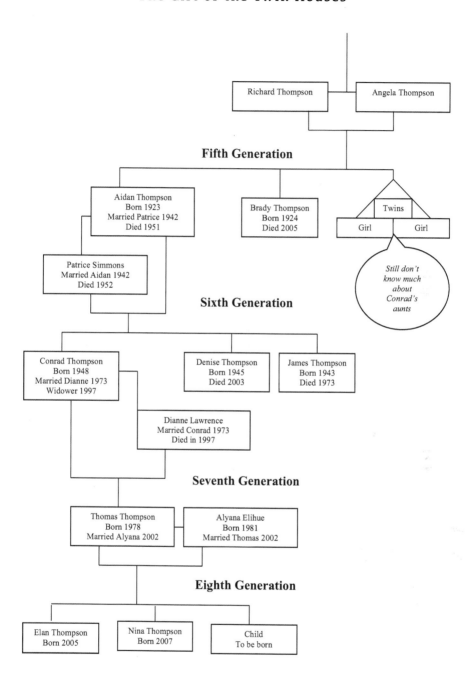

Richard Thompson | Angela Thompson

Fifth Generation

Aidan Thompson
Born 1923
Married Patrice 1942
Died 1951

Brady Thompson
Born 1924
Died 2005

Twins
Girl | Girl

Patrice Simmons
Married Aidan 1942
Died 1952

Still don't know much about Conrad's aunts

Sixth Generation

Conrad Thompson
Born 1948
Married Dianne 1973
Widower 1997

Denise Thompson
Born 1945
Died 2003

James Thompson
Born 1943
Died 1973

Dianne Lawrence
Married Conrad 1973
Died in 1997

Seventh Generation

Thomas Thompson
Born 1978
Married Alyana 2002

Alyana Elihue
Born 1981
Married Thomas 2002

Eighth Generation

Elan Thompson
Born 2005

Nina Thompson
Born 2007

Child
To be born

CHAPTER 18

Heather Lewis
1915–1940

"The house looked lovely, and the woman who sold it to me was so sad, with such need to get away from her painful memories that I just couldn't resist. I bought it right then and there. I was sure I could talk James into it." Heather spoke quite directly.

I'd been organizing the frames and the pictures in my attic when I saw the photograph of an elegant family standing in front of my porch. They didn't look like they belonged there. They looked like four tourists posing for the camera in front of a quaint little house.

I hadn't heard any more stories since Ethan's account and didn't expect one today. Needless to say, Heather's authoritative voice took me by surprise.

"James would not care anyway," Heather went on. "It was my money, and he knew it. I think it was the money that killed our marriage. He didn't feel manly enough since he was not the primary breadwinner. The bread just came to him ready to enjoy, and he had forgotten how to take pleasure in it, given that the bigger portion came from me."

"How long did you own the house?" I dared to ask.

"A long time. I do not exactly know. After a while we just forgot about it."

I heard myself gasp. "Forgot about it?"

"Are you going to listen or are you going to interrupt me? I have no patience for that, you know." She continued without the courtesy of waiting for an answer. "As I was saying, James was just too weak. It was not my fault that I had inherited a lot of money from my family. My father had built an empire from scratch, and I had inherited its proceeds as the only child—just a simple fact of life.

"I married James when I was only eighteen—a good match, by all accounts. We were both born into wealthy families and were accustomed to lives of luxury; consequently, the match seemed perfect at the time. What we did not understand was that we should have had something more in common. Pity.

"When my parents died, the money just poured in. James was rich as well and enjoyed the freedom the money brought, but obviously he resented my superior status. Or so I thought.

"I became pregnant right away and had my two children. I did not know any better then. After the second was born, thank God, I dried up. Having two was hard enough. I do not know what I would have done had I had more children.

"Of course, they had nannies, but that is not the point. It is what a pregnancy does to your body. Prior to the pregnancies I was beautiful, some would say perfect. But after the children ravaged my body, I lost that sharp look about me. No one noticed, and obviously it did not get in the way of enjoying men, since they're always so willing and ready to please and be pleased. But I didn't look as I wished to look.

"Anyway, one day I was extremely bored and angry with James, who kept insisting that I ought to spend more time with my offsprings, when I decided to take some time away from everyone. I was tired of being told what to do or not do. Spending a little time by myself would give me the strength to deal with him and the children upon my return.

"The train ride was spectacular. I liked making use of the very thing that brought economic bliss to our family. The Cascades, as usual, were stunning, and being within them, even while sheltered in a train compartment, felt quite invigorating.

"I do not remember how I ended up in the picturesque little town or the house itself. Details of that nature do not seem to stay with me. I only recall sitting in the living room with the owner of the house signing the papers over a cup of coffee. I thought this quaint little house in the middle of nowhere would make a wonderful vacation home for the children.

"There was so much for them to do around these parts, with the horses and the farm; they would be properly entertained. James would have no choice but to stop pestering me about paying attention to them. We could just send them off with their nannies, a couple of maids, and a butler to tend to them. There was something magical about this place, and all would be happy. Most important, I would be free of the burden.

"My little escapade turned out to be just what the doctor ordered. I'd come with no purpose, and now here I was, doing something for the family.

"But in the end, my selfish, spoiled little relations did not agree with me and furthermore did not even recognize the effort I had put into acquiring the house.

"James thought that my actions were foolish and refused to consider sending the children to this part of the world on their own. They were too little, he said, and could not be sent away. So, we did not send them or go there ourselves and just forgot about the house."

I gasped again, but this time I was careful not to interfere. Heather paused for a moment in her narration. I could feel her thinking, remembering what had taken place. A million questions were crowding my mind. How could she forget the house? What happened to the animals? Is Heather the woman to whom Rachel sold the house? Did Rachel come back or did she stay in the house since Heather did not return? How about Angela—did she know the house had been forgotten?

"Then, one day out of the blue I thought about the house again." Heather was talking to me again, and I silenced my mind.

"Summer. I think it was around 1928. Yes, I think so. It was a dreadful year, and I was bored with nothing to do, nothing to occupy my mind. James was off sailing again, and the children were getting on my nerves. So I just ordered us packed, and when James returned, I announced that our entire little family, including him, was going on holiday to the house in the Cascades.

"After we got there and discovered the shortcomings of the house, James was so angry he stopped speaking to me. When I bought the house I did not pay any attention to the number of bedrooms nor whether it had any servant quarters. Why worry about that? I thought all houses had servant quarters. But this house did not. It only had three bedrooms. That was the very first obstacle to our happy holiday.

"James was beside himself and began to bark orders to settle us in. Every time I tried to intercede he stared at me, his eyes filled with fury, and his face would get terribly red as he pointed his index finger at me. I never knew what he meant by pointing that finger at me, but he looked so fierce that I decided it was best to just let him have his temper tantrum.

"He sent the butler to the neighbors to ask if there was a way to house our servants, at least for the night, before going back home on the next train. Of course, there was nothing. The neighbors were just a simple family who could hardly make ends meet.

"The lady of the house, a nice woman called Angela, walked over with her kids to see if she could be of assistance. I am usually not good with the names of people who do not travel in my social sphere. Come to think of it, I am not good at remembering names of people who are in my social sphere, either. Why crowd my mind with useless information? But I do remember Angela's name. The reason I remember her name is for a very simple fact. In the end, I thought she was an angel for solving all of my problems, and her name of course says so. Simple.

"She was young and probably my same age, yet she was quite wise. There was something about her that made you trust everything she said and did. There was a special sense about her. You liked her right away. That is a feat hard to achieve with someone like me, yet I was immediately partial to her.

"First and foremost, you didn't have to tell her anything about what you wanted or needed or what was acceptable. She just knew. With great ease she simply took control of the situation. First, and I cannot imagine how, she calmed James to the point that he agreed to go out for a 'discovery walk,' as she called it, with our children and hers. I couldn't believe my eyes when James walked into the wilderness of the little valley with six youngsters.

"'Aidan, my eldest, is ten. He'll guide you,' Angela said to James. Then she turned to her children, and said, 'Kids, this is Mr. Lewis and his children.

This is Michael. He's eight, like you, Brady, and his sister, Alice, is seven, just like your twin sisters, Casey and Deidre. Take good care of them.'

"And off they went into the wilderness without any hesitation. I think I even heard James laugh as they crossed the valley.

"Then, quite efficiently, Angela worked with our servants to set them up in the barn. It was such a horrid place for them to spend the night, but Angela made it sound so normal and so comfortable that none of them complained. Because it was summer, she assured us they would not be cold, but the place looked revolting to me. They, however, did not seem to mind at all, and anyway, it was just for one night.

"Along with the servants, she took care of the inside of the house in an attempt to make us comfortable. I had bought the house with all of its furnishings, and to be honest I had not noticed how ugly and old they were. I had trouble just thinking of sitting on the dilapidated sofa, let alone sleeping in the master bedroom, if you could call it that.

"The children's bedrooms were just as bad. One was furnished with a little bed, an old sewing machine, and a bunch of knickknacks. The other bedroom, however, was more troublesome. It contained some old furniture and was decorated with cheap lace and doilies in such poor taste that it was simply unacceptable.

"Somehow Angela knew how I felt about that particular room and took care of it. She was so efficient. They moved some of the old furniture out of that horrid little room into the attic, and then she put away all the doilies and changed the lace curtains for some plain curtains of her own. By the time she was finished, the children's rooms were spare but tolerable. The main bedroom looked quite acceptable for one night. I could not tell you what she had done to create that change. It just looked different.

"She also handled dinner arrangements, inviting all of us, and I do mean all of us, including the servants, to dinner with her family in her home.

"I could not believe we would sit at the same table to eat dinner with the help, but James would not have it otherwise. 'These are unpretentious folks,' he told me, 'and this is the way they do things. Just be gracious for once in your life.' He said it with such conviction that I took offense at the implication that I was not gracious, but he would not dignify my anger with a good fight. He just ignored me.

"Angela's little home was quaint also. It looked just like ours, so I immediately understood why she knew her way around our house.

"She offered us no cocktails, and conversation was not sophisticated at all. Not surprising, given the fact that we were out in the middle of nowhere, in the home of some horse ranchers and farmers, having dinner right along with our servants.

"But I was pleasantly surprised. I enjoyed the food, and to my amazement, I took pleasure in learning about the personal lives of our maids and butler. This latter part was a clever ruse by our charming hostess, Angela.

"She kept the conversation going by asking little innocent questions of us all, making small, clever comments that made us feel at ease, and as a result, before we knew it we had shared our lives.

"I wanted to take notice of her technique so that I could use it at my dinner parties if the conversation stalled, but she caught me in her web of charm, and before I knew it, I had shared my own history with these strangers and our servants.

"I felt so vulnerable when I finished. I could not believe I had spoken about my childhood and teenage trials and tribulations in front of everyone. James even looked taken aback. But I should not have worried. Angela had a remedy for that as well. Somehow she knew how I felt. Immediately she turned what I thought was too much information about me into just the opposite, by offering herself as prey. By the time she was finished telling us about her family's history, I don't think anyone remembered anything I had said. Actually, compared to Angela's story, mine was unmemorable.

"We all slept quite well, I might add, a rather surprising fact, given that James and I had not shared the same bed in years. I do not recall how it had come about, but one day we were both sleeping in separate rooms, leading separate lives. That night, however, we had no choice but to share a room and a bed.

"After the nice dinner with Angela, and once the children were tucked in, and the servants were in the barn, James and I faced the unavoidable moment of having to cohabitate.

"We awkwardly undressed, put on our nightwear, and got into bed. He felt so warm, considering that I was chilled to the bone. Satin does not blend well with rough living. He had not spoken a civil word to me all day so I did not expect him to start then.

"But he did. 'I asked Angela to care for the house for us.' His voice echoed in the darkness of the bedroom.

"'Why would you do that?' I asked him.

"He didn't hesitate when he answered. 'We will not return here any time in the near future, and I think this house needs to be cared for by the care-taker of her twin.' He said it with such certainty, it took me a minute to think it through. I thought that he had lost his mind, speaking of the house as a person, and sounding so corny. But something stopped me from blurting that out. Instead, I thought about what he said, and somehow found it to be a reasonable solution.

"'How much did you offer to pay her?' I asked instead.

"Once again he answered without hesitation and with a sense of absolute resolution, leaving no room for any argument. 'I told her I would pay whatever she wanted. But she turned me down and said it would be her pleasure to do so. She said she loves this house and caring for it was the least she could do. I also asked her about the animals.'

"I remember gasping, and then I whispered, 'Oh, I didn't think of the animals...how awful of me...I'm sorry. I...' and I couldn't finish the sentence. I felt so terribly guilty.

"James went on though. 'Turns out they've been caring for them since you bought the house. I asked her to take them all to her place.' He paused, waiting to hear my reaction. I imagine he thought I'd explode with anger or something like that.

"But I didn't. Instead I asked, 'What did she say to that?' An unusual re-sponse coming from me, considering that normally I simply state my opinion.

'She thanked me,' he answered, 'and told me it was nice that I cared for the animals enough to give them a proper home.'

"He didn't say anything for a few moments, and then I felt his hand touch mine. Under normal circumstances, I would have just yanked my hand away and gone somewhere else in the house, far from him. But I did not do any of that. Instead I welcomed his touch."

Heather paused, and I heard her sigh. She was silent for a while, remembering. An instant before I would've prompted her to go on, she started again.

"Then he whispered, 'Heather, I don't think we should sell this house as we agreed earlier. Let's just wait and see. This place is special.' He sighed so deeply I could feel his emotions as if they were inside of me. I did not know why I was feeling these sensations. I had never felt so susceptible. It is not in my nature.

"With my hand still in his, I asked him what he meant. I thought that my curiosity was more directed at finding answers about my feelings than concern for him, and yet my question seemed to imply the opposite.

"He took a moment to respond, and then he spoke softly. 'The walk with the children was delightful. Angela's children are healthy, content, and infectiously happy. They are well read, well educated, and charming. You should have seen our children. They acted like they were in a candy store, not to buy something, mind you, just to enjoy it. The Cascades are so extraordinary, and this little valley with its farm and house cast a magical appeal. I can understand your impulse to buy the house. I would have done the same. Sorry I lost my temper.' He sighed and so did I.

"Then he kissed me. I kissed him back, and before I knew it, we were making love. I do not ever remember making love with James. I remember having sex with James. Never making love. That one night in that little house, we found love. Simply exquisite.

"When we were done, we did not say a word. We were both crying. Crying for the lost years, the lost feelings, and the lost potential.

"We fell asleep in each other's arms. Another first.

"The next morning the smell of freshly baked cinnamon rolls and coffee woke us up. We simply smiled at one another. We were peaceful at last.

"Angela, of course, had brought the ingredients to our house, baked for us, and had fixed a full breakfast of delicious farm eggs and bacon with fresh orange juice and the 'best coffee in the Northwest,' as she told us. We sat as a family to enjoy her breakfast. Never before had we sat with our children to breakfast, and it was a strange feeling to have them and James around during this part of the day.

"I said, 'Angela, you should not be cooking for us. Let me call for the servants. Please sit with us.' But Angela would not hear of it. Instead, she told me, 'Heather, they're not nearby. I invited them to have breakfast with my kin early this morning. I thought it would be all right with you if they took a bit of the morning off from their regular work, could see what we do around these parts to keep up the farm, and care for the horses. Richard and my kids are showing them around. Hope it's OK with you. I'm going to leave you now to enjoy your breakfast with your family. We'll all be back in a couple of hours to help you pack. Enjoy your morning.'

"We did as she said and had a glorious time. I actually enjoyed talking with our children. Michael had grown up to be a nice-looking, intelligent little boy, and Alice was prettier than I had ever been, and smarter. How could I have missed how pleasant my children were? I asked them about their walk with their father and Angela's children, and they entertained us the entire time. It was so lovely that I wished it would never end.

"But end it did. We knew we could not live in this little house for more than one day. It was just not feasible, and not one of us wanted to damage the memories of the most perfect day and night we had spent in the heart of the Cascades. Not even our young children. They did not fuss about our eminent departure, did not complain, and did not argue. They too wanted to keep the recollection of this special place intact.

"As promised, Angela helped us, and as we were leaving, she insisted on taking our picture. She wanted to 'preserve the memory,' she told us. So we eagerly complied.

"James made all the arrangements with Angela to care for the house in our absence, and Angela invited our kids to come and vacation here with them, so I promised to write to her and keep in touch.

The Gift of the Twin Houses

"I had made a similar promise many times to other friends and acquaintances but never kept it. Politely, I said that I would write to them because it was the correct thing to say, but I never did it. This time, though, I kept my promise.

"When I first started writing to Angela, I was nervous. I just did not know how. I had never written to anyone, mostly because I did not think it was a worthwhile endeavor. It took a big hunk of time out of my day. But something had changed me, and I wanted to write. After all, I would be writing to a special woman, someone who I trusted, and someone who understood me. After I wrote her the first letter, my nerves disappeared, and a few years later, I knew why I kept my promise. Writing to Angela helped me get through the pain of James's death.

"When we got back, James and I kept our love afloat and did not fall into our old patterns. Without even discussing it, we moved into one bedroom again. It was pure bliss between us. We never lost the magic of the night amid the Cascades, a memory that will be eternally with me.

"We both found ourselves much more involved with our children, going on outings, doing homework, or just having our meals together as we had done in the little house in that precious valley. I discovered how much I liked being a mother. I had something to offer to my children and found that to be quite stimulating, I'd found the person I was meant to be and was determined never to let her go.

"Both children did vacation with Angela each summer, and all of us exchanged wonderful letters filled with joy and the tales of our activities during our days apart.

"Then James died in a sailing accident. He loved to sail, and in the end he died doing something he loved. Angela helped me find comfort in that. She also helped me keep in the forefront how we had reunited and found love. She helped me treasure those feelings for the rest of my life, as I remained faithful to James and our love.

"Angela cared for the house as she promised, never asked for anything in return, and would not accept a thing from me. It was her destiny, she wrote to me. I tried to visit her when the children went out there for their annual holiday, but I knew that James's absence would be too noticeable, and I did not dare spoil the memory of our magical night there. So I never saw Angela again. We just faithfully wrote to each other.

"In the end I convinced her that my destiny was to help her kids go to college. Why not use the same ploy she'd use on me? To my astonishment she agreed. So Aidan, Brady, and her twin girls, Casey and Deidre, went to the University of Washington along with my children. They had become such good friends over the years that it all worked out perfectly.

"I never knew how her kids or how my own children turned out, but I would imagine they all did all right. I got cancer and died before I should have.

"Angela would have objected vociferously if I had written to her what I was planning to do, and therefore I never did. I just wrote it in my will.

"The house went back to its rightful owner. The woman who loved it and would care for it, along with the memories it held of us who had been transformed by it."

Then, as quickly as she had appeared, Heather vanished.

CHAPTER 19

The Bond

THE NEXT COUPLE of days I focused on Conrad's clan, which left little time to spend in my attic. Christmas loomed, and I busied myself making the ornaments with the children, getting presents, cooking, and baking.

Conrad talked me into making several tarts for the store, and they were selling fast. Word spread about Sarah's delicious "French tart," and everyone wanted one.

"I don't know if I can keep up with demand," I told Conrad and Tom as I witnessed the six tarts I'd just brought to the store sell in less than five minutes.

"Your next batch will do for a couple of days. I'm going to build demand by holding some back. Are you off to make more ornaments with the little ones?"

"Not today. We're all done with the ornaments, and I need to tend to the house. I found a couple of my mother's handwritten recipes and I'd like to try them. Would you like Caesar salad and chicken Marsala for dinner?"

"Getting fancy. I like it. You know I'll enjoy anything you make."

"I'll need some anchovy paste. Also, do you have any Marsala wine?"

"Anchovy paste I have. Don't know about Marsala wine; I'll take a look." He went to the store's cellar.

Tom had just finished with a customer and joined me. "I can't tell you how much Alyana enjoys your company."

"We've just clicked, haven't we? She's quite special."

"It's her Native American heritage. She's tuned into the world in a unique way."

"I didn't know that's her heritage. How interesting."

"Well, I don't know that's her own heritage. It was that of her adoptive parents. Not knowing her own true heritage, she's chosen to believe it is. Same for our kids."

Conrad returned from the cellar with a bottle in hand.

"No Marsala wine, but this is a good sherry. Will it do?"

"Yes, I'm sure."

"Tom's been telling you about Alyana?"

"Yes, a bit."

"Has he told you about the kids' names?"

"Didn't have enough time, Dad. You came back too soon," Tom chided.

"Go on then, tell her."

"Her adoptive parents named her Alyana, meaning 'forever flowering,' and she is, isn't she? Elan stands for 'friendly one,' and Nina for 'full of grace.' Dad's name stands for 'wise counsel.' I'm the only one lacking a name with Native American meaning."

"His mother named him Thomas in honor of all the great men in history that have borne that name. Quite special, don't you think?" Conrad asked me.

"C'mon, Dad, you made that up. On the other hand, Sarah, your name stands for 'princess,' and our kids love knowing a princess that makes delicious tarts." Tom smiled and left to tend to several customers who had just come into the store.

"Same time for dinner, your highness?" Conrad asked.

My turn to smile, nod, and wave good-bye.

I don't remember ever having such a good time during the Christmas holidays. Even though I'd enjoyed Christmas with my nana and my parents, this season didn't feel the same. I'd been born into their traditions and customs, and they automatically became my own. This time new routines and practices were emerging, born out of a natural combination of my happy memories, Tom's, Conrad's, and Alyana's. Together we were crafting our family's very own Christmas.

My appreciation increased with every new experience, so when I returned to the house, I stepped into the attic to thank Angela for the great gift she had bestowed upon me of the memories she'd left behind. This time I didn't search for a story. On the contrary, I was quite content reliving the old stories as I went about my chores; I required nothing. They'd become my silent companions, and today I daydreamed about their family traditions during the holidays. But as usual, the attic had other plans for me. As I walked about, I came across the story of Angela's twin girls, Casey and Deidre.

I found a package hidden behind one of the trunks. Obviously I'd not looked behind this particular trunk before. The contents were wrapped in coarse paper, and the package was dusty and forgotten.

It surprised me that this trunk had escaped my attention. I felt certain I'd done a thorough cleaning of the entire room several times, yet I didn't remember seeing this package. Regardless of what I remembered, the dust that covered it told the truth. It bothered me that I'd neglected a part of my attic. Could I have been so absorbed in the stories that I'd overlooked certain corners? Whatever the reason, first I apologized and then told my attic that it wouldn't happen again.

I carefully opened the wrapping. It protected an old photo album that was in good condition. The coarse paper had sheltered it quite well. I glanced through it and perused the many photos that showed Angela's pride and love for her twin daughters. It was, however, a spotty record of the passage of time in their lives. There were photographs of Angela and Richard with their babies, photographs of the girls when they were little, some when they were in their middle years, and some as they blossomed into beautiful young women. After that, there appeared to be a lapse in the sequence of photographs, with nothing till they were older.

Something in their eyes had changed as they aged, and I wondered what had occurred, but the album was silent. It didn't relate the stories of the photographs. No matter, I could wait. In due time they would come out. By now I knew that the memories came to me in the order they wished to be heard. Maybe they came in the order I could appreciate them better. Whatever the reason, I decided not to rush them or force them out.

After I properly thanked my attic and Angela, I took the album with me and sensed right away I had done what I was expected to do. I dusted the album and placed it in the living room near the Christmas tree so that it would get acquainted with its new surroundings away from the corner in the attic.

I went about my chores in the house, and around noon, Conrad surprised me by paying a midday visit.

"Thought I'd take the afternoon off. What do you think? Are you up for some adventure?"

"Like what?"

"Just do something we normally don't do in the afternoons in the middle of the workweek."

"What do you have in mind?"

"Come, let's go in the living room."

His playful and childlike demeanor was delightful and made him look younger and even more handsome. Filled with anticipation, I happily followed him.

"OK, you sit right here." He eased me onto the sofa. "Then, I'll just get down on one knee, get this little box from my pocket, open it, and ask you a question. Sarah, will you marry me?"

I gasped and lost complete sight of him. My eyes were filled with tears, and I could not see anything or speak. I think I held my hands over his, or reached out to hold them. Whatever it was, I did something that clearly sent him the message that I'd accepted his proposal. The next thing I remembered was his arms around me helping me stand, feeling a ring slide onto my finger, and then being kissed and cuddled.

I don't know how long we stood there kissing and embracing each other. My tears were unstoppable, shedding years of loneliness, years that saw my youth and my dreams of love pass by, years of hidden emotions, of isolation, of disappointment and regret.

Time either stood still or passed by without notice. I really couldn't say. I wasn't fully aware of my surroundings. We were cocooned in the intimate moment of total surrender to one another. Suspended in a space that knew nothing of fear or distrust that offered only unconditional affection, devotion, and tranquility.

He eased me onto the sofa and held me in his arms as my tears subsided. We were silent, enjoying the tender comfort of the love we shared.

"I thought I would never marry," I finally said.

The Gift of the Twin Houses

"That's 'cause you were waiting for me, just as I've been waiting for you." He caressed my face and hair. "The only difference is that I knew you'd come."

"Angela?"

"Yep."

"How did she know? What did she say?"

"After Dianne left us, she'd look into my eyes and wink. Then she'd say that my soul mate would arrive one day, and here you are, in my arms for the rest of our lives. Soul mates." Slowly, he kissed my eyes, my cheeks, my nose, and my mouth.

"How do you know it's me?" I whispered between kisses.

"You know well enough it's you. Since we first met, you've known we were meant to be together."

I envied his conviction and wished to find that certainty within me soon. In the meantime I just gave myself to the moment.

We held each other in the warmth of love, and at length my tears subsided, my eyes cleared, and at last I looked at the ring around my finger. The exquisite gold band had been crafted into thin tree branches interlaced with each other, clasping a delicate bird's nest that cradled an octagonal diamond.

"The ring is stunning, and it fits me perfectly. How did you know my size?"

"I've held your hand in mine. I designed it with the Cascades in mind since we both like them so."

"You designed it? Oh…Wow! It's gorgeous!"

"This is your engagement ring, and I wanted it to be one of a kind, from me just for you. Because…well…I hope you'll agree to wear my grandmother's wedding ring. She so much wanted you, and only you, to have it."

"Me?" Startled, I sat up, breaking our embrace.

He laughed and eased me back into his arms, kissed my head, and caressed my hair.

"My turn to tell you a story. When I wrote to tell Grandma that I wanted to marry Dianne, she asked me if her middle name started with an *S*. Of course it didn't, and I never heard from her what it all meant until just before she died. She took off her wedding ring, gave it to me, and told me that this was the ring my soul mate should wear when we married. She'd shared many years of love and devotion with this ring and wished the same for her. Then she told me her name…Sarah."

I gasped, and my hands rushed to my mouth, protecting the emotion that flowed through me.

"The wedding ring is an intricate gold band, rare in its construction. It's in excellent shape, as if time and use had never touched it. She gave me my grandfather's ring to wear. When I had it sized to fit me, since my hands are a bit larger than my granddad's, the jeweler couldn't believe his own eyes. Both rings are made of individual pieces of gold joined together forming a circle. The jeweler had a hard time matching the design in Granddad's ring to make it larger for me, a challenge he eventually overcame with great pride. As for yours, my grandma and you wear the same size."

"Where do you suppose they got those rings?"

"Don't know. How could they afford them? They were such simple folk."

"Did they leave behind a will?"

"More like a letter, with their property passing on to me and my aunts."

"No mention of the rings?"

"No. Grandma had already given them to me, so no need to include them. I do have a letter she wrote that you're supposed to open on our wedding day."

"A letter for me?"

"It is addressed in her own handwriting to Sarah. I'd say that now that you have accepted my proposal and will be my wife, you are the Sarah she wrote to."

"How long do I have to wait to read it?"

He laughed so hard I could've sworn that the little ornaments on the tree shook and joined in his fun.

"Seems to me you are more interested in the letter than in asking about when we shall wed."

"Oh." I giggled. "I guess you're right. When do you want to set the date for? What about Alyana and Tom? What will they think of you asking me to marry you?"

He chuckled, "They helped me prepare the proposal. Alyana suggested I get down on one knee. Tom did it for her, and she thought it was special. Was it?"

"Oh yeah!"

"Good. They'll like to hear that. Let's find a calendar," he said, and as he scanned the coffee table, he noticed the album. "I see you found another treasure left behind in that attic of yours."

"It's an album with the photos of your aunts."

"May I?"

"Of course. It's yours. Your grandmother left it for you here in your house."

"This is your house, not mine."

"This house belonged to Angela. Heather Lewis willed it to her. Although come to think of it, I don't remember seeing your name or Angela's on the deed. That's strange. I don't remember to whom the house belonged."

I must've looked bewildered as I sat on the edge of the sofa staring at my future husband because once again he burst out laughing.

"You sure look funny when you worry like that. You furrow your forehead and you pucker your lips. It makes me want to kiss you."

"Well, what are you waiting for?"

We kissed, laughed, and relaxed back onto the sofa as we looked through the album of photos.

"I'd like to know how you found out about the Lewis bunch when you're ready to tell me."

"I can tell you right now if you wish."

"It can wait. I think this moment is about my aunts. You see, my aunts lived in this house after they finished college. My grandmother gave them the house. The last name on the title was of Casey's late husband, Tarkington. I only had the power of attorney to sell it for them if the right person came along."

"No wonder it didn't sound familiar. Why did they sell their house?"

"We're about to discover that, aren't we?"

"Through this photo album?"

"And those questions you know how to ask."

"Did Deidre ever marry?"

"No. Never."

"Why?"

"I know some of the story but not all of it. Maybe if we look at the pictures we can piece the whole story together. Want to share your secrets with me?"

I smiled, and without an ounce of fear, I relaxed and opened myself up for whatever wished to appear before me. Together we were about to join our stories of his twin aunts.

Their childhood had been a happy one, as they were loved by Angela and Richard and their older brothers, Aidan, Conrad's dad, and Brady. Angela and Richard made a good-looking couple. Angela's photos showed her as a tall brunette with a light complexion, a radiant smile, captivating dark eyes, and a composure that conveyed distinctiveness. Richard was a bit taller than his wife, of darker complexion, as virile as Conrad, and just as handsome. Their children were all attractive, well dressed, and all exuded self-confidence. The twins were born in 1925, and clearly the youngest of the bunch. Brady was one year their elder and Aidan was three. The photographs showed a happy family, content with life, with many cheerful pictures of the twins and their brothers all through to their teens. There were photos of the entire family and photos of just the twin girls engaged in play or work, always together, always eyeing each other, always sharing the experience of the photograph.

Then the pictures stopped for several years, with no photographic memories of the time they spent away from home while in Seattle attending college, having joined their brothers at the University of Washington.

"Casey and Deidre moved in with Heather Lewis and her daughter, Alice. The boys had their own place near the university where they lived with Michael, Heather's son," Conrad added.

We did find a graduation photograph of the twins in their nursing uniforms.

"Grandma said that since they were little they knew they would dedicate their lives to the care of others," Conrad explained.

The Gift of the Twin Houses

Casey met her husband in the hospital where they were first assigned. We found a photograph of Casey and Horace in their wedding garments but no sign of Deidre, Angela, Richard, or their sons.

What happened next no one really knew, but the pain was apparent in all their faces. The twins came back home with a baby girl but no husband. They lived in what was now my house with Sophia, Casey's daughter.

"Are you sure Sophia is Casey's daughter?" I asked.

"Everyone thinks so."

But the photographs told me a different story. "I think that Sophia is Deidre's child. Don't you see that in their eyes?"

"No, not really. As far as the family is concerned, that was never an issue since they both behaved as Sophia's mothers." He paused to glance at the photographs, and then he looked at me.

"This ability of yours is something else. We never doubted that Sophia was Casey's."

"Maybe I'm wrong."

"I'm not sure. You've tapped into that part of the universe that shares the truth. That's what Grandma used to call it."

"Did she?"

"Looks like you're picking up where Angela left off."

"You think that's what's happening? Where did she leave it? What's missing?"

The uneasiness of the thought that I had tapped into something Angela had left undone startled me and made me recoil. Instinctively I stood up and walked away from Conrad.

"No need to run away, Sarah."

The kindness in his voice reassured me, and I returned to the sofa and his embrace. I still felt apprehensive and uneasy, and he was well aware of it.

"I'm not sure what's in store for me," I said. "At times it feels like I'm on the verge of uncovering some deep pain or something really awful. It frightens me, and I pull away. I'm not used to it. Feels strange. It scares me."

"Still no need to run away. No harm can come of it. Why not just trust it and see what will come?"

"You're right. I should. But somehow, I'm still too insecure." I took a deep breath, hoping to inhale some of his valor.

He held me in his arms, I settled down, and we continued to remember the lives of the twin aunties as we looked through the album.

"I sense that part of what I have to unearth concerns your aunts."

"Then let's see what we find out."

The photographs of their later years with Sophia showed them going about their happy lives as if nothing had come to pass. Only the lost twinkle in their eyes spoke of untold heartache.

"My grandma said that the truth of what had happened in Seattle remained buried in their hearts, never allowing the slightest whisper to escape and harm Sophia or me and my siblings. Angela's advice to them was that the past didn't define them, that it only helped shape the future they were destined for."

Conrad spoke with admiration and compassion about his aunts, and the good they had done for all the folks in these parts. "They tended to the sick and the elderly and, along with Angela, were revered for their kindness and unselfishness. In fact, the twins were the ones that eventually were able to reunite Angela with her mother, Rachel. It turned out that Angela's momma had never reached her cousin in Montana after selling the house to Heather Lewis. For many years no one knew what had happened to her. She'd just disappeared."

"Frightful."

"We didn't think so at the time. Grandma Angela told us that she knew her mother was at peace and that one day they would be reunited, so she never made a fuss over it. She simply waited for the right time, and eventually that moment arrived. Her daughters brought it to her."

"How?"

"For years the twins inquired about Rachel everywhere they went and with everyone they encountered. They were convinced that by spreading the word about their search for their grandmother Rachel, they would find her or at least discover what had taken place, why she had never reached her destination. They researched the many routes to Rachel's cousin in Montana and traveled them, inquiring about her each step of the way. In the end, one of their patients told them that he'd met a nun, Sister Rachel, during a recent train ride to Montana. He wasn't sure if this might be the same Rachel they were looking for, given that she was a nun and couldn't be a grandmother, but thought he'd mention it nonetheless on account of the similarity of the name."

"What happened?"

"The twins didn't hesitate and immediately followed up. Their efforts were rewarded when they met their grandmother."

"What kept her from reaching her cousin's?"

"Rachel entered a catholic convent on her way to her cousin's. On the train to Montana, she'd sat next to a nun and decided right then and there that a life devoted to God and to the service of others would bring her the peace she sought."

"Why not tell Angela where she was?"

"She didn't know where Angela had gone to. She sent a letter to her cousin explaining what had happened and where she was, but the letter never reached its destination. Rachel had accepted the silence as penitence for quitting on her daughter."

The very last photograph in the album was a picture of Rachel in her habit, sitting next to her daughter, Angela. Behind Angela, and holding her hand, stood her husband, Richard. They were in front of their Christmas tree, surrounded by Rachel's grandchildren and great-grandchildren.

"Look," I said, "It's just like our Christmas tree."

"Indeed."

"Do you think it's all right to take this photo out of the album and place it in one of the frames next to Angela's fourteenth birthday picture and her pa's photo?"

"Don't ask me; you're the caretaker of the memories."

"Then let's go to the attic to see if we can find its frame."

When we entered the attic, the setting sun immersed the room in striking golden rays.

"Man, oh man! No wonder," Conrad exclaimed.

Just as before, we looked into each other's eyes and knew all that needed to be said without uttering a word.

It took us no time to find the frame Angela had picked for this photograph, and as the sun disappeared, we left the attic and made our way to Angela's old room.

We placed the family picture of Momma surrounded by Angela, Richard, and their children and grandchildren next to her pa's.

Conrad put his arm around my waist as we took in the photographs. "This is a nice room. The photos fit in. Are these your folks?"

"Yes, and my nana."

"Good-looking family. Interesting how the pictures go together, your family and mine."

"Yes, they are at ease here. Every time I look at these pictures, I feel as if they reach out and caress me. The memories they suggest are filled with warmth and joy. Their honesty is disarming."

"You're in good hands."

We turned out the lights and made our way down the hall. As we passed my bedroom, I felt Conrad's hold, and at once I realized the significance of where we were.

I tensed and stopped as I succumbed to millions—no, billions—of misgivings. Conrad immediately tightened his grip on my waist and tilted his head to touch mine.

"Sarah, please don't fret. There should never be fear or tension between us. If you are not ready, we'll wait."

"Thanks, it's just that I—"

"I get it."

An awkward silence fell between us, and I felt an emptiness in the pit of my stomach.

In spite of my refusal to make love, Conrad never let go of my waist, but I noticed some hesitation on his part as we made our way down the stairs. His kiss good-bye was loving and tender yet different.

I felt shaky, unstable, and insecure through and through.

The Gift of the Twin Houses

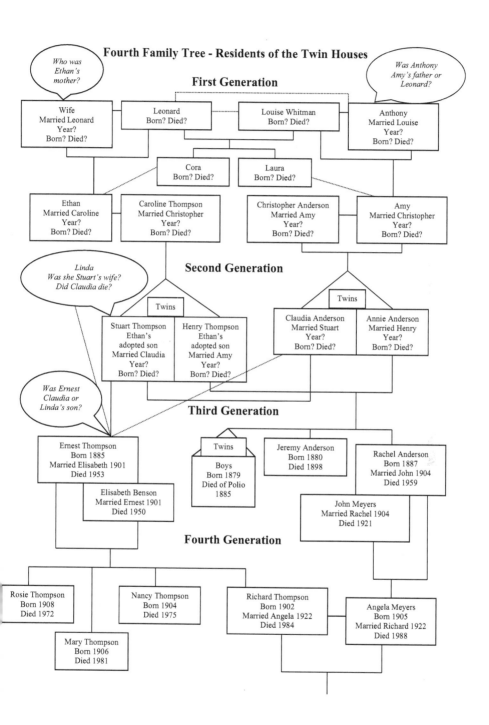

Fourth Family Tree - Residents of the Twin Houses

First Generation

Who was Ethan's mother?

Was Anthony Amy's father or Leonard?

Wife
Married Leonard
Year?
Born? Died?

Leonard
Born? Died?

Louise Whitman
Born? Died?

Anthony
Married Louise
Year?
Born? Died?

Cora
Born? Died?

Laura
Born? Died?

Ethan
Married Caroline
Year?
Born? Died?

Caroline Thompson
Married Christopher
Year?
Born? Died?

Christopher Anderson
Married Amy
Year?
Born? Died?

Amy
Married Christopher
Year?
Born? Died?

Second Generation

*Linda
Was she Stuart's wife?
Did Claudia die?*

Twins

Stuart Thompson
Ethan's
adopted son
Married Claudia
Year?
Born? Died?

Henry Thompson
Ethan's
adopted son
Married Amy
Year?
Born? Died?

Twins

Claudia Anderson
Married Stuart
Year?
Born? Died?

Annie Anderson
Married Henry
Year?
Born? Died?

Was Ernest Claudia or Linda's son?

Third Generation

Ernest Thompson
Born 1885
Married Elisabeth 1901
Died 1953

Twins

Boys
Born 1879
Died of Polio
1885

Jeremy Anderson
Born 1880
Died 1898

Rachel Anderson
Born 1887
Married John 1904
Died 1959

Elisabeth Benson
Married Ernest 1901
Died 1950

John Meyers
Married Rachel 1904
Died 1921

Fourth Generation

Rosie Thompson
Born 1908
Died 1972

Nancy Thompson
Born 1904
Died 1975

Richard Thompson
Born 1902
Married Angela 1922
Died 1984

Angela Meyers
Born 1905
Married Richard 1922
Died 1988

Mary Thompson
Born 1906
Died 1981

V. & D. Povall

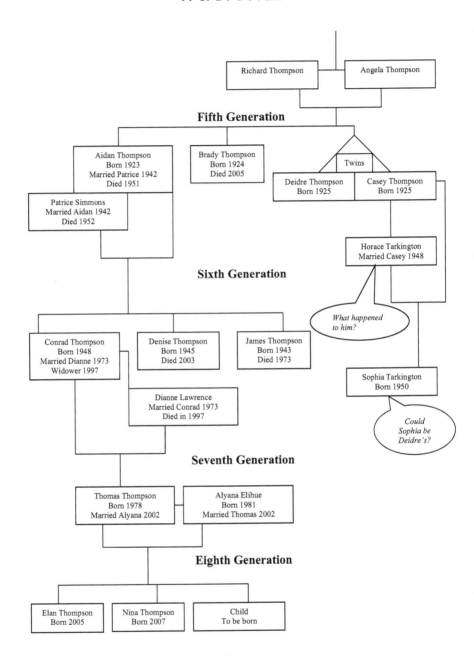

Richard Thompson | Angela Thompson

Fifth Generation

Aidan Thompson
Born 1923
Married Patrice 1942
Died 1951

Brady Thompson
Born 1924
Died 2005

Twins

Deidre Thompson
Born 1925

Casey Thompson
Born 1925

Patrice Simmons
Married Aidan 1942
Died 1952

Horace Tarkington
Married Casey 1948

Sixth Generation

What happened to him?

Conrad Thompson
Born 1948
Married Dianne 1973
Widower 1997

Denise Thompson
Born 1945
Died 2003

James Thompson
Born 1943
Died 1973

Sophia Tarkington
Born 1950

Dianne Lawrence
Married Conrad 1973
Died in 1997

Could Sophia be Deidre's?

Seventh Generation

Thomas Thompson
Born 1978
Married Alyana 2002

Alyana Elihue
Born 1981
Married Thomas 2002

Eighth Generation

Elan Thompson
Born 2005

Nina Thompson
Born 2007

Child
To be born

CHAPTER 20

Slippery Road

I DON'T KNOW how long I paced the living room after he left, or the dining room, let alone my bedroom. As the night went by, my anxiety grew. The old Sarah had taken hold of all my senses, and I could do nothing to bring back peace and calm. Chaos had set in, and terror traveled through my veins.

The instant the morning awoke, I drove away from my house, away from my valley, away from my newfound self, and away from Conrad.

I drove following the signs toward Seattle, but with no specific direction, just away from it all, escaping. I couldn't bear the shame of middle-aged virginity. What would he think of me? How pathetic I'd become, an old maid, a forgotten woman, an abandoned body. How could I confess that I had no sexual experience with men? He would find me repulsive, desolate, pitiful, ridiculous.

What was I thinking when I accepted his marriage proposal? With marriage comes sex. I should've put two and two together. But no, I just gave myself into the happiness of his proposal. Never thought of sex. How could I've forgotten about sex? What will I do now?

Escape, pure and simple escape. It worked before, and it should work now.

This time however, I had no precise destination, except to follow the road before me, and the signs toward Seattle, all the while asking myself a myriad of questions and absent from my surroundings.

Then, the snow stopped me. I don't know how long it had been snowing, but I suddenly noticed that the roads were covered with it that and visibility had diminished to a few feet. I had reached Leavenworth and saw the faint lights of a hotel off the highway. I made my way toward it, parked the car, and checked in.

I settled into a small, quaint room with Bavarian decor. The warmth of the heater welcomed me. I took a deep breath and allowed myself to relax a bit. I opened the curtains and sat by the window to watch the snowfall. Only then did I notice it was dark again. I had lost an entire day in the labyrinth of my frightened mind.

As reality set in, I imagined Conrad worried sick about my absence. The cynical Sarah quickly concluded that if he'd indeed been worried, he would've called me on my cell. Since I hadn't received a single call, obviously he had retreated after my refusal. The trusting Sarah, however, sneaked a quick doubt, so I picked up my cell and discovered that I'd turned it off. As soon as it came on I saw there were over fifteen messages, all from Conrad. Fear or not, I should've at least had the civility to call and tell him not to worry. Gathering all my courage, I dialed his number.

"Hi," I managed to say.

"Finally!" he shouted. "Why haven't you answered your cell? Are you all right? Where the hell are you?"

"I'm all right. I'm at the Bavarian Lodge in Leavenworth."

"What on earth are you doing there?"

"I'm all right. I promise. No need to worry about me."

"What got into you leaving like that?"

"I'm…well…I'm OK. I'll call you in the morning. Don't worry."

"Don't worry? How could I not worry? I don't know what made you leave and behave like this, but now I'm in charge. I'm coming to get you. You stay put. I'll be right over."

"No! Please. Conrad, please no sense in coming out tonight so far from your home. I'll wait till the snow stops, and I'll come home then. I'll be all right."

"I'm already out. I figured you were scared and had bolted. I've been combing the highways searching for you. What room are you in?"

"Four zero seven, but—"

"I should get there in a few." With that, he hung up.

My selfish escape had worried him to such a degree that, regardless of his own safety, he'd been searching for me in the middle of a snowstorm.

The Gift of the Twin Houses

Sarah, what can you possibly tell him when he shows up to justify your selfish actions?

Time flew by as I worked myself into a frenzy, and before I could come up with any type of sensible explanation, he knocked on the door of my hotel room.

The minute the door opened, he pulled me to him and held me tightly in his arms. Without letting go of the embrace, he stepped into the room and shut the door behind us. He held me for a long time, easing all his fears and tribulations.

"I didn't mean to scare you," I whispered.

"Well, you did."

Then, he held me arm's length and stared into my eyes. " What got into you?"

"I think I was heading for California to see my friends."

"You think? You're not sure? Drive all the way to California without telling anyone? Whatever for?"

I stepped away from him. I couldn't look at him; my shame was so deep that to steady my nerves I stared out the window at the falling snow. "I thought I needed their advice."

"About what? Couldn't you do it over the phone?"

"I didn't think of that."

"Sarah, look at me."

I turned toward him and saw his beautiful eyes pleading for an answer.

"What's the matter? What's happened? Please tell me."

"I'm afraid."

"Of what? Of Angela? The stories you hear, the—"

"No," I interrupted, "it's not that, although that's still unsettling."

"Then what?"

I knew I couldn't hide it from him, so I took a deep breath, lowered my eyes, and confessed. "I've never experienced intimacy with a man."

There, I said it. My shame, fully exposed stood between us. As strongly as I wished to take back my words, I knew it had to be said sooner or later. After all, I had accepted his marriage proposal. Nonetheless, terror consumed me. My heart beat so fast and intensely, I thought it might burst right out of my chest.

As he walked toward me, I stopped him. "Conrad, please don't come closer or I won't be able to tell you what...well, what I need to say."

He stopped in spite of his desire to hold me in his arms. I could feel his need to reassure me, to give me strength, to support me. But I needed to be strong for my own sake and to be honest with him.

"I accepted your marriage proposal without thinking of what would come next."

"Do you want to wait until after we are married? Is that it?"

"No. It's not about being prudish. It's about...it's about...it's about...well not knowing what to do. It's so...embarrassing."

Conrad continued to respect my request for space. He simply smiled. "So you have little experience. There's nothing to be embarrassed about."

"Yes, there is. Please hear me out." *Might as well put it all out there.* I took a deep breath and looked into his eyes. "I was left at the altar many years ago, innocence intact, and never got close to any man again. My fiancé blamed my fear of intimacy when he dropped me."

"Sarah—"

"Everything I feel about you is new, and I don't know how...well... Anyway, what happened so long ago wasn't fear of intimacy. It was fear of my extrasensory capacities. I didn't want my fiancé, or anyone else, to know about the abnormal connections I felt. So I did sort of distance myself."

" OK, but—"

"Growing up with this kind of supernatural stuff around me had a completely different effect from what you experienced with Angela."

"I get that."

"I kept it well under wraps. No one could even guess. So, in time it evolved into what he so aptly called fear of intimacy. I just couldn't get close to anyone, afraid I would be discovered and cause pain and anguish as it had done when I was little. So I distanced myself...I'm not sure I can—"

"No need to fear that with me."

" I know. I'm not afraid of that anymore."

"Then what? We can wait until we're married."

"Oh, it's not that either. Believe me it's not about time or a piece of paper that says it's OK to have sex."

"Well, what is it? I'm at a loss here."

"It's about...well...I don't want to disappoint you...What if...what if...I can't go through with it? Or worse, what if you don't like me? Now you've asked me to marry you and you've told the kids, and if you don't like me, if I don't satisfy you sexually, after all, I've no experience...well...you're stuck with me, and then...well, then...there's no way out, and you're trapped."

Smiling, he walked toward me. I tried to stop him again, but he just kept walking.

"You can't stop me," he said. "You know I can't resist kissing away your fears when you frown and pucker your lips."

He caressed my forehead and kissed it and then kissed his way down my nose till he found my mouth. His kiss was gentle, and I was aware of the delicate pulsations that conveyed his love and devotion.

"Stop tormenting yourself or I'll keep kissing you until the frowning goes away, or until we stop all these worrisome thoughts of yours."

He then kissed me long and hard.

"But Conrad, I'm a...*a virgin.*"

He kissed me again with such passion that my knees buckled.

"There is nothing on this earth that will ever make me change my mind."

Then he gently lifted my chin toward him and kissed me so softly that it felt as if the most delicious, sweet, soft butter was melting between our lips. It was exquisite.

"I love you, Sarah, more than I ever thought possible. I've never felt as deeply about anyone as I feel about you. Don't ask me to explain why or how come because I wouldn't know what to say. I'm trying to get a handle on it myself. I just know that when I'm with you, I'm whole, I'm alive, I'm excited. There's something about you that penetrated my senses and my soul from the first time I laid eyes on you, and since then, it's taken over me. There isn't anything that will ever make me change my mind about wanting to spend the rest of my life with you."

Our kiss this time was more penetrating—a kiss hungry for the full submission of our bodies.

I gathered all my courage and led him toward the bed, my legs trembling with every step.

"C'mon, then," I whispered, "let's dive into it and live with the consequences. Whatever they may be. No matter what happens, it's better if you know what you are getting into before we get married."

"You're sure? No need to rush to prove anything."

"I'm sure. Just remember, I don't know…well I've no idea what to do to… how to…well…to give you pleasure. I might fail miserably. How about that for a consequence?"

"The consequences will be what we make of them. We want to be together, don't we?

"Yes, but—"

"No more buts. And more important, no need to force anything between us." He smiled while caressing my cheek.

I knew I needed to plunge into it and should take the initiative to let him know he could move forward, so I unbuttoned his shirt and caressed his muscular chest. Pure delight rushed through me. I felt myself relax as he quietly unbuttoned my blouse. When we shed our upper garments, we held each other in a warm, delicious embrace, the feel of our exposed skin penetrating our consciousness.

His hands gently explored my bare arms, my back, and my sides, and as they caressed my skin, they conveyed pleasurable shivers through all of me. His touch felt velvety soft, filled with tenderness and sincerity, and I allowed myself the pleasure of giving into the sensations without concern or embarrassment. I didn't recoil when he reached my breasts. He caressed them, cupped them, and kissed them with such gentleness that I felt like a precious gem in the hands of its greatest admirer. He simply made me feel beautiful, sensual.

We shed the rest of our clothes and lay down on the bed. Strappingly virile, his entire being emanated strength and forcefulness, yet his touch was as soothing as the petal of a rose. With kisses and caresses we explored each other's bodies, admiring their uniqueness, their imperfections, their peaks, and their valleys. We danced to the song of love, having found our own rhythm and cadence, accompanied by the melody of his voice as he whispered, "I love you," or "You're so beautiful," or plainly, "Sarah, my Sarah."

I remember murmuring his name and whispering that I loved him, my chorus to his beautiful song.

"You may hurt a bit when I come in," he said. "I'll be gentle, but let me know if it's too much."

And it wasn't. For a second I did feel tightness, but immediately it gave way to a perfect cuddle. I relaxed into the sensation of togetherness, of oneness, and as we moved in unison, our breathing joined in.

I could feel him going in and out, a caress within me, and with each thrust my contractions increased, hungry to possess every bit, devouring his manhood. He knew I wanted all of him, and at once he responded by sliding his arm under my lower back, and pulling me toward him as he thrust inward, deeper and deeper each time. I not only fully admitted him, but with each thrust I pulled him toward the deepest recesses of my being.

Together we reached the peak of pleasure, of immense joy, of utter delight.

Afterward we cried, in silence, holding each other tightly, unwilling to let go of the intimacy of our love and passion.

"Thank you," he whispered, "thank you for waiting for me. Thank you for giving me the gift of the purity of your body."

All I could do was sigh.

We lay in each other's arms savoring the memory of our first time, enjoying the warmth our bodies shared.

"Sex is a lot better than I ever imagined."

"This wasn't sex, Sarah; this was love." He drew me closer.

I buried my head in his chest so that I could experience his scent again. It was intoxicating. I found something beyond appealing about his smell. When he'd reached climax, it had changed. His breath had become a bit colder, and his scent turned muskier, a combination that increased my reaction and propelled me through my own climax.

"What a deep sigh," he said. "What about?"

"Thinking of us. I hope you're right that nothing can keep us apart."

"Still doubtful?"

"I can't help it. I sense there's something stirring, something unaddressed."

"Just promise me one thing. No more running away from me."

"I won't run away, but I might need you to...well, I don't really know what."

"Good. Angela never ran away again either."

We laughed, and for the first time in my life, I enjoyed the shared intimacy, the feeling of total and complete surrender of my defenses, of absolute trust.

"So, when do you think we should tie the knot?" he asked.

"Whenever you wish, but the sooner the better. I don't want to be apart from you. Without you I'm bound to craft horror stories and shy away from whatever Angela has in mind for me."

"How about if we marry between Christmas and New Year's?"

"What do you think Tom and Alyana would say to that?"

"I ran it by Tom, and he's all for it. I'm sure Alyana will be OK. We can ask them later. Anyway, it takes three days to get a marriage license here in Washington, and we'll need to decide on the ceremony."

"I like it. Our Decembers will be filled with fun celebrations."

"I thought, if it's all right with you, we should give my house to Tom and Alyana for Christmas, and we could live at your place. OK if I move in with you?"

First, I covered him with kisses, and then I slowed down enough to speak. "Thank you for not asking me to leave my house, and thank you, thank you, for bringing the family close to us. With Alyana's baby on the way, she'll have her hands full, and I'd like to help her. They're such a wonderful couple, and I love their little ones."

"How about if we help them move in before the ceremony?"

"Before? Wow. That's fast. I don't know. I really don't. Could we do so much in such little time?" I answered with extreme preoccupation at my inability to even guess what we, the couple, should do. I could feel the old worrisome Sarah breaking through.

"You're so darn cute with your worries." He kissed my nose. "C'mon, let's go find something to eat, and we'll celebrate our union while we plan the wedding. I'm starving."

"Oh no. We'll have dinner all right, but we'll celebrate our union in our home. It's the decent thing to do for her."

He just laughed and kissed the tip of my nose again. I loved it when he did that. It made me feel like a charming, coquettish young girl. Isn't it wonderful how a gesture can evoke such feelings of adolescence and happiness? Well, it did the trick, and all my worries disappeared. At least for the moment.

By the time we got dressed, the snow had stopped falling, and we made our way down the block to the restaurant.

Conrad called Tom and Alyana to reassure them that all was well. He asked them to join us for Sunday brunch to plan the wedding together.

As usual, we eased into effortless conversation as we sipped a glass of wine, ate a simple dinner of meat and potatoes, and enjoyed the background Christmas music.

"It felt so good, I can't imagine why I feared it so."

"I'm relieved I didn't hurt you, this being your first time."

"No, it didn't hurt at all. Actually, it felt delicious. Some time back, a friend of mine got married after being a widow for many years. She felt embarrassed to ask her doctor, a man, if she needed something or if she could even do it. So I offered to ask my own doctor, given that she's a woman. My doctor said that when women, young or old, go without sex for years, their bodies react to renewed lovemaking as if they were adolescents. She told me that she had many women patients who had that very reaction to sex even in their golden years, because it's all about the emotion of love and desire for one's partner. It stimulates the hormones, even in us older types, and the body reacts accordingly. It certainly worked for me at my age. Go figure."

"What age? And you're not 'an older type.' You're perfect."

"All your doing. I certainly feel young with you."

"So do I."

After dinner, hand in hand, we took a nice short walk, enjoying the peace and quiet that a cold night brings after a snowstorm. We decided that it made no sense to wait till Christmas for him to move in with me, so as soon as we got back home, we would bring his things over to my house—or rather, to *our* house.

We spent the night ensconced in our charming Bavarian room, cuddled in each other's arms under the warmth of the comforter, and made love every time we woke. I used to think it impossible to actually fall asleep in the arms of another person. It looked nice in the movies, but the skeptical Sarah thought it would be uncomfortable. Nice to prove her wrong.

Bright and early the next morning, we went downstairs to breakfast, and I felt as if the entire world knew what had happened and envied me. We walked into the restaurant, hand in hand, a couple in love, a radiant twosome, comfortable with the intimacy between us, and exuding such bliss that everyone in the restaurant turned to look at us and smiled. We smiled back.

We went back to our room to gather our belongings, and as we reached the door, Conrad turned to me and smiled. "One more time?"

"One more time."

And, like adolescents, trying to grasp the very last opportunity before going home, we took off—well, we practically tore off each other's clothes, jumped on the bed laughing, and had an unforgettable quickie.

CHAPTER 21

The Twin House

SLOWLY, WE MADE our way back home. Conrad followed me in his truck, closely watching over me. The roads were covered with snow, and the plows continued to push it aside. How stupid I'd been, and how relieved I felt now that Conrad had rescued me from my own folly. In these weather conditions, I don't know if I could've made the trip back on my own without the reassurance of his presence behind me.

We were stopped several times while they cleared the roads. By the time we got home, the evening shadows of early winter nights made their presence known. We were starving, so we first prepared a quick meal by reheating the leftover chicken and shared our bliss with our house. We told her Conrad would be moving in, and she communicated her joy with her familiar cracks and cricks.

After dinner, we made our way to Conrad's house to pick up a few things.

As we entered, I sensed that his house wanted me to be aware of the memories that were important to him and needed to be cared for along with those of her twin.

Understanding what had been requested of me, I told him, "I'm sure there are mementos, furniture, photographs, and special items you'd like to take with you from here."

"Would you believe I haven't thought of that?" He stopped in the middle of the living room. "I'd have to mull it over, but right now, other than my personal belongings, some photographs, and knickknacks I like, most of everything else should remain here with Tom and Alyana. You'll see their little home in a few days when we go for Christmas Day. It's pretty sparse. They'd been waiting to buy a home, so they've been saving up."

"Why didn't they move into my house when they married? It remained empty, didn't it?"

"They were not the ones destined for that house. You were…*we* were, you and I, now that I think on it. C'mon, let's go upstairs to my room to get a few things."

I'd never been to the upstairs of this house, of Angela and Richard's home. I walked behind Conrad with trepidation, not wanting to disturb the history it held, worried that somehow it might disapprove of my taking Conrad away. But soon I realized I had nothing to worry about—the house didn't object. She understood the path we were taking to be the correct one, the one destined to be.

The upstairs displayed much of Angela and a good deal of Richard, Conrad, and Tom. There were feminine traces here and there, but since Angela's absence, the masculine tones were more vivid and palpable, and I understood Alyana's comment about the feel of this house. Manly overtones permeated every room, a clear continuum in space and time of the influence of Leonard, its designer, builder, and first inhabitant. How he'd been able to achieve masculine tones for his house and feminine ones for Louise's remained part of the puzzle. Perhaps the result of his devotion to her.

Conrad's bedroom had been his grandparents' at one point and, I imagined, Leonard's. It was furnished beautifully by a double bed with stunning wood head and footboards, late 1880s by my estimation. The armoire and dresser were of the same period and the same type of wood, as were the small table, the rocking chair, and the two armchairs. I stood mesmerized by the simplicity and power that emanated from each piece and by the ensemble as a whole.

"I can see your admiration of my grandma's proudest possessions. She talked my grandpa into getting each piece, a year at a time. When they gathered them all, he told me he'd understood why she insisted so. He said that in this room they felt in unison with the woods and nature as a whole, as if a bit of the Cascades had entered their room. He loved to be next to Grandma when she sat in her rocking chair to knit or read. He read his newspaper or just chatted with her, their private time and space. We children knew to leave them be."

"I can imagine it." I spoke so quietly it sounded almost like a whisper. Then I saw a guitar resting against the dresser. I walked toward it and caressed its strings.

"Is this Angela's old guitar?"

"Yes. How'd you know? Wait, what am I saying? Of course you know these things."

"You play?"

"I do."

"Did Angela teach you?"

"In a way. My dad took to playing it when he was little. Guess he loved to hear Grandma play it and wanted to do it himself. Soon after we moved in here, I took to it just as easily as he did."

"On her fourteenth birthday, I heard Angela apologize to her guitar for not being able to take it with her, and she told it she knew it would be loved. Guess she was right."

"Without a doubt. Thanks for telling me that. I always felt a special connection between the guitar and Grandma."

"Has Tom learned to play it as well?"

"Yes. He has his own at home."

"Will you bring this one with you?"

"Of course. I've been teaching Elan and Nina. It plays easier than other guitars, so it's simpler for little ones to learn."

"Where did you sleep when you were young?"

"James and I slept in the room down the hall, and Denise slept in the one right next to this one. Before that, my dad, Aidan, slept in my bedroom with my uncle Brady, and my aunts, Casey and Deidre, slept in what later became Denise's room. Go take a peek if you want. When Tom's mom, Dianne, moved back here with me, we lived in a house not far from here. After she left I moved back into my old room, and Tom inherited my sister's room. Some of the old furniture is still there, but much of it is newer. This bedroom set here is the only one that has not succumbed to the modern world."

I walked down the hall to Conrad and Tom's former bedrooms. They held simple furnishings, nicely mingling the old and the new. I imagined the twin aunties as little girls, Conrad's sister, his brother, father, and uncle. So many memories were held in these rooms. I wanted to know them all. I wanted them to come to me and make me part of their history, their world, and I heard them say yes, they would come and visit.

Suddenly I saw Leonard and his son, Ethan, in this house. Then the image of Ethan's sons, Stuart "the cowboy," and his brother, Henry, showed up. I caught a glimpse of Henry as he left this house and moved to mine when he married Amy's daughter Annie. Then I saw Stuart marrying Annie's twin sister, Claudia, the birth of their baby girl, and the sadness he felt when they both died. Then I saw another woman alongside an older Stuart with a baby boy. The images were clear enough, yet confusing, until I understood their meaning. They offered glimpses of the people who were related to one another while pointing out those who weren't. But why or how did I know that?

"Lots of generations have passed through these rooms," Conrad said as he put his arms around me.

"I just realized that Leonard knew the truth. Amy was not his. Louise must've conceived Amy with her husband, Anthony."

"Doesn't matter much now, does it?"

"I think it does. And I think I'm supposed to do something with this information. Don't know what though."

"When the time comes, you'll know."

"I guess."

"C'mon," Conrad said as he took my hand.

"Wait, do you have an attic?"

"Twin houses all the way. Upstairs. C'mon."

As we climbed the stairs, he turned to me. "Nothing like that attic of yours. This one holds old furniture, and that's about it."

"Your grandmother didn't care for it like she did for mine?"

"Maybe it lacked the same significance. I don't know why. This attic is where Grandpa Richard used to keep the things he didn't care to put in the outer shed. Things he might need during the winters without having to go out in the snow."

The Gift of the Twin Houses

We reached the attic, and he opened the door for me. I stepped in, and in an instant I understood the role this room had played in their lives. It reflected Leonard's personality through and through. A room created to ensure that both households would be safe and well cared for. A rational room, a room designed for practical uses, leaving all the emotions to be dealt with by the attic of its twin.

I made my way into the attic and around all the old, forgotten, dusty furniture, admiring each piece, imagining it in the house instead of abandoned in this room.

"I haven't been in here for years," Conrad said.

"There are some nice pieces. Why store them here?"

"We never wanted to get rid of the old stuff as Tom and I got newer or more useful things."

"Will you bring some with you to our home?"

"Well, I wasn't planning on it. Tom and Alyana may want to use them or better yet, they might want to sell them and make a bit of money."

"Would you mind if we take a look at what they don't want before they sell it? Maybe we'll want to keep it."

"Sure."

I moseyed back to him and out of the attic. He closed the door behind us, and as we made our way down the stairs, I sighed.

"What's the matter?"

"Did you see the old wooden double crib under the table in the right corner?"

"No, I don't recall a double crib."

"I wonder who the crib belonged to."

"I can take a look at it and hazard a guess as to when it could've been made."

"Will you?"

"Yep."

We walked down the hall past the small bedrooms, but before we reached the stairs to the lower floor, I stopped to look at Angela's room once more.

Conrad put his arm around my shoulders and we stood in silence observing his old room.

"I moved into this room after my grandma passed away. It was comforting."

"Do you want to move this furniture to our house?" I asked.

He remained silent for a while. Then he took a deep breath, exhaled, and tightened his hold around my waist. "I hadn't thought about it, but now that you mention it, it feels right."

"I think Angela and Richard would want us to."

"Well, there's one way to find out. Do you want to try the bed?"

With a wink, the perfect little gesture I had come to love so much, we entered the bedroom.

Angela sighed with delight as she quietly left the room and closed the door.

"Why close the door?" he asked. "We're alone."

"I didn't close it. It closed on its own."

"Did it?"

CHAPTER 22

Sarah

PERFECTION FILLED OUR second night together. We made love several times, cuddled, talked, kissed time and time again, and thoroughly enjoyed each other. Hard to believe how easy it had been for me to give myself to Conrad, how wonderful it felt to share this intimacy with him, and how uninhibited I felt. Considering that I'd never allowed a man to go further than a good-night kiss, it amazed me how much I craved Conrad's hands all over my body, and how unafraid I felt that he would find any flaws.

"I love your cinnamon skin," he told me. "It's as smooth as fine velvet." Then with each kiss and caress, I melted away. These emotions, the sense of comfort and lack of timidity, were all due to him. He made me feel special. Through his eyes I looked beautiful and enchanting, and with that, he'd conquered all my inhibitions. His gaze caressed my face, my breasts, my buttocks, and I saw delight in his face. No pretense in his actions or his words, he was genuine and without a doubt sincere in his admiration. He saw me as a sensuous, desirable woman, and consequently, so did I.

In turn, I saw him strong, with enormous sex appeal, and possessing an uncanny ability to combine tenderness with unbridled passion. I think that the adoration he saw in my eyes also made him feel dazzling and powerful. From our point of view, we were a stunning couple.

The sun peeked through the curtains as we woke up, and in the quiet of the early morning, he held me in his arms, and we glimpsed into my past.

"With a French nana and a Spanish mom, I'm sure you're used to traveling," Conrad said. "You'll be OK with a sedentary type like me? You know I didn't inherit the adventuresome streak from my dad. I'm more like my mother and my grandfather."

"Nothing would please me more than to grow old with you in this valley, surrounded by our family, and cared for by our twin houses. I'm not much of a traveler. I take more after my dad. He found his calling as a corporate attorney and was content to stay put and look after it, just as I did with my teaching."

"And your mom and nana?"

"My mom had no use for travel, as it disturbed our routine. She enjoyed her work and caring for all of us. She lived vicariously through her books, so she didn't like to wander about. Nana had had enough travel in her youth and delighted to be in a country that didn't push her to become someone she didn't wish to be. She preferred staying put. She loved her life in Boston, and after retirement, she involved herself in many community improvement projects. We all liked Boston and didn't seek to travel. We did go to Mexico often though."

"Where in Mexico?"

"Mostly Monterrey, a city in the northern part of Mexico where my father, Ernesto, was born. We visited with his family. But we also traveled to other cities and towns in Mexico."

"Ah, you inherited your cinnamon skin from him."

"Also from Nana and her family, who were olive skinned. I inherited my complexion mostly from my mom. My dad's term of endearment for my mom was *Canela*, which is cinnamon in Spanish."

"*Canela*," he said in perfect Spanish. "You're a veritable United Nations. You spoke Spanish or French at home?"

"Mostly English, Spanish for comfort, and French with Nana."

"Your parents raised you well, except for making you hide your abilities."

"They meant well, but once convinced that it was dangerous, they wouldn't budge. They held firmly to their convictions, same with Nana. It's part of my genetic makeup."

"I haven't seen that in you."

"Until recently, I behaved much like them. Their influence took firm hold on me. Nana tried to chip away at the cocoon they built around me, but she wouldn't stray from their teachings. It's interesting how I can actually recognize a genetic trait and then suddenly choose not to follow it. I certainly like it better now that I am open to new experiences."

"Good, 'cause I like that in you."

He bathed me in kisses, and before we knew it, we were making love. Oh, what a delight to indulge our senses early in the morning when our bodies were warm and cozy under the comforter. This time our lovemaking became a waltz, our bodies softly joining in perfect rhythm, delicious waves of tenderness and excitement flowing through us in perfect synchronicity.

It was slow and soothing, like a soft breeze in the freshness of the morning. Our climax was unhurried, a deep explosion of pleasure, roving little by little, generating immense desire every step of the way.

We stayed in a warm embrace for a while before saying anything, and I realized how much pleasure all these new experiences with my husband-to-be meant to me. Then all of a sudden, a gush of tears erupted. Years ago I'd closed the door on the notion of ever having a husband or a family of my own, and I'd hidden the key that could open those dreams deep inside me. Unbeknownst to him, Conrad had just found it. The door had been opened, and years of repressed sorrow were now uncontrollably gushing out. So I let them flow. Time to cleanse the past and allow my new life to emerge. This was the moment to remove all skeletons from my closet.

"I think I finally understand how broken I've been."

"You don't have to explain."

"I do."

"Please, don't go on just because you think I want to know why you've cried so. The past is just that, gone. What matters now is that I love you."

"But I'd like to share it with you." I went on. "It's not every day that one finds oneself."

"Then, by all means."

"The pain and then the fear of being different, of being evil, or of being a witch, as they had called me, controlled me all my life."

"Since six."

I smiled. "Yes, just six. It's understandable that without hesitation I accepted my family's desire to eliminate that horrid part of me."

"Not horrid."

"Not for you or Angela, but my family thought it terrifying at that time. It scared the daylights out of all of us. Supernatural stuff is not only foreign for most people, but also scary. Hard to explain, how it happens or why it happens. Particularly difficult for people like my parents, who needed concrete evidence to be able to manage its enigma. Even my nana, as intuitive as she was, couldn't offer any help on that score."

"I'm sure they researched it."

"I would think so. Never asked. By the time I could, I didn't even think of it. I'd gotten used to the person we had crafted."

"Crafted?"

"That's how I see it now. Influenced by the push for self-reliance, logic, rational thought, and independence, coupled with the strong opinions of my parents and grandmother, I lost my true self. Someone crafted in their mold emerged. So, I never really paid attention to me or what I wanted or needed, let alone who I was. I just accepted their representation of me and shut down the Sarah I could've been, the Sarah that I am today."

"I'm glad to have you."

"You have no idea how glad I am to have you." And of course we kissed for a long time before I could go on.

"As I think back, something pushed me to go west to college and to remain in California after I graduated. I never went back home after I finished college. I settled on my own, away from my family."

"Opposite coast. As far as possible from them."

"Yes, interesting isn't it? Nothing to do with not loving them, I simply followed their teachings of independence. They themselves saw my move away from them as a natural result of my upbringing, and in turn, I felt quite comfortable on my own. It seemed to me that I'd achieve the path they had hoped for me, and they were proud of my accomplishments."

"This permanent move happened before or after you didn't get married?"

"After. The engagement happened as I finished college. We met there."

"What's his name?"

"Patrick."

The Gift of the Twin Houses

"And?"

"Marriage seemed like good idea at the time; finish college, start a family, be normal. But in the end, I couldn't get close to him. I liked him enough. A nice young man, but I sensed that if I opened up to him, the images would reappear. So, I shut myself up and thought I could go through the marriage like that, encased in my own fortress. After all, my entire life had been just like that, so a marriage under those circumstances could work. But he didn't agree. I do wish he'd said so before not showing up to the wedding."

"He just didn't show up?"

"I'm sure he wanted to hurt me, and he succeeded. Afterward, I never wanted to feel that pain again, so I fell into a routine of restraint and detachment and became quite adept at being aloof. The Sarah who controlled her life didn't allow intimacy and therefore stayed safe. I loved being a teacher, so I threw myself into my work. My students were so fragile they—"

"Fragile? Why?"

"My field was special education. Most of my students had one or more disabilities. They needed so much attention that they absorbed all of my awareness, and I plain forgot all about me. I lost myself in the persona my parents crafted. Not till I came here, and entered our home, did I start shedding the shield in hope of finding my true self."

"Maybe your true self is in somewhere in the mix of the two. What attracts me is the blend of the self-reliant and the spiritual Sarahs."

"Maybe that's it. That's who I am, a bit of both. Time will tell."

We kissed, and for a while, as the sun entered the room. We held between us the lessons of the past that now brought hope for our future.

When we finally got out of bed, a new experience awaited. We showered together. Not only a sensual experience, but lots of fun. We drew immense pleasure from the familiarity of lathering each other, washing one another's hair, and cleansing our bodies. Erotic and exhilarating, though at times it tickled, and we burst out laughing. The joy of running my soapy hands along his entire body was thrilling. The hair on his chest, arms, and legs tickled my palms and sent little shivers through me. His manhood responded to my touch even though we'd just made love. How exciting to see him so ready to pleasure me again.

His foamy hands felt soft and rough at the same time. Conrad's delight and pleasure were so apparent that any insecurity I might've felt of letting him explore my body washed away. When his hand slightly opened my legs and glided in between, my body quaked. He trembled, instinctively reacting to my response. We took our time, thoroughly enjoying the pleasure of this most intimate and private exchange.

CHAPTER 23

Generations

AFTER WE DRESSED we went back to our house, and together we fixed a fun improvised brunch. With the leftover bread, we made eggs in a blanket, and we thought the children would get a kick if we also made pigs in a blanket by wrapping cocktail wieners in bacon and baking them till crisp. We also whipped up hash brown potatoes mixed with a bit of onion and garlic, and for dessert we added a nice fruit salad topped with whipped cream or vanilla yogurt.

"I like this feast," Elan announced, and they all joined in, cheering the culinary prowess of the bride and groom-to-be.

"Sarah," Tom announced, "welcome to the family," and everyone raised their glass of orange juice as they cheered. "We call my dad Papa, so Alyana and I thought, if it's OK with you, we'd like to call you Mama. You know our history with our moms. It's fitting for you to be our mother now that you'll marry Papa."

It happened again, the inability to speak because my tears took over. I smiled, and Conrad reached for my hand and said, "I've learned that this reaction means yes."

We all laughed together.

Little Elan stood next to me, put his arm around my shoulder, and wiped the tears from my cheek. "Why are you crying? Don't cry."

"I'm crying with happiness Elan; they're tears of joy."

"We're celebrating that Sarah and Papa are going to be married, she's going to be our mama," Alyana explained.

"Good. We'll make ornaments at Christmas and eat Mama's apple cake. Yum." He gave me a big hug, kissed the tears on my cheeks, and then my eyelids. "There," he said as he climbed on my lap. "Mommy says that kissing the tears on your eyes makes you feel better. Are you better, Mama?"

"I am, darling, thank you."

Of course Nina didn't want to be deprived, so she wiggled out of her chair and climbed on my lap as well, kissing my cheeks and eyelids. "There, Mama," she said when done. "Better."

Dotingly, I hugged my grandbabies.

It turned out to be another perfect day. We took walks out in the snow, made snowmen, played games, talked, laughed, and enjoyed a great family day. After we put the little ones down for a nap, it came time for Alyana to rest a bit, and in the calm of the early afternoon, we planned our wedding.

We agreed on New Year's Eve. Conrad said that the world would be celebrating our wedding vows right along with us. Tom and Alyana thought it a fun idea, and as for me, it reminded me of my parents' engagement stories, so it turned out to be the perfect day for our wedding.

Conrad reached for my hand and announced, "Sarah and I want to give you an early Christmas present."

"C'mon, Dad, you're the ones getting married. You guys should be the ones with presents, not us."

"Listen up, son. We'd like for you to have the twin house."

"What?" Tom's face drained of all color.

"This house? But—" Alyana in contrast was beet red.

"No, not this one, the one where Tom grew up. We want to have you nearby."

"Dad, are you sure? You've lived in that house all your life. It's your home."

"My home is with Sarah, in this house where your grandma grew up. You're inheriting Granddad's house. It stays in the family, just as Grandma said it would. It's what Sarah and I want, not only for you, but for us as well. We need you close by."

"Papa, this is so unexpected," Alyana said. "Tom and I can't even begin to tell you how much this means to us." She glanced at her husband with an inquisitive look. Tom nodded his approval back, and Alyana went on. "We got word from Doc yesterday that we're going to have twins. That's why I'm so big."

"Twins," we both said in amazement.

"A boy and a girl from the looks of it," Tom added. "We've been worried silly about how we would all fit in our small house. But now you've...well, you've solved the problem."

"Good," Conrad said. "How about if we move you right after Christmas? It'll be great if you can be here by the time we get hitched. Can you handle it?"

"We'll manage all right," Tom said as he eyed his wife, who concurred.

"I'll start moving my stuff over in the next few days. We'll move you in well before the twins are born. All the furnishings are yours to do what you wish with, except for Grandma's bedroom furniture. Sarah and I want to bring it here. Other than pictures, some knickknacks, and my stuff, we don't plan to take anything else."

"Dad, it's too much. You can't leave behind all the memories. You're sure you don't want them here with you?"

"Not unless you two don't want them. If there's furniture you wish to replace with newer or more modern styles, just let us know. We'll bring the old stuff over here if it's to remain in the family. Anything we don't keep, you can do whatever you wish with."

"But what about the desk?" Tom insisted.

"Well...let me think about that."

As I watched the exchange between father and son, the kindness and respect that Tom showed captivated me, as well as the deep understanding of the significance that the house and its contents had in their lives. Angela's influence was palpable in these wonderful men.

Alyana and I glanced at each other as if we'd just shared the same thoughts. We smiled and sat back, listening to father and son come to terms with what really mattered to them.

"Alyana," I whispered, "if you and Tom find something you like in this house, please feel free to take it with you. As you know, this house had some furniture when I bought it. You're welcome to it, if Conrad agrees. It would give us great pleasure if we could help you get started in your new home with everything you need."

"Boy, Sarah, what a Christmas present you've given us. I'm in shock. I still can't believe we'll be moving close to you guys in a few weeks and into the house we love so dearly."

"We have a wedding and a move to plan, let alone prepare for twins," announced Conrad. "Tom and I will take a stroll down to the old house, reminisce, and take inventory. We'll leave you girls to make your own plans, and then we'll compare notes."

We *girls* did just that, young and carefree, a bride and her bridesmaid filled with anticipation as we planned the wedding. Alyana offered to help me look for my dress, and together with Tom she offered to take care of the invitations. We had all agreed to invite only our closest friends, about twenty people. I only had a couple of girlfriends I wanted to invite and hoped they would be happy for me and come, but they were unlikely to travel all the way from California on New Year's Eve. The invitation to my wedding would be enough of a surprise to them. At least I knew they'd call to congratulate me and get the skinny on my husband-to-be. They'd want a picture of Conrad and ask about all the particulars surrounding him and his family. They would do what good friends do in order to make sure that their pal doesn't make a mistake and marry without their scrutiny and approval of the groom.

"I wish my parents and my grandmother were still alive," I told Alyana. "They would be so happy to see me married to Conrad."

"I know what you mean."

"You felt the same when you married Tom?"

"Yeah. I wished my adoptive parents were alive to walk me down the aisle. I thought they'd be happy to see that I'd turned out all right. But in the end, it didn't matter, 'cause it's really about you and your husband, and when that special day comes, all you can think about is him."

"You're right. I'll focus on Conrad, and let go of the past."

"I didn't mean that. Hold on to the past, just don't let it drag you back. You have memories of your own parents and grandmother. That's precious. I wish I had that richness myself."

"Oh, I didn't—"

"It's OK. I don't dwell on the fact that I'm adopted."

"But—"

"What I tried to say is that what matters is what we make of our new lives. Our past has crafted who we are, but the present and future are what we chose to make of them."

"I get you."

"Our two men have amazing stories of their heritage in this valley going back many years. Now, you and I are stepping into their history, bringing with us our own. Your heritage is plentiful, while mine is somewhat spotty, but they are our histories nonetheless."

"Indeed."

"In the end, we'll have richer tales to share with my kids. I can't tell you how happy I am you've joined our family."

"So am I."

"Your background is so varied, and that's what parents are all about, giving their kids and grandkids, even great-grandkids, the gift of their lives, their histories, their knowledge, and their love. I can't wait for everything you'll be sharing with us. Let alone the many stories Papa will tells us."

"What do you mean?"

"Now that you've brought him back to life, he'll be reminiscing about his childhood, his teen years, and all that followed."

I reflected on the wisdom of Alyana's advice and embraced the memories my parents and grandmother had given me.

"Why so quiet? Did I say something that bothered you?"

"No, no. I was thinking how wise you are for someone so young."

She laughed. "Ah, not wise, not at all."

"You sure can pinpoint what's important."

"That because I was adopted."

"Oh?"

"I instinctively know what matters most. That's why I want my kids to truly appreciate the treasures that their father's family has hidden in these houses and in this valley."

"I know what you mean."

"Do you?"

"Has Conrad told you that I've been finding some great photographs in the attic that tell the stories of his ancestors?"

"He's just told us that you've got the gift Angela had and that you're now tuned into your destiny."

"That's an odd thing to say."

"C'mon, Sarah, you know how special our men are. Grandma Angela had a great influence on them. I don't even think they realize they make comments like that."

We laughed with the knowledge that our men had indeed a particular ability to sense the world, and that they did not bother to hide it or think of it as abnormal or unmanly.

"It's kind of fun to watch them go about their daily lives aware that there are other dimensions of consciousness. They have an uncanny ability to perceive nature and its inhabitants in a way that most normal folks don't."

"Alyana, I seem to have tapped into one of those dimensions myself. It appears as if I've entered into a new realm of consciousness where I can understand the rhythm between today and years past."

She smiled, and I exhaled, relieved that the truth flowed out of me without hesitation or fear or the anguish associated with admitting I possessed extrasensory abilities.

"That was a deep sigh," Alyana whispered.

"I was thinking how at ease I am with you. How effortless it is to tell you about these oddities of mine."

"Oddities?"

"Yeah. Hearing the stories of the old abandoned photos in my attic is bizarre to say the least, don't you think?"

"No, not really. You've got a gift that enables you to perceive what most of us can't. Maybe that ability seems odd to folks who don't understand it. I think it's awesome."

Smiling, I reached for her hand. "Thank you."

She brought the back of my hand to her lips and gently kissed it. "No need for that," she said softly.

"Ever since I arrived here, I've been a completely different person. I have a sense of belonging, of being where I need to be."

"It doesn't surprise me. As far as we know, Papa's been waiting for you for a long time. Tom says his grandma kept saying that one day Papa's better half would come to complete him."

"Why say that to her grandson? I wonder how it affected his perception of his mother."

"As far as Tom was concerned, Angela was his mother. He has little recollection of his birth mother other than she was sickly and detached. He saw her as someone whose illness required her to be away from those she loved."

"Hard to believe, don't you think?"

"Angela made sure that Tom didn't resent his mother's absence, and along with Papa, gave him plenty of encouragement to be happy. He grew up with no resentment of her absence whatsoever, and with the understanding that she'd gone due to an illness that made it impossible for her to be with her son and husband. A simple fact of life, with no need for negative emotions tied to it."

"Angela was an extraordinary woman. I wish I'd met her."

"I'm sure you've already met her. She is very present in our lives."

"You sense her presence?" I asked tentatively.

"She visits me in my dreams, and sometimes she whispers during the day, guiding me, or coaxing me toward the right path."

"Does it scare you to feel these things?"

She laughed delightedly. "No, not at all. I guess I didn't tell you that my adoptive parents were Native American. Their ancestry came from the Okanogan and Methow First Nations."

"Tom mentioned it."

"I grew up well aware of the spiritual guidance of our ancestors."

"You grew up sensing the dead?"

"In a way. We sense nature and the natural rhythms of the earth and, if we're open to it, we discover that our ancestors are part of those rhythms, part of nature."

"I never thought of it that way."

"Angela and her twin girls, Casey and Deidre, were well known by the various First Nation tribes in our region. I knew of Angela way before I married into her family."

"How?"

"They cared for the sick alongside the medicine men and women of the different tribes. Not only did they understand our history and traditions, but they also were respectful of and tuned into our spirituality. You do know that Sophia married an elder of the Mi'kmaq First Nation and settled in Nova Scotia."

"No, I didn't. Conrad and I spent time looking at the photo album of Casey and Deidre, but we never got to chat about Sophia."

"I thought you knew how this house came to be yours."

"Well, I know that it belonged to Casey until I bought it. I also know that the house and I have some spiritual connection. But to be honest with you, I don't understand why you kids couldn't have moved here."

"Well, I don't know the exact reason myself, but I do know that after attending Sophia's wedding ceremony, the twin aunties didn't come back home. They were invited to join the Mi'kmaq Nation and stayed in Nova Scotia with their daughter. Angela told Papa that this house should remain empty while waiting for its rightful owner. Someone she knew would come soon. The house needed to pass to a person who understood the house and its memories. She told him the twin houses would be joined again, so he needn't worry, just care for them, and be open to the future that awaited him."

"Wow. It's hard to believe."

"And yet here we are today, stepping into the future that Angela laid out for us."

"Without a doubt, even if it's beyond belief. Do you know if Sophia and her mothers stayed in contact with Angela?"

"As far as I know, they did. Ask Papa about it. He'd love to tell you."

"What's she going to ask Papa?" little Elan asked as he sauntered into the living room. Sleepily he climbed onto his mother's lap. Alyana covered him in little kisses and caresses.

"Mama wants to know all about your great-aunties."

"Oh. Ask Papa to read you one of their stories," he said.

"Sure," and I smiled, "which one should I ask him to read?"

"The one about the wolves and the beaver."

"Can't you tell it to me?"

"Yep, but Papa tells it better. I'll hold your hand so you don't get scared."

"Is it scary?"

"No, but sometimes you think it is going to be. I'll hold your hand."

Little Nina was also awake and wobbled toward her mother, rubbing her sleepy eyes. Elan made room for his sister with the ease of their familiar after-nap routine. Alyana welcomed her with kisses and caresses as well.

"Papa," Alyana explained, "has a little book where his aunties wrote some of the stories they heard while among my people. I think they used to read the stories to Sophia when she was little."

Suddenly the image of the twins reading to Sophia in this very living room in front of a Christmas tree invaded my mind. The vision was so vivid that I could've sworn they were right in front of us.

"Yes, I can sense them as well," Alyana whispered, and smiled. "It's our ancestors opening the path to the memories of our land."

Elan and Nina didn't question our exchange; they lay on their mother's lap, content with the warmth of her love, enjoying her soft caresses, and the delicate breeze emanating from her rhythmic breath as it softly stroked their hair.

I smiled back, watching my destiny evolve before me.

CHAPTER 24

The Truth

AWAKE AT TWO thirty in the morning, I tiptoed out of our bedroom, quietly closed the door, and made my way down to the kitchen, feeling well rested and ready to take on the day. I made a cup of coffee and went upstairs to visit with my attic.

As I entered I realized that I didn't know where to find the light switch, or even if one existed. Having always been in the attic when enough natural light came through the window to illuminate my way, I was at a loss in complete darkness. Not even the faint whisper of moonlight through the window seemed enough.

I tiptoed back to the kitchen, grabbed a flashlight, and returned to the attic. I didn't find a light switch on either wall flanking the entry door. I shone the light around the other walls and found nothing. I then shone the light on the ceiling and discovered the absence of a light fixture. How could there be no electricity in the attic? There must be an outlet somewhere.

Starting from the entry door along the wall on my right, I began a slow and deliberate search for the outlet, combing every possible space, and finishing with the wall on the left of the entry door. Nothing.

How about the floor? What if the outlet is in the floor instead of the wall? Starting on the right again, I meticulously zigzagged through the entire room. Nothing. *How peculiar.* Then, I remembered seeing an old floor lamp leaning against the left-hand corner of the attic behind one of the trunks.

The floor lamp, that's it. I brought it out from its corner and placed it by the armchair. *But where's the plug?* I grabbed the cord and searched again for the mysterious outlet. The cord was long enough to reach the entry door and beyond. I went out of the attic and, cord in hand, hunted for a spot on the outer walls to plug it in.

I found an outlet, right under the heater's vent. Exhilarated, I rushed down to the kitchen and grabbed a light bulb, hoping that the floor lamp was in sufficient shape to work. I screwed the light bulb in, and then carefully plugged the lamp into the socket. The light came on. Still kneeling in front of the outlet below the heater's vent, I noticed a small compartment to the right of the vent. A square metal door kept it tightly shut. A small round handle hung from the middle of the upper part of the door. Both the door and the handle had been painted over many times, from the look of it. I tried to pry the handle loose, but it had been painted over so many times that it wouldn't budge.

I dashed to the downstairs hallway closet to find a tool that would help open the compartment. In minutes I returned, chisel in hand. I covered it with a towel to muffle the noise, and I hammered it in between the metal door and the wall. Not wanting to wake Conrad, I worked slowly and deliberately, chiseling away all around the metal door, detaching it from the wall. Once I'd released it on all four sides, I pulled it, and the small plate came loose.

I shone the flashlight and found a tin can hidden all the way in the back of a cubbyhole. Enthralled with my discovery, I pulled it out and took it into the attic, now illuminated by the soft light of the old floor lamp.

No sooner had I sat down on the armchair than I heard Angela speaking with Louise Whitman.

"Today I'll tell you the truth that Leonard never knew," Louise told Angela.

"Why keep it to yourself until this moment?" Angela asked.

"Stubbornness, I guess. Just needed to have something that was mine and mine alone."

"You must have cared about Amy and how it could impact her."

"She was always strong, unique, different. I knew she would be all right whether she knew the truth or not."

"Didn't you think of her children? What if her kids married within the family?"

"I did not think any of my daughters would marry."

"You were wrong," Angela said with such dryness in her tone that it startled me.

"I was wrong about many things," Louise whispered back. "That is why I kept the records. To set it straight."

I looked at the contents of the tin can and found Amy's birth certificate, as well as the birth certificates of her sisters and Ethan.

I gasped when I read the birth record of Louise and Leonard. *Twins,* born in Boston in 1815 to Janet and her husband, Horace Whitman. "Oh my God! They were twins!" I blurted out.

"Twins," I heard Angela whisper to me. "Twins."

The paper was so fragile, I feared the documents would disintegrate in my hands if I held them too long.

"Sarah," Angela coaxed, "read them out loud. Their trueness will set the record straight."

I did as she asked. "Cora Whitman, born in New York on June 22, 1833, to Louise Whitman, mother, and Leonard Whitman, father." I paused to catch my breath. "Laura Whitman, born in Philadelphia on August 14, 1838, to Louise Whitman, mother, and Leonard Whitman, father." When I held the next one, I couldn't help myself and gasped as the birth certificate shook in my hand.

"Read it out loud," Angela persisted.

"Amy Rochester, born in Boston on July 6, 1843, to Louise Rochester, mother, and Anthony Rochester, father.

"Now, the final one."

"Ethan Whitman, born in Boston on January 4, 1842, to Adrianne Osborn Whitman, mother, and Leonard Whitman, father."

"Thank you," Angela told me, before she turned her attention back to Louise, who resumed talking.

"Leonard never knew how I recorded the births of our daughters, or of Amy." Louise told Angela. "But when you read these records it becomes clear what we did...who we had become."

The Gift of the Twin Houses

"I see."

"You see only what I chose to show, Angela. Appearances are what you make of them. No one knew my daughters were Leonard's. No need for that, really."

"How did you manage to keep it a secret?"

"For my first two pregnancies, I went away from friends and family. We lived in Boston, so I traveled to London and made up a husband, writing to all acquaintances of the happy nuptials and the impending birth. I returned from Europe just in time to deliver Cora in New York. When I arrived in Boston, I was a sad widow with a baby girl. For Laura, I first went to Paris and wrote of a wonderful second marriage and new pregnancy. This time I chose Philadelphia for Laura's birth. Difficult to trace, I thought, but it did not matter, no one ever doubted me. Back in Boston, it all appeared to be quite natural and heartbreaking, now twice a widow with two little girls as the remnants of a couple of marriages that ended in tragic deaths. People felt sorry for me. 'Poor, sad Louise, such bad luck.' It helped hide the truth."

"Why not have your babies in Europe? Why come back to New York and Philadelphia?"

"I wanted their birth records to be on American soil, where they were conceived, and recorded in a manner all could understand."

"Why all the cover-up if you wished the records to speak of it all? Why not just tell Leonard the truth when he guessed that Amy wasn't his?"

"I didn't want to confess I'd been intimate with Anthony. Leonard was a better lover thinking I had only been his." Louise laughed, a dry, cold laugh that chilled my bones.

"There is more to this truth you seek," Louise went on. "Leonard got married, only for appearances, he told me, assuring me that he would be faithful to me. But shortly after their nuptials, Adrianne was with child. I could not bear the thought of him making love to another woman. I withheld myself from him."

Angela sighed, her hand folded on her lap as she watched Louise walk about the room. They were in *my* living room. Well, the living room in our house but in Louise's time.

"Leonard pushed me toward Anthony for appearances also. I did not resist. I was in so much pain by Leonard's betrayal. He lied to me and made love to Adrianne. Can you believe it? Made love to her and got her pregnant. I wanted to hurt him in the same way. So I married Anthony, and we conceived Amy."

"It would've been better for him to know the truth."

"No. It would not. As long as he thought I had been only his, he would never suspect that I was the one who told Adrianne about us. I killed his wife when I told her that truth. He would never have forgiven me if he'd known. History proved me right."

"Why did you tell her?"

"Ethan was a beautiful baby, and I was insanely jealous of her. I wanted to hurt her. Especially when I gave birth to Amy, another girl. I broke. I saw myself as a failure, so I lashed out."

"Why didn't Adrianne tell Leonard what you had done?"

"He was not there. He was attending to some business away from Boston. She killed herself within an hour of my departure from her home. I had already left Boston when it all happened. I did not wish to wait for the outcome of what I had done. After I told her, I left Anthony, took Amy, and moved to New York, away from everybody."

"Only Amy?"

"Amy had purity. I thought it would do me good. But it did not. Leonard came after me and whisked us off to this godforsaken place."

"You don't hate it as much as you say."

Louise smiled, walked toward Angela, sat nearby, and reached for her hands.

"Our conversations have helped. I am more at ease."

"Leonard has forgiven you. It's time for peace within you."

"He has, but I have not just yet. Too many deaths on my shoulders weigh me down. If you think on it, I am hideous. What I have done to those I should have loved is unforgivable."

"Louise, no need for melodrama."

"It is not melodrama!" She stood up facing Angela. "I will put the facts before you, and you will have no choice but to agree with me. The first one to go was Adrianne, the truth so unbearable that death turned out to be a better option. Followed by Mother, broken by the same truth, withering before my very eyes, with not an ounce of compassion ever coming from me. Anthony drank himself to death, unable to cope. The last one to go was Leonard, the man I loved, and love, so dearly. He chose a painful death in order to sever all connection with me."

"Is that so?"

"You know it is. In one of my temper tantrums, I blurted out what I had done to Adrianne. My true nature revolted him. He could not bear the truth. Do you understand now?" She turned toward the windows and stared at the closed curtains.

"Yes, I understand, but you've come a long way. You are now owning up to your actions, you're facing your demons, and you're making amends."

"One slow step at a time."

"Better than no steps at all."

"You are, as usual, correct." Louise sighed and returned to Angela's side. "Ethan has been wonderful to Leonard, telling him all about his life, and Amy's, and the children and grandchildren. I like to hear the stories now that Leonard allows me to listen in."

"That's good."

"It was so sad to hear about Amy's daughter, Claudia, dying in child-birth with little Jennifer. I had difficulty seeing how deeply hurt Ethan looked when he told Leonard of their deaths, and of Stuart, his beloved son, running off to Canada to escape the pain...so distressing to feel the anguish in Ethan's heart. I cried for him and for Stuart."

"Did you hear yourself just now?"

Louise turned to face Angela. "Stop your implications, and just tell me what you mean. I hate it when you do that."

"You expressed sadness and cried. You cared for Ethan."

"Oh, that. Well, all *your* doing. This need of yours for the truth has me cleaning house."

I saw Louise smile at Angela before she continued. "I like this business of the truth. It is liberating. I particularly enjoy hearing Ethan talk to Leonard. No one talks to me, not even Amy. But I do not blame them."

"Ethan and Amy will be happy to hear that."

As quickly as they had appeared, they vanished. I waited to see if they would return, but what needed to be said had been said, and they didn't come back.

Still shaken, I carefully placed the documents back in the tin can, turned out the light, and went downstairs.

The sun had risen and Conrad had left for work. He'd left me a note on the kitchen table.

Hope you had good news from the attic. Went by, but you were so engrossed that I went to work. If you need to talk, just come by. Love, Conrad.

I picked up the phone and called the store. "Good morning, darling," I said when Conrad answered the phone. "Sorry I didn't see you off this morning. Got up real early and didn't want to wake you."

"Good morning to you too. All OK? Need to chat?"

"I'm all right. A very unsettling story."

"I have a minute if you'd like to run something by me."

"I saw Angela in our living room talking with Louise Whitman."

"Nothing new there. You've seen other stories with Grandma."

"Except she was speaking with someone who was born in 1815."

"Ah. Got it." And he paused for a while. "This one is more complicated than just a quick phone call. Anything in the conversation that shook you up?"

"Yes. But I need to think on it. It can wait until tonight."

"OK, see you then."

My hands trembled as I replaced the receiver.

Incest. What should I do with this truth?

CHAPTER 25

Lineage

AFTER A QUICK shower, I packed the photos and records of the Whitman clan, and in less than thirty minutes, I showed up at Alyana's doorstep.

"Sarah, what a pleasant surprise. I was just about to put the kids down for their naps. Come in."

"So early? It's only eleven."

"They both woke up really early this morning. They were full of energy, so now they're tired and ready to lie down."

I followed Alyana into the tiny bedroom where both children were already in their beds, their eyes half shut. We kissed them and tucked them in, and by the time we reached the door, they were both asleep.

"Want something to drink?" Alyana whispered as we made our way to the room that combined their den, dining room, and kitchen.

"Thanks. I also woke up early this morning, around two thirty, and heard an interesting story in my attic. Thought I'd run it by you, and see what you can make of it."

"Sure thing. Let's nibble on some cheese, veggies, and crackers while we chat, and I can put my feet up."

In no time she arranged a tray of goodies and made some iced tea. We settled in the den and pushed some of the toys aside to give us room on the sofa.

I began the story with the first photograph of Louise Whitman, and then I showed her the picture with Louise, her daughters, and her mother in front of my house, and then Leonard's and Ethan's photo. I followed with the photograph of the three sisters, and the one of Annie with her father Christopher and her baby son Jeremy. I showed her the sepia photographs that came to life with Ethan's narrative for his father. I ended with the conversation I had heard between Louise and Angela and showed her the birth records in the hidden tin can.

"Great story," was the first thing Alyana said.

I nodded in agreement, having enjoyed the account myself. Listening to my own storytelling, I realized how much I'd learned from them, how well I told the tale, almost like a writer crafting an interesting yarn that captures the imagination of others.

"What do you make of the conversation between Louise and Angela?" I asked. "Louise was born in 1815. How could she be having a conversation with Angela?"

"It's believed by many of my people that where the spirits of our ancestors live, time as we know it doesn't exist. They're not in this life, or dimension, if you wish. I think you've tapped into that place through Angela. She wants you to know this story. Have you wondered why she's letting you in on all the ancestry of the twin houses?"

"I've thought and thought about it, but I'm still puzzled."

"Did Papa find out if Jeremy was Grandma Angela's uncle?"

"Yes, he was. Jeremy was born in 1881 and died in 1898 in a mining accident. That's how ownership of the house ended up with his little sister, Rachel, Angela's mother. Jeremy's older twin brothers died of polio."

"So that's where the twin gene comes from, Angela's lineage. Nice to know. But wait…Ethan was Leonard's son, right?" Alyana asked.

"Yes. He adopted twin boys, Henry and Stuart Thompson, who married Amy's twin girls, Annie and Claudia. Annie, Jeremy's and Rachel's mom, married Henry Thompson. That's where Conrad's last name Thompson comes from."

"But what about the other twin?"

"From what Louise said today," I answered, "Claudia, her twin sister, married Stuart Thompson, but she died in childbirth along with her baby. We now know that the cowboy in Jeremy's story was his uncle, Stuart Thompson."

"According to Jeremy's story, the cowboy runs off to Canada and comes back injured to be cared for by his brother and sister-in-law the year Rachel, Angela's mom, is born."

"Looks that way. Conrad told me the family records show that Stuart married a Linda Saunders in 1884. Their son, Ernest, Conrad's great-grandfather, was born in 1884 in Conrad's house. Sorry, your new home," I clarified, and Alyana smiled.

"Why wasn't his wife, Linda, in Jeremy's story? Why was Stuart cared for by his brother in his home instead of his own with his wife and child? Wait. When was Rachel born?" she asked, a puzzled look about her.

"In 1887. I know you're wondering why the cowboy's wife, Linda, or their son, Ernest, who would've been three, didn't appear in Jeremy's story either. I've wondered myself, and the best I can come up with is that Jeremy just made some parts up and omitted others. He did make up the little girl, Elisa, in the story."

"That makes sense. He told you he made her up so the kids at school wouldn't think he was writing about his own family, didn't he?"

"He sure did. If he purposely omitted Linda and little Ernest, then the rest makes sense. We know that Ernest married Elisabeth in 1901. Richard, their son and Conrad's grandfather, was born a year later in 1902. His sisters were all born about two years apart from one another."

"Boy, you know your genealogy! How can you keep up with all these names and dates in your mind like that?"

"Well, to be honest I've created a cheat sheet. I've been drawing a family tree and filling in the blanks as the relationships emerge. Odd, isn't it?"

"Not odd, amazing. It just clicks for you. Definitely you've tapped into the history of the twin houses. Anyway, going back to who's who. Grandpa Richard's line comes from Ethan's adopted sons, Henry and Stuart Thompson. Grandma Angela's line comes from Amy Rochester. Right?"

I jumped up, my hands at both sides of my head, making sure my thoughts wouldn't disappear. "Oh my God! I get it! Angela wants me to know the legitimacy of her family's lineage. She wants me to know there's been no inbreeding."

Alyana eyes widened. "Oh…"

"Even though Ethan was Leonard's son and Amy was Louise's daughter, they were not conceived by their incestuous relationship. Only Cora and Laura were theirs, and they never married or had children—"

"That we know of."

"In the story of the three sisters around the kitchen table, Cora was forty-nine and Laura was forty-four. They were alone and bitter. Only Amy had children."

"Interesting." Alyana smiled and tapped the sofa next to her for me to sit back down.

I complied. We smiled and both sipped our teas as we processed the information.

"What do I do with it? Other than sharing it with you, Tom, and Conrad, which is important enough as it is, do you think I'm supposed to do something else?"

"Maybe, maybe not. Time will tell."

After a deep sigh, I relaxed, leaned back on the sofa, and took Alyana's hand in both of mine. "Thank you. I can't tell you how much it means to me to be able to speak with you of these strange experiences. Anyone else would think I'm losing my mind."

"We know better, don't we?"

"Yes we do."

"Interesting that the twin gene comes from both Angela's and Richard's lineage."

"From Louise through Amy on Angela's side and from Ethan's adopted twin sons on Richard's side. Two completely different and separate families."

"Now all joined in me and Tom. Angela's telling us our twins will be fine."

We smiled and continued to hold hands as we relaxed on the sofa.

I returned home relieved, feeling as if a heavy weight had been lifted from my shoulders. All of these stories, which at first appeared to be quite unrelated, had come full circle to create a tapestry of family heritage that needed to be shared with present and future generations.

I assumed that now the house would release the tug that kept insisting something needed to be unearthed. It seemed that I now possessed the information Angela wished me to have, so the uneasiness as to what would come next would be gone.

But I was wrong. The house remained constant in her desire to continue unearthing its secrets.

Conrad's arrival that evening brought with it a needed sense of closure. He delighted in hearing of my visit to Alyana and its outcome.

"I don't think that I ever thought it necessary to figure out who was related to whom, or how the twin houses came to be. I just took it for granted. The houses were here, been in the family for generations, and we've all enjoyed living here. Granted, some more than others. What a story...to think that Grandma Angela wanted us to know where we all came from. Who would've thought of incest, of all things? Why didn't she tell us directly before she passed on? Everyone is gone, so there's no sense in keeping it all secret."

"Don't know. Maybe she didn't know the whole story?"

"I don't think so. She knew it all right."

"Maybe she knew enough just to marry Richard safely."

"No...it's not like her."

"Why, then?"

Conrad furrowed his forehead as he thought things through. "She must have had other plans. I'm sure she knew the whole story all along."

I reached over, kissed his forehead, and caressed his cheeks. "You also look kissable when you worry. I don't think I'd seen you furrow your forehead before."

He smiled and pulled me to him. We sat on the sofa in silence, watching the Christmas lights dance about in rhythm with the crackling fire nearby.

"Could be she wanted the story to come from you," Conrad whispered as he caressed my hair. "She wanted you here, by me."

"Why go through all that trouble? It would've been easier just telling you all."

"Easier, maybe. As significant? I don't think so."

"What do you mean?"

"What about you coming to terms with your own abilities, with who you are today?"

"You think she wanted that for me?"

"She knew you'd come. Why not?"

We filled our evening with reflections, sensitive to the voices of the past that wished to convey the truth that had been hidden for so long, wondering what remained to be uncovered.

The Gift of the Twin Houses

Fifth Family Tree - Residents of the Twin Houses

First Generation

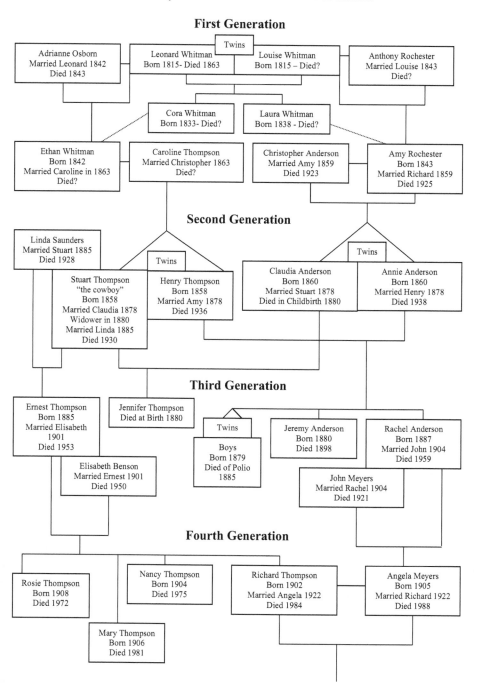

Twins

Adrianne Osborn	Leonard Whitman	Louise Whitman	Anthony Rochester
Married Leonard 1842	Born 1815- Died 1863	Born 1815 – Died?	Married Louise 1843
Died 1843			Died?

Cora Whitman	Laura Whitman
Born 1833- Died?	Born 1838 - Died?

Ethan Whitman	Caroline Thompson	Christopher Anderson	Amy Rochester
Born 1842	Married Christopher 1863	Married Amy 1859	Born 1843
Married Caroline in 1863	Died?	Died 1923	Married Richard 1859
Died?			Died 1925

Second Generation

Linda Saunders				
Married Stuart 1885				
Died 1928		**Twins**		

Stuart Thompson	Henry Thompson	Claudia Anderson	Annie Anderson
"the cowboy"	Born 1858	Born 1860	Born 1860
Born 1858	Married Amy 1878	Married Stuart 1878	Married Henry 1878
Married Claudia 1878	Died 1936	Died in Childbirth 1880	Died 1938
Widower in 1880			
Married Linda 1885			
Died 1930			

Third Generation

Ernest Thompson	Jennifer Thompson		Jeremy Anderson	Rachel Anderson
Born 1885	Died at Birth 1880	**Twins**	Born 1880	Born 1887
Married Elisabeth			Died 1898	Married John 1904
1901		**Boys**		Died 1959
Died 1953		Born 1879		
		Died of Polio		
	Elisabeth Benson	1885	John Meyers	
	Married Ernest 1901		Married Rachel 1904	
	Died 1950		Died 1921	

Fourth Generation

Rosie Thompson	Nancy Thompson	Richard Thompson	Angela Meyers
Born 1908	Born 1904	Born 1902	Born 1905
Died 1972	Died 1975	Married Angela 1922	Married Richard 1922
		Died 1984	Died 1988

Mary Thompson
Born 1906
Died 1981

197

V. & D. Povall

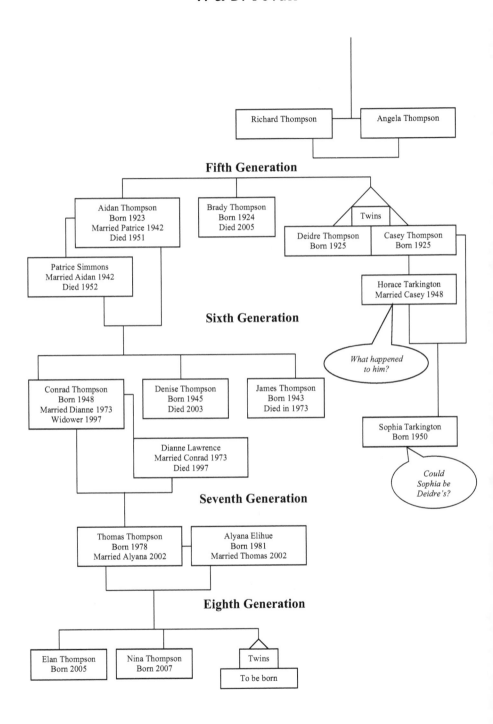

CHAPTER 26

The Intruder

Several days passed with no word from the attic. With so much to do in preparation for the holidays and the wedding, I didn't particularly miss it.

Early one morning, Conrad had left for work, and the house felt ill at ease. Something was disturbing us. Something kept tugging at us and getting in the way of our routine.

I couldn't focus on my household tasks, didn't have the urge to bake or even cook the meals for the day. I just felt out of sorts. I could sense that the house was equally at odds by the many pops and snaps that kept breaking the silence of the morning. So I gave us some time off.

I stopped trying to do the things we didn't want to do, poured myself a cup of coffee, and went up to my attic. Maybe if we sat quietly for a while, we'd come to terms with what bothered us. Perhaps my presence in the attic would suffice to settle us down.

Today the attic looked gray and sad. The sun didn't shine; instead, an icy, misty rain was showering the house and the valley. It had been a while since I'd spent time in the attic, and just the thought of being there made me feel better, even in the grayness.

Attempting to ease our discomfort, I walked around the room, running my fingers along its furniture, its trunks, and the boxes of photographs with stories that remained to be told.

A loose floorboard cracked under my foot. How strange, I thought, bearing in mind I'd walked throughout this attic many times. Maybe I'd never stepped on that particular board before. Unusual though, considering how loose it was. I placed my cup on the little table by the armchair and examined the floorboard.

I removed it to reveal a small rectangular tin can and a dusty baby blanket. Cautiously, I took them out of their hiding place and brought them with me to the armchair. I opened the little tin can, and its contents startled me. On my lap were the photographs missing from the album of Angela's twin girls.

My heart pounded, and my hands trembled. Unsure if I were allowed to peek into their secret, I looked around. I didn't want to know anything not meant for me. I had stepped, literally stepped, on a well-guarded secret and didn't wish to disturb a past intended for burial.

I leaned back in the armchair, my hands softly resting on the can and its contents, closed my eyes, and asked permission.

After a while, my heartbeats slowed down, and my hands warmed up. Peace settled within me, and I came to terms as to why I'd been so out of sorts all day. The house had been calling me to the attic and the hiding place under the floorboard. A story needed to be heard. A story as sad and gloomy as the gray skies filled with drizzly tears.

Casey strolled into the attic. A young woman right out of the 1940s, a cheerless beauty, her eyes bathed in sorrow. She stood behind me, her hand resting on the back of the armchair, looking at the items on my lap.

"It's a sad story," Casey whispered. "One that shouldn't be repeated, one that should be buried. A true story that should never have happened. It's because of its horrible truth that I've placed it in this tin can. The photographs and newspaper articles, my son's birth certificate, along with Sophia's, are all part of this truth. I've hidden them under the floor in the attic. I don't think we'll ever look at them, but its trueness must be kept."

"Do you mean for me to see it?" I asked, hoping she wouldn't recoil and force me to put it all back under the floorboard.

She nodded and walked around the attic, her hands distractedly caressing the items they touched. "It is a truth that will be with Deidre and me through eternity. Sophia may want to know it one day. It needs to be kept so that it will bear witness."

"Is that what you wish me to do?"

She didn't answer, just continued her stroll around the room, stopping here and there for no apparent reason.

"It is a wretched story. A tale of selfishness and pride, a story of pain so deep that it changes who a person is. An event that wants to be forgotten but can't be.

"I met Horace Tarkington at the hospital in Seattle where we worked. He was a surgical intern. Deidre did not trust him from day one. She advised me to stay away from him. But it all took place during a time I needed to find my own independence, my separateness from Deidre, and I stubbornly closed myself to her."

"What about Angela? Did she mistrust him as well?"

"Mother felt there was something broken inside him. But I took her meaning as a challenge to fix him instead of as a warning to walk away from him. I was a nurse after all, and it was my duty to help others. I convinced myself I could heal whatever was damaged inside him, so I married him."

"I saw the picture of you and Horace outside the church, but were your sister and mother there? I don't see any pictures here of your wedding."

She looked at me and smiled. A bitter smile, directed inwardly. "We took a picture outside the church, and I sent it to Mother. She put it in that album of hers. Best I could do at the time. You see, we were several years out of the Depression and a couple after the end of the war when Horace and I got married. Money was still scarce, and my parents couldn't travel to Seattle. At least that was their excuse. Mother must've known what was to come. Heather Lewis and her children, Michael and Alice, were there, so were my brothers and several friends. Deidre was physically present, but she didn't partake of the festivities."

"No photographs?" I asked again.

"I destroyed all of the wedding pictures. I tore and burnt all the photos that reminded me of Horace. Maybe I shouldn't have, but I did."

Casey was silent for a while, and I didn't interfere. I sensed she needed a bit of time to come to terms with those memories.

"Justin was born about ten months into our marriage, a delight, a lovely child that brought much happiness to what had quickly turned into a painful marriage. Horace was indeed broken inside, truly broken. He had within him a tear that no one could fix, certainly not me. Living through the hell of my marriage taught me one of the most important lessons in my life...humility.

I thought myself capable of tending to any type of illness, especially anything that needed fixing in my husband. I was wrong. Very wrong."

"What was the matter with him?" I dared to ask.

"He'd been repeatedly abused by his father when he was a child and had come apart. His mother never intervened, and he resented it. Pour soul, she'd been beaten and abused as well, and Horace couldn't shake off the grief or the hatred for her compliance, so he chose to become his father. He put on a nice façade for the outer world to see, but in the privacy of our bedchamber, he gave in to his violent, vicious self. Just as his father had done."

Casey was silent again, and I didn't say a word. I imagined the worst and didn't want to accept my dread. I sat in silence, waiting for Casey to speak again.

"Deidre came back to me as soon as I returned from my honeymoon and tended to my wounds, physical and emotional. She wanted me to leave him, but I couldn't. My vows kept tugging at me. He was the father of my unborn child, and I kept hoping he would come around and leave behind the horror of his past. Hope dies last, they say, and I was heading in that direction myself.

"I barely survived the last beating, which brought with it the early birth of Justin. As a result, the true nature of my husband became known. He was dismissed from the hospital, and he left town.

"Deidre and I moved into a little apartment nearby the hospital, and I was able to make a bit of money working in the clinic a few hours a day while Deidre cared for Justin between her full-time shifts at the hospital. Maybe if I hadn't left for work that day, things would've turned out differently. We'll never know.

"When I opened the door to our apartment, I saw Deidre sprawled on the floor bleeding, her clothes torn, her legs scratched, her face contorted with pain. Horace was holding Justin in his arms. He had taken his diapers off and was…"

All of a sudden, the image of Casey standing at the entrance of her small apartment took over my senses. I saw her, clear as day, standing by the door, the look of shock etched in her lovely face.

Transported to her apartment, I was present, witnessing everyone and every move.

I saw Casey yank little Justin from his father and kneel close to her sister, desperately searching for signs of life.

In horror, I saw Horace slap Casey and then kick her in the stomach. Even though she rolled to one side, Casey didn't let go of Justin. She held her baby protectively against her.

I saw Horace pull and pull on the baby, frantically trying to yank him away.

Casey would not yield.

Horace then drew her up and with a closed fist, punched her on the chin with such violence that she and Justin crashed against the wall. Like rag dolls, both Casey and her baby slumped to the floor.

Horace approached them.

Deidre came from behind, the poker from the fireplace held high above her head. She hit Horace over the head. He dropped to the floor. She pummeled him repeatedly until the last breath left his body.

I saw Deidre rush to her unconscious sister and pick up Justin's lifeless body.

The images faded as I returned to the attic and to a silent Casey.

Still shaken, I sifted through the contents of the little can and found Justin's death certificate. A piercing pain gushed through my entire body.

"Justin was almost a year old when he died. Horace, his own father, killed him."

I gasped.

"The police understood." Casey went on. "The hospital staff and doctors understood; everyone understood what had happened, and they felt sorry for us. Sorry that he'd harmed us, sorry that he'd killed his own son, sorry that he'd raped Deidre. But no one felt sorrier than me. It had all been my doing, my arrogance, my selfishness."

"Casey, you shouldn't blame yourself. You didn't know. You were young, full of hope, a nurse. It's admirable that you insisted in honoring your vows."

I tried to comfort her, knowing full well there was nothing anyone could say that would help her shed the guilt.

"No one felt sorry for Horace. At least no one told us they were sorry he'd died in the struggle. At the time it didn't matter to me...I felt such agony with the loss of Justin that I had no room to grieve the loss of his father.

"We left Seattle as soon as we knew Deidre was pregnant. We moved near Tacoma, where Sophia was born. Deidre went into the hospital using my name as the widow Tarkington. No questions were asked. None needed, really. He was, after all, the father of her baby. Sophia was born legitimately, and for her sake, we decided to forget the pain and sorrow."

"Did you?"

"You've seen our photos. What do you think?"

"Impossible to forget."

"Impossible. But we could pretend. Shortly after Sophia was born, we came home. Mother knew something awful had happened to us, but she never pried. She embraced us, as she'd always done, and helped us settle into our new lives. We never spoke of it. We never hinted that there'd been anything wrong. Sophia grew up with two loving mothers and doting grandparents who loved her as much as they loved her uncle Aidan's kids, Conrad, James, and Denise. When Heather willed the twin house to Mother, she gave it to us to live in, and we poured all of our love into our home and into Sophia, whisking away any remnants of the man who had conceived her."

"Does Sophia know who bore her?"

"Sophia grew to be a special little girl with a great ability to communicate with nature and the world, just as our mother did, as you do. I think she knows in her heart that Deidre is her natural mother, but as far as she's concerned, she has two moms, so it doesn't really matter. She knows her father died in an accident before she was born and never asked for more details. I think she sensed when she was little that we didn't want to remember the pain associated with his death. For all I know, she's seen it in one of those visions of hers."

"Did you ever forgive him?"

"In time we were able to let go of the anger. We began to understand how he'd suffered himself, how his own life had been hell, and so in the end we were able to forgive him. It was important to us for Sophia to grow up surrounded by love and kindness. We didn't want her to feel any type of resentment emanating from either one of us. That, coupled with our father and mother's devotion, enabled us to live content lives."

"Is this little baby blanket Justin's?"

"Yes. We never mentioned Justin to anyone. We just kept him in our hearts and memories, praying for him, remembering him every year on his birthday, and mourning him every year on the day of his death. I would sneak away to the attic, take out his baby blanket, and hold it in my arms while I looked at the photographs on your lap. He was such a lovely little boy. I wonder what his life would've been had he lived? Probably a life as precious as Sophia's."

With that last thought, I felt Casey leave.

I sat in the attic for a long time looking through the photographs of Casey, Deidre, and Justin. I wondered who had taken those pictures and imagined that it must've been one of their friends from the look of happiness in their eyes. It couldn't have been Horace.

Justin and Sophia's birth certificates were there, as well as a photograph of Deidre in the hospital with little Sophia in her arms. I realized I held the only picture that told the true story of Sophia's birthmother.

I remembered Alyana saying that after they'd gone to Nova Scotia for Sophia's wedding, they didn't return. I imagined that Angela had packed their things and shipped them there. Obviously, Casey hadn't told her mother about the secret hidden under the loose floorboard.

I left my attic, taking the small tin can and baby blanket with me. I cleaned them both and carefully put them away in a small packing box, placed it in the bottom drawer of my dresser, and carefully covered it with my sweaters.

I knew I couldn't share this story with Conrad, and it pained me, but it was not for me to share. His aunts would have to decide if they wished him to know. I needed to respect their secret.

When Conrad came home from work, he immediately knew that something had happened, but with his customary respect, he did not pry.

"From the look on your face, you've been up to your attic," he said. "C'mon. Let's go out to dinner and take a nice stroll down Main Street. It looks beautiful all dressed up for Christmas."

"We don't have to. I'll whip up something in no time," I protested.

"No sense in arguing. My mind's made up. C'mon."

He dragged me to the coat rack, slid on my snow boots, put on my coat, buttoned it, kissed me, and pushed me out of the house.

"You need airing," he said. "It'll be good for both of us to walk down Main Street and take in the cold air. We'll enjoy it."

He was right. In no time the heaviness in my heart lifted, and the joy of walking hand in hand down the street with my future husband engulfed me. As I relaxed, I understood that Casey did not intend to sadden me or lay a heavy burden; instead, she'd shared her most delicate secret with the soul mate of her nephew, the woman Angela had chosen to care for her family's memories.

It was now up to me to figure out how to give her back her memories without violating the secret.

Back home, we had just stepped into the foyer of the house when Conrad's cell rang.

"Hello." What followed was an interminable pause, during which his countenance became somber. "When?" he said, followed by another long silence. "Well, at least that's good." Another pause. "Yes, of course. Let me know if there's anything else I can do." Another prolonged silence. "We'll be ready. Give my love to your mom. Love you both." He hung up and turned to me.

"What is it?" I asked.

"My aunt Casey died this morning."

The Gift of the Twin Houses

Sixth Family Tree - Residents of the Twin Houses

First Generation

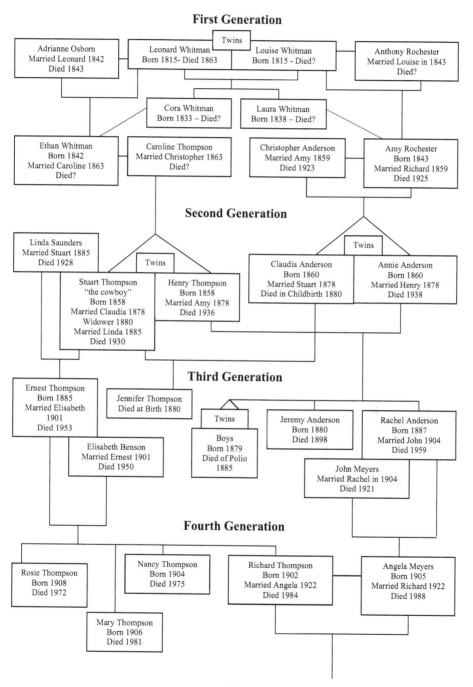

Twins

| Adrianne Osborn Married Leonard 1842 Died 1843 | Leonard Whitman Born 1815- Died 1863 | Louise Whitman Born 1815 - Died? | Anthony Rochester Married Louise in 1843 Died? |

Cora Whitman
Born 1833 – Died?

Laura Whitman
Born 1838 – Died?

Ethan Whitman
Born 1842
Married Caroline 1863
Died?

Caroline Thompson
Married Christopher 1863
Died?

Christopher Anderson
Married Amy 1859
Died 1923

Amy Rochester
Born 1843
Married Richard 1859
Died 1925

Second Generation

Linda Saunders
Married Stuart 1885
Died 1928

Twins

Stuart Thompson
"the cowboy"
Born 1858
Married Claudia 1878
Widower 1880
Married Linda 1885
Died 1930

Henry Thompson
Born 1858
Married Amy 1878
Died 1936

Twins

Claudia Anderson
Born 1860
Married Stuart 1878
Died in Childbirth 1880

Annie Anderson
Born 1860
Married Henry 1878
Died 1938

Third Generation

Ernest Thompson
Born 1885
Married Elisabeth 1901
Died 1953

Jennifer Thompson
Died at Birth 1880

Twins

Jeremy Anderson
Born 1880
Died 1898

Rachel Anderson
Born 1887
Married John 1904
Died 1959

Elisabeth Benson
Married Ernest 1901
Died 1950

Boys
Born 1879
Died of Polio
1885

John Meyers
Married Rachel in 1904
Died 1921

Fourth Generation

Rosie Thompson
Born 1908
Died 1972

Nancy Thompson
Born 1904
Died 1975

Richard Thompson
Born 1902
Married Angela 1922
Died 1984

Angela Meyers
Born 1905
Married Richard 1922
Died 1988

Mary Thompson
Born 1906
Died 1981

207

V. & D. Povall

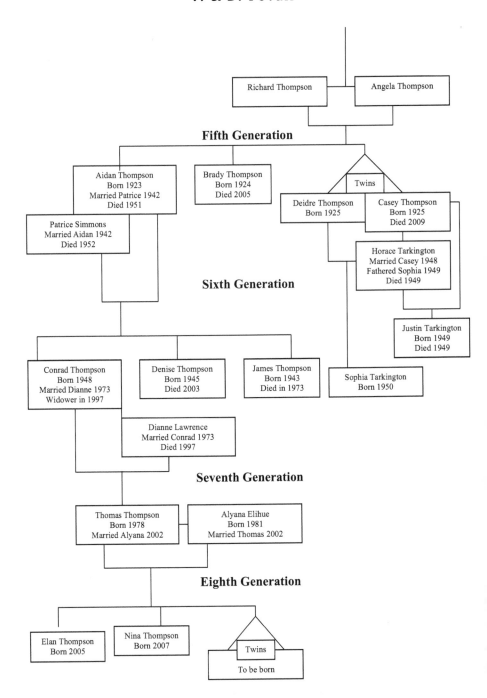

Richard Thompson — Angela Thompson

Fifth Generation

Aidan Thompson
Born 1923
Married Patrice 1942
Died 1951

Brady Thompson
Born 1924
Died 2005

Twins

Deidre Thompson
Born 1925

Casey Thompson
Born 1925
Died 2009

Patrice Simmons
Married Aidan 1942
Died 1952

Horace Tarkington
Married Casey 1948
Fathered Sophia 1949
Died 1949

Sixth Generation

Justin Tarkington
Born 1949
Died 1949

Conrad Thompson
Born 1948
Married Dianne 1973
Widower in 1997

Denise Thompson
Born 1945
Died 2003

James Thompson
Born 1943
Died in 1973

Sophia Tarkington
Born 1950

Dianne Lawrence
Married Conrad 1973
Died 1997

Seventh Generation

Thomas Thompson
Born 1978
Married Alyana 2002

Alyana Elihue
Born 1981
Married Thomas 2002

Eighth Generation

Elan Thompson
Born 2005

Nina Thompson
Born 2007

Twins

To be born

CHAPTER 27

Heritage

CASEY WISHED HER ashes to be scattered in the wilderness surrounding her childhood home, so Deidre and Sophia would arrive a couple of days after Christmas to fulfill her wish. The loss of his aunt had dampened Conrad's usual high spirits, but he busied himself making all their travel arrangements and looked forward to seeing them both. He was determined not to allow the unexpected news to undermine the cheer of Christmas for his grandchildren and encouraged us to do so as well.

I, on the other hand, was having a more difficult time dealing with these events. Undoubtedly, Casey had come to me moments after her death to share her secret. That in itself was unsettling. Why did she visit me? What did she expect me to do?

The few days leading up to Christmas were filled with not only my quandary as to what to do with Casey's possessions but also the anticipation of spending the first Christmas with my new family.

As if that were not enough, the house and I were excited with the prospect of Deidre and Sophia coming to stay and wanted to welcome them with all our love. All in all, it promised to be an unforgettable week.

Tom and Conrad had moved Angela's bedroom set into our house and transferred my old one into the room where I kept my unpacked boxes. That room now needed to be readied to receive our guests and grandchildren when they stayed with us.

The first order of things on this day was to unpack all of the forgotten boxes and decide what to do with their contents. I looked forward to this activity, wondering how the new Sarah would react to her own memories. Filled with expectation and hope for new discoveries, I entered the room.

Unable to decide which box to open first, I unsealed all of them at once, and then stepped back, waiting to see if any of them would ask to be attended to first. I found this particular behavior somewhat out of the ordinary for me. Why couldn't I just move systematically through each box? I'd always been a well-organized, practical person, had labeled all the boxes, knew what each contained. Yet now I felt indecisive, all of a sudden I feared finding something unexpected.

I was experiencing the same emotions as when I'd first stepped into the attic. I had a premonition that something was about to happen.

I waited, but none of the boxes asked to be emptied first. I went to the closest one and began to take out its contents, grateful to have only nine boxes to deal with. Something kept tugging at me, and I didn't know what, so the faster I got through them, the sooner I'd encounter whatever may catch my attention.

The first box contained many of the knickknacks I'd gathered through my life, buying them either on a trip or on a weekend shopping stroll through an outdoor mall. I liked to promenade through the outdoor malls, feeling the fresh air and the sun as I gazed at the many displays. The items I took out of this box did not affect me at all. I simply remembered when and where I purchased them, and the recollections were pleasant. I noticed they were all nice, decorative possessions such as flower vases, small figurines, a couple of ornamental plates from Italy, a handful of little statues, ornamental boxes of all sizes from Mexico, and many more such items. I couldn't understand why I'd put them away. They were not only beautiful but also irreplaceable. I placed them throughout all the rooms in the house and knew I would enjoy telling the stories of their origin to my grandchildren.

After I emptied the first box, the other ones were not as ominous. I'd found a purpose, and as a result, unpacking each item and finding its place in the house became an enjoyable prospect. What a delight to find in several of the boxes the books that either my nana or my mother had enjoyed, which I now looked forward to reading again. Somehow, now that I had welcomed my gift and cherished the stories of the past, my family's books brought with them not only the tale within the book but the memory of its readers and their reactions to the book.

By the time I finished unpacking the last box, I realized that I was crying. I don't know when I'd started crying. They were noiseless tears, slowly rolling down my cheeks and dropping on my lap. I think the tears must've started when I held in my hand the things that belonged to my parents and my nana.

The ache wasn't about the items themselves but about their loneliness, about their abandonment.

Nana had died shortly after she turned eighty of natural causes. She'd told us over the years that when she turned eighty, it would be time for her to move to her next life. She didn't want to risk being a burden and not be able to care for herself. She'd mentioned that so many times to us that as her eightieth birthday approached, we were all prepared.

That year I visited with her all summer long and was able to stay there all through the fall, thanks to a sabbatical to conduct some research at the University of Boston. I lived with my nana all those months up to the time she passed away. It was a peaceful death, with all of us around her, and she felt happy and content. All her affairs were in order, and in the end, we had no doubt in our hearts as to her satisfaction with how she'd lived her life. How she knew she would die after her eightieth birthday remained a mystery. This premonition of hers was not logical and didn't make any sense. My skepticism had run rampant after she became ill, and I'd interrogated all her physicians to ensure it wasn't something she had done to herself. But they all confirmed that she had died of natural causes. She'd caught a cold that turned into pneumonia, which caused her death. Nothing more.

As she prepared for her eightieth birthday, she taught us the value of not burdening your family with the decisions of what to do with your possessions when you are gone. Guided by Nana, my mother, father, and I went through all of her belongings. She told us about them only if we asked. She intended to give us whatever possessions we really wanted while she was still alive. She wished to donate the rest to some of her trusted charities or to individuals of her choice.

No one in my family has ever been a gatherer, so it was not a hard task. We each took with us what we wished, and I helped her give away the remainder. When all was said and done she felt relieved that everything had found a home and a future.

I'd heard some of my friends talk about how hard it had been to go through their loved one's possessions after their passing, and how awful it felt deciding what to do with their clothes or their collections or their relics. My nana took care of that for us. She made it easy, and as I unpacked her effects, I realized how selfish I'd been when I put them away. My neglect of them was inexcusable.

My parents told me that they'd learned an important lesson from Nana and would do the same for me when their time came. The turn of events that followed, however, was so unexpected that they were never able to execute their plans.

My paternal grandmother was next to go, followed by her husband a short year after. Both died of complications from existing maladies, heart for my grandmother and cancer for my grandfather. My father, their eldest son, inherited their estate in Mexico much to the chagrin of his siblings. With Nana gone and the winters in Boston growing colder, my parents decided to move to Monterrey.

My father had already retired from Gillette, and caring for the family estate was a good way to keep his young mind occupied. I think he also longed for his birthplace, and my mother was happy to accommodate his hankerings. My mother missed Nana terribly, and everything around Boston reminded her of her absence. They both loved Mexico, so the decision to move south proved to be a simple one.

I helped them with the move to Monterrey during my summer break from teaching. That's when they asked me to take anything of theirs that I liked. I just couldn't do it. I believed they needed to take all of their possessions with them. After all, those things represented their lives in the United States and would help them reminisce with fondness about their time in Boston.

I felt quite adamant about it, mostly thinking of my father's comfort. My paternal grandparents' estate was filled with expensive and beautiful things not only from Mexico but also from around the world. Therefore, a bit of Boston and the simplicity of their own belongings would be a nice reminder of what was important to them. In the end, other than some of my mother's books and a handful of knickknacks they boxed and mailed to me later on, I didn't take anything with me.

Maybe I had started crying when I remembered how much I would regret this decision in later years, but at the time it felt right.

After their move to Monterrey, I visited my parents every summer. I enjoyed spending time with them, and I loved Mexico, its architecture, its colors, its food, and its people. I have fond memories of those trips. However, in terms of possessions, that's all that remains from my parents.

They died in a car crash five years after they moved to Monterrey. The horror that ensued began but a few minutes after the funeral with the reading of their will. The vultures descended upon the estate. Watching the sibling rivalry and the fight for control was revolting. I didn't want to have anything to do with these people, even if they were my aunts and uncles. I had nothing in common with them, and after observing their despicable behavior, all I wanted was to be as far from them as possible. That is exactly what I did. I told my lawyer to give my portion of the estate, whatever it turned out to be, to the Catholic Charities in Boston under my parents' names. I left Monterrey after giving those instructions and never went back. Nor have I ever had any contact with my father's siblings. I was notified of the donation when it happened, and that part of my past came to an end.

Now it had resurfaced, and deep sadness enveloped me. The tears had stopped, but as I placed each memento of my past life throughout the house, it pained me to remember. Each item brought with it a memory of how it had come to be in my possession, my life in Boston, my trips to Mexico, a purchase made or gift received from Nana, Mom, or Dad. How sad that I possessed so few things of my familial heritage. Now I understood why I'd packed them away. I'd told myself that my life was cluttered and needed a bit of scarcity. But in reality I had hidden the pain of the sudden loss of my parents and the aftermath of the greed that followed.

I finished unpacking all the boxes and readying the room in a daze, not remembering the details. I finished right before dinnertime—simple tasks that should've taken but a few hours had obviously taken much longer.

The minute Conrad came in he said that he felt a sense of melancholy permeating the house. He walked in the kitchen just as I was taking the bread out of the oven. After I closed the oven door and placed the bread on the counter, he held me tightly in his arms.

I cried quietly in the safety of his embrace.

"Remembering your folks, I guess, from the look of the lovely things you've spread around the house."

I nodded.

"C'mon, lets open a nice bottle of wine, and I'll build us a fire and light the Christmas tree, and you can tell me all about your day."

Like a small child that has been hurt and needs tender loving care to feel better, Conrad took me under his protection and gently guided me out of my sorrow.

"Well, Sarah, it looks to me as if, in terms of your possessions, you have what really matters to you, and from what you've told me, what really mattered to your parents and your nana."

"Yes, but it's so puny compared to your heritage."

"Ah, my cinnamon beauty." He said it so gently I felt as if I could dissolve in his arms. "No sense in comparing. All families are different. Your family was made up of folks who came from different parts of the world and left you with many assets that aren't physical. Just look at you speaking Spanish, French, and English. That's an impressive legacy."

"It isn't really, just luck to have my parents and grandmother." No sooner had I finished that sentence than I felt the weight of remorse lift.

"That's my girl," he said, and kissed my nose.

I smiled. Conrad, my future husband, had made me whole again, helping me appreciate the richness of the legacy from my parents and Nana. I finally understood that their bequest shouldn't be valued in the quantity of their possessions but instead in the quality of their history, in the influence on those of us who had come in contact with them, and the inspiration that the recollection of their lives would bring to future generations.

"All this talk about Mexico has me hankering for Mexican food," Conrad said.

"How about chicken enchiladas in green tomatillo sauce?"

"Can I help?"

"Yeah, you can fix the margaritas. I might need a couple. This is my first time making enchiladas. My mom's recipe is quite simple, and I was planning on making them one of these days. Let's just fix them tonight."

As usual it turned out to be an evening of love and enjoyment.

The only thing that weighed me down was the impending meeting with Deidre and Sophia. The suddenness of Casey's visit still had me reeling, and I wondered how much more my "gift" would reveal in the days to come.

Most alarmingly, I feared that more unsettling scenes awaited me.

CHAPTER 28

Visitors

CHRISTMAS EVE PAVED the way to the creation of a whole set of new traditions for all of us, and the house was in high spirits.

Conrad closed the store at noon on Christmas Eve, and the entire clan had come to our house in the late afternoon to join in the preparation of an early dinner. We roasted a leg of lamb with the recipe my nana had brought from France. I'd shared with them how every Christmas Eve my family enjoyed a delicious dinner with the leg of lamb as its centerpiece, accompanied by mashed potatoes, buttered green beans, and freshly baked bread. The leg of lamb was roasted in the oven, speckled with cloves of garlic, bathed in milk, and then adorned with rosemary. A salad of cherry tomatoes mixed with diced cucumbers, chopped Greek olives, thinly sliced onions, and sprinkled with virgin olive oil and red wine vinegar accompanied the meal. The spread reflected the beautiful red, white, and green colors of Christmas. They all wanted to taste this meal, so we'd agreed to prepare it together.

As we fixed each dish, I acquainted them with its French name. I loved to watch every one of them practicing speaking French. Elan and Nina thought it to be a fun game. He had the best pronunciation, but his sister was not far behind. I could see how much I would enjoy teaching them about the languages and customs of France, Spain, and Mexico.

Around two in the afternoon, as we were baking the bread, a surprise came knocking on our door. One by one, many families living in our town came by the house with gifts or homemade goodies, not only to wish us a Merry Christmas but also to congratulate us on our engagement.

Many of these people I'd never met, and I liked visiting with them and getting to know them. The house smelled delicious and looked radiant in her

The Gift of the Twin Houses

Christmas colors and lights. Every time the bell rang, it sounded more and more melodious as it announced with joy the arrival of more well-wishers.

Being someone who typically shied away from social functions, I found myself, to my surprise, utterly at ease talking with every person who came to the house. I had a sincere interest in them, their families, their histories, and their traditions of the season. Conversation between all of us came easily, and we spent a pleasant afternoon discovering one another. Not only did I feel welcome among them, but also I felt that they were earnestly seeking my friendship. A new experience for me, given that never had I encountered such a warm welcome into any type of social environment, and their sincerity and openness was disarming. Conrad and his family were highly valued and loved in these parts. I'd stepped into a world where people not only respected the decision and choice he'd made for his future wife but also embraced it fully, as if they shared in the decision itself.

It was particularly fun to hear Conrad tell them all about our "French Christmas Eve Dinner" as if it were the title of a movie or book. He took such pride in describing the menu that it was impossible for folks not to want the recipe for each dish. Tom took charge of writing it all down, freeing Alyana to help me in the kitchen while we cooked and visited with our guests. Elan and Nina were great hosts, helping their dad and granddad entertain our visitors.

By five o'clock the guests were all gone, and we sat down to dinner. It tasted delicious, much better than I remembered, maybe due to the fact that this time my family and I prepared it together. We ate and reminisced about how much fun the afternoon had been.

When Nina was done with her dinner, she left her seat and crawled onto Conrad's lap.

He gently stroked her hair. "All right, little one, what was your favorite part of fixing Christmas Eve dinner with Mama?"

"The food word game."

"It wasn't a game," Elan interjected. "We learned French food words. Like at school but fun. I liked saying the words and making the food. That was the best."

"I liked the meat taking a bath in milk," Nina told her granddad.

"You never thought you'd see meat taking baths in milk, did you? Can you remember how to say milk in French?" Alyana coaxed her daughter.

"*Lait.*"

"A bath and a shower," Elan added. "Mama sprayed it with that big stick with the bubble at the end."

"A long, long bath and a shower." Alyana smiled.

"You're right. First the meat took a two-day bath in the milk while it marinated in the fridge, and then while we roasted it in the oven, I sprayed it with milk. Altogether the meat was well bathed and showered."

"The French word for meat is *agneau*, right?" Alyana asked.

"Yes. You guys are great!" I smiled proudly from ear to ear.

"How about you, Elan?" Tom asked.

"Mashing the *pomme de terre* and then mixing the *beurre*. I like how you make the *r* in French. It's like a roar in your throat."

"Like a lion," Nina added.

"You both learn fast. We'll learn more words as we make other foods. Would you like that?" They nodded their approval in unison.

"OK," Conrad said, "I vote that we make this an annual meal," and he raised his hand as if in school. The grandchildren immediately raised their little hands, and of course, their parents did as well, laughing. I couldn't have been more pleased.

"Mama," Tom said, "you sure have the gift of listening. I've learned a bunch about some of these folks in just their short visit with you today. Considering that I've known many of them all my life, I'm amazed how much I didn't know about them and how easily they just opened up to you. That's not easy in these parts. The Northwest is where folks settle to get away from others. People don't usually share as they did with you today."

"It's the storyteller in her," Conrad said. "She's curious about their stories, and she listens with such sincerity that they just unwrap their lives."

"C'mon, how could you not listen when folks are talking?" I chuckled.

"For starters you could do what most people do. They ask you a question, and as you start to answer, their attention goes elsewhere," Alyana said.

Conrad nodded. "You have what Grandma Angela had: sincere interest in people. It comes with your abilities. I'm sure that's why you became a teacher. You care."

After I reflected on Conrad's assertion, I arrived at the same conclusion. I enjoyed teaching because it allowed me to share knowledge.

And yet, here I was keeping a secret that concerned them all, because it was not mine to share.

We took our desserts, milk, and hot cocoa to the living room to partake in another of my family's Christmas Eve traditions, to open one present we'd placed for one another under the tree. Elan and Nina chose which present we would each open with a little coaxing from their parents.

The joy on their little faces turned out to be the best gift of all. After we each got our present, Nina decided to sit on my lap and open hers and help me open mine. I think she enjoyed opening the presents more than the presents themselves.

Our gifts were simple but filled with meaning. Tom and Alyana gave me a splendidly crafted dream catcher decorated with beautiful feathers and beads.

"For your bedroom, Mama," little Nina said.

"Do you know what it does?"

She nodded and continued playing with her own present, a little doll her mother had sewn that wore the exact same dress Nina was wearing.

"There you have it, Mama." Alyana chuckled. "Aren't children precious on how they relate to us? You asked if she knew what it did, and she told you she did. In her little mind, she answered. No need to say more."

"Don't you wish we didn't lose that clarity as we grow older?" I asked. "Anyway, I'd still like to know more about the dream catcher."

"Dream catchers," Alyana answered, "are a symbol of unity among the various First Nations. Many say that over the years they've been overcommercialized, so some of my people don't use them anymore. In the old times, they were created by hand, making a hoop from the branch of a willow and then weaving a net in the middle that looks like a web. Handmade dream catchers, like this one, are made with sacred feathers and stones. The ones you see in the stores that are mass produced just have trinkets."

"This one was made by an elder in Alyana's tribe just for you newlyweds," Tom said. "Alyana told her all about you guys, and she made it for you and Papa to hang over your bed in your new bedroom."

"It'll catch all the bad dreams and only let the good ones through. We'll always wake up happy and content with each other and the world around us," Conrad added, and winked at me.

The dream catcher was not only stunning but a symbol of the greatest gift of all: the opportunity for me to learn from Alyana about the First Nations of our region, their traditions, beliefs, and spirituality. I had so much to look forward to.

Tom and Alyana gave Conrad a letter with the offer of a two-week vacation away from the store after the wedding. He smiled mischievously at me, and of course, I blushed.

Elan's gift was a book I'd chosen for him. He loved to have stories read to him, and I thought that giving him a book with the stories of Mother Goose would pay homage to his great-grandmother Angela. After all, she'd chosen this book as one of the two books she took with her when she left home at fourteen, and I could only imagine how much she must've loved the stories within it. Reading them with Elan would bring a bit of Angela closer to us.

Tom and Alyana's gift was a bonus check from Conrad. It must've been much more than they expected because all Tom could do was shake his head, hug his father, and hold on tight to Alyana's hand. She in turn cried. I hadn't seen her cry before, but I knew her tears were tears of joy and love for my future husband. What a treat to witness the love they all shared with one another.

After we finished dessert and opening our presents, the grandchildren were happy to go home, eager to go to bed in anticipation of the arrival of Santa Claus.

Conrad and I eased into our evening routine of recounting our day as we washed the dishes and cleaned the kitchen.

"Now that I have a two-week vacation, where do you want to go for our honeymoon? Want to go to Boston?"

The Gift of the Twin Houses

"Are you kidding? When do we leave?"

"We need to get married first in order to have a honeymoon."

"I meant how soon after the wedding, you silly man."

"I know what you meant. I get a kick out of teasing you. I like the little crease that pops up on your forehead. You look cute." He kissed my forehead. "Anyway, I think we'll have the kids moved into their new home a couple of days after Christmas. Tom and I have talked about closing the store to make the move in one day. Deidre and Sophia will have arrived. So barring any surprises, we can leave the first day of the New Year."

"Great!"

"Are you up for a train ride? We can go from Seattle to Boston. I like the idea of being cooped up with you in a train. We'll spend some time there so you can show me your old stomping grounds."

"You've thought of everything. It sounds perfect." This time, I kissed him.

Our honeymoon started that very evening as we slept under the protection of our dream catcher on the bed that once belonged to the woman who'd brought us together. We were both tired, the kind of exhaustion that comes from giving oneself completely to the demands of a day filled with excitement and new discoveries. Our lovemaking, in response to the fatigue of our bodies, was tender and soothing. We were so at ease with each other that, without a word, our actions, strokes, and responses became one. Long gentle kisses and delicate caresses showed the way to a togetherness of immense pleasure as if we were cradled by tranquil ocean waves swaying into peaks of ecstasy.

We fell asleep in each other's arms.

Christmas day turned out to be just as magical as the day before. I'd gotten up around four thirty to bake the muffins and pastries. I felt in tune with the house and her happiness to have celebrated Christmas Eve with us. The silence of the early morning of Christmas day enthralled me, and I felt embraced by the warmth of my house. Conrad must have sensed that I needed that time to myself because he didn't put up much resistance when I left our bed. He was right; with the arrival of Deidre and Sophia, my turmoil about their secret had increased, and I needed to think. I still had no idea how to handle it. I could only hope that Angela would lend me a helping hand.

Conrad and I arrived at Alyana and Tom's small rental house around seven thirty in the morning with freshly baked muffins and breakfast pastries. Even though there were many boxes packed and ready to move into their new home, we were quite comfortable.

Alyana brewed coffee and made hot cocoa. Conrad always arrived this early to make sure he'd be there when his grandchildren woke up and ran into the living room to see what surprises awaited them under the Christmas tree. His recollection of their little faces lighting up with the wonder of what awaited them under the wrapped presents was infectious, and I couldn't wait to be a part of that. It filled me with excitement and anticipation. I'd never experienced the look of a child facing the magical surprise of the overnight visit by Santa Claus.

An hour later, the faces of our grandchildren entering the living room and discovering the presents under the tree turned out to be as marvelous as Conrad had described it. The sparkle of happiness, wonder, and marvel in their little faces saturated the entire household. We shared their exhilaration as we each opened a present, one at a time, taking turns as everyone watched, and rejoiced in the gift that each received. It felt as if we all had received many gifts.

Nina loved unwrapping presents so much that she got to do it for all of us. It was great fun to watch her face fill with anticipation to see what was hidden under the wrap, and then she would excitedly tell us what was inside before she finished tearing off the paper. Her descriptions were delightfully funny.

The rest of the day was filled with the enjoyment of being together, playing games, having fun out in the snow, great food, and packing as much as we could in preparation for the move into their new home.

The day after Christmas turned out to be a busy one at the store for Tom and Conrad and just as hectic for Alyana and me as we packed the family for the move. Conrad promised the little ones that he would move the Christmas tree without having to take it down, so we carefully wrapped it in bed linens. By the end of the day, the entire family was worn out but also exhilarated with the prospect of the move.

The Gift of the Twin Houses

Early the next day, we were ready to start packing our cars and trucks when friends showed up. Unexpectedly, every single person who had come to visit us on Christmas Eve came to assist us with the move. With their help we moved our little family to their new home in less than four hours. The men took care of loading and moving all the boxes and furniture, while the women helped unpack and got everything ready in the house.

We focused on the kitchen first, knowing that by lunchtime we would all be starving. Everyone had brought their Christmas leftovers, and we celebrated the first meal in Tom and Alyana's new home with great friends and a wonderful variety of delicious foods.

By the end of the day, all the boxes were unpacked, the furniture was all in place, and Tom, Alyana, and the children were ready to comfortably spend the first night in their new home. We were all so exhausted we could barely stand.

However, sleep didn't come easy for me. My anxiety about the impending arrival of Deidre and Sophia kept tugging at me. I had no clarity as to whether I should reveal the visit from Casey, let alone what to do with her secret.

Unable to sleep, I decided to take Justin's baby blanket and the small tin can with their painful memories to the attic. Maybe together, in the silence of the night, I would learn what needed to be done.

It was a beautiful, clear night, and the light from the moon and the stars made it easy for me to ease upstairs without the need to turn any lights and wake Conrad up. The attic was bathed in silvery tones, and as soon as I entered, it cracked its familiar welcome. I smiled, sat in the armchair, and gave us time to think and feel.

No one came to visit, no one whispered a word, and yet all of a sudden I knew that I had to return the secret to its hiding place.

It wasn't easy to do so. Part of me felt that I had to keep it in the open, that Casey needed the truth to be told. But a stronger urge pressed me to conceal them again.

I sensed that the permanent burial site for Justin's baby blanket and the aching past of Casey and Deidre were yet to be revealed.

CHAPTER 29

The Meeting

I STOOD BETWEEN the fireplace and the front window staring out over the snowy valley. Conrad had left for the airport in Seattle early in the morning to retrieve Deidre and Sophia, and I expected his truck to trundle toward the house at any moment. My hands felt like ice, and I kept burying them under my armpits to keep them warm, with questionable results. The fear had permeated my being since learning they would be coming to stay with us. A fear, I now realized, born of the prospect of meeting in the flesh someone who formed an integral part of the cast of characters Angela had arranged for me to meet. Someone who, until days earlier, was no more than a tenuous figure seen in a vision that offered the comfort of knowing that its reality was far removed from the present. Now, the present was emerging from the past and coming face-to-face with me.

All the recriminations of my childhood now resurfaced with renewed urgency. Suddenly, my family's concerns over my special gift seemed like undeniable wisdom. Why had I come here? Why in heaven's name had I given in to that inexplicable urge to uproot myself and come to this far corner of the world? And worst of all, why had I chosen to visit the attic and rummage through boxes of photographs of people I didn't even know?

I wanted to run away again, but I knew it was too late. My involvement with my house, with Conrad, with the photos, and with Angela all pointed to this moment, and I understood that with such involvement came responsibility.

Each time I relived Casey's revelations, a cold shiver raced across my skin. All my efforts to avoid such repetition had so far proved futile, but I kept trying. Now, as the moment of truth approached, the images raced into my mind with increased vigor. I had hoped that replacing the tin can and baby blanket under the floorboard was the right thing to do, and it would persuade the images to cease. But they persisted.

Conrad's truck appeared in the distance. I felt my heart race as my breathing sped up and my mouth went dry. "OK, Sarah. This is it. I hope Angela knows what she's doing, because I sure don't."

The truck pulled up a few feet from the front steps as I made my way to the door and stepped outside.

Conrad came around to open the passenger door and flashed me a smile and a wink of reassurance as he went by.

"Watch your step; it's kind of icy still," he said to Sophia, offering her the support of his hand. She was a beautiful woman, with a smile full of promise and optimism, and as she looked up at me, her eyes flashed with affection and serenity. With the urn that sheltered Casey's ashes nestled safely under her arm, she rushed toward me. Her resemblance to Angela was astonishing.

"Sarah. How wonderful to meet you." The genuine joy in her voice lifted my spirits and brought a smile to my face. She embraced me without an ounce of hesitation.

Conrad's voice brought my attention back to the truck. "Easy now, Aunt Deidre. I got you."

There she stood. Tears tried to force their way into my eyes, but I pushed them back as I heard myself sigh. Tiny and frail, Deidre still had strength and resolve etched into her eyes and the weight of unlocked secrets carved into her face. She looked up at me and nodded almost imperceptibly. Conrad proffered her cane and she grasped it without removing her eyes from me. He placed his arm around her and guided her up the steps. As they reached the porch, I stepped back to give her more room.

"Aunt Deidre—" Conrad began.

"I know, I know," Deidre interrupted. "This is Sarah."

I searched desperately for something to say. All I could muster was a feeble, "Welcome."

She reached up and placed her hand ever so gently upon my cheek and tears pooled into her eyes as she smiled. It was too much for me, and my own eyes flooded as I wrapped my arms around her. After a moment, I stepped back and mumbled, "Come out of the cold."

I pushed the door open and Conrad smiled at me again as he led her into the house. Her house. My house. Our house. I ushered Sophia in and followed close behind.

I shut the door behind me and watched as Deidre approached the stairs and stood there, as if frozen in place, staring up the stairs toward the upper floor. Sophia handed the urn to Conrad and then touched the old woman's elbow.

"Are you all right, Momma?"

Deidre nodded.

"C'mon let's rest a bit," Conrad suggested, but Deidre didn't move.

I glanced at Conrad who seemed as lost as I about what to do next. Quietly he stepped into the living room and placed the urn on the mantle. Just as quietly he returned to the foyer.

At long last I managed to find my voice. "Can I get you something to drink? I have some hot cocoa if you like. Or maybe some coffee?"

Without changing her gaze, Deidre shook her head. "I have avoided this moment for far too long. I may lose my resolve if I wait any longer." She turned to Sophia and pulled her close. "Let's go upstairs."

With one hand locked onto the banister and the other on her daughter's arm, she climbed step by painstaking step without ever looking down, the old feet remembering exactly where to land in spite of the passage of time. It was mesmerizing.

Conrad and I were unable to decide if we should join them or not, so we remained in place as they climbed. When they reached the second floor, Deidre paused.

"Come on up, you two. I can't do this alone," she said, a tremble in her voice.

By the time we reached the attic, Sophia was helping Deidre settle into the armchair. The old woman's eyes searched the floor for the secret hiding place.

"I know it seems odd, but I can't remember which board it is," Deidre murmured.

Sophia placed her hand on her mother's hands. "It's OK. It doesn't matter."

Deidre shook her head and a deep anguish colored her voice. " It is important…and now I don't know which one it is."

I took a deep breath and gathered all my courage. I pointed. "It's that one."

The look of bewilderment on Deidre's face made me regret my statement as soon as I'd made it. Her eyes stayed locked onto me for so long that I felt compelled to go on.

"Casey told me. The day she died."

I removed the floorboard and took out the tin can and the baby blanket. I handed them to Deidre, but she held up her hands rejecting them, shaking her frail head, and looking away.

Sophia reached out and took them. "It's OK, Momma. We don't have to go through this. I've felt the pain both you and Momma Casey experienced."

Conrad looked at me, perplexed, a look that pleaded with me to do something. But I didn't know what to do or what to say without violating Casey's trust, so I shook my head.

Deidre looked at me and said, "She told you?"

I nodded.

Deidre sighed, and looking at all of us, she said, "It's time for the whole truth."

"Let's go downstairs, Aunt Deidre." Conrad said. "We'll be more comfortable there."

We did as he suggested.

"We always intended to return," Deidre said, taking the cup of coffee I held out to her and placing it on the table. "But, somehow, we just never did. Never even spoke of it until just before she died." She poured a hefty spoonful of sugar into her cup and stirred it. Then, she slowly sipped her coffee before continuing. "We both hoped that if we left it alone, the pain would disappear one day." She stopped breathing for a moment and then went on. "Of course, it never went away."

"I'm glad you're here now," Conrad said.

"Casey asked me to bring her back. She wanted to be buried with what was left of her son, Justin."

"I'm glad we're all here and that this secret is out in the open," Sophia whispered as she touched her mother's hand.

I glanced at Sophia. "You never knew."

"Not the whole story. Not the details. I noticed the furtive, involuntary glances they gave each other sometimes and knew they wanted to hide it from me. I respected their wishes. As I grew older I sensed the violence, the pain, but the fear I felt in them made me withdraw."

"Did you ever wonder about your father? Who he was?" Conrad asked.

Sophia glanced at Deidre. "I asked them once about my father. They told me he had died before I was born but very little else. I could see it made them nervous, that they didn't really want to talk about it. Eventually, I just gave up."

"How does one tell a child," Deidre whispered, "that her father did such terrible things? How could I tell her that I killed him to save us all? How could I tell her about violence like that? No child deserves to hear such horrific things about her father." Deidre's head tilted, her eyes saddened, and her face became clouded with despair as she looked at her daughter. "I'm sorry." She began to sob.

Sophia rushed to her mother and knelt before her. "No, you don't apologize for loving me, for protecting me. You and Momma Casey gave up every chance of happiness to keep me from suffering. You don't apologize, you hear me? You hold your head high. You smile and you rejoice in the happiness you made possible for me. You cherish the strength and the courage that allowed both of you to do what had to be done, even at your own expense. Look at me." She lifted her mother's face to hers. "I am you. I am Momma Casey. And both of you are me. I smile because of you. I live because of you. I am a woman with a full life, with joyful memories, and with a bright future because of you. And you must never apologize for that. I am forever grateful for all you've done, and I will love you forever for that. I am proud of what and who I am, and you are proud of what and who I am. Always."

Deidre caressed her daughter's face. "I love you."

Through my flowing tears, I glanced at Conrad. His face glistened with moisture. He caught my eye, and I motioned for us to leave the room. As quietly as we could, we made our way to the kitchen. Behind us, gentle sobs bonded daughter and mother more closely and more deeply than ever.

As for Conrad and me, we melted into each other's arms.

CHAPTER 30

The Commission

THE BURIAL CEREMONY was simple yet meaningful. Deidre remembered their favorite tree where they spent endless hours in childish play, climbing it, playing with its leaves, and reading under its shade. She had visited their tree with Conrad and pointed to a branch they used to sit on as they shared many a story. Before the ceremony, Conrad had dug a small burial site, and we all gathered under their favorite branch to openly acknowledge the existence of Justin and bury his belongings along with his mother's ashes.

Alyana asked one of the elders of her tribe to perform the burial ceremony, and the ritual brought with it a sense of closure.

"We shared our private stories when we sat on that branch. I think she'll be happy here," Deidre murmured. She turned to Sophia. "When my time comes, I wish to join her."

"I'll bring you back, Momma. I promise."

I clung to Conrad, somehow overly conscious of this moment of mortality.

Two days later, my friends Iris and Sonia came knocking on our door, and the whirlwind of out-of-town guests, along with the preparations for the wedding, propelled us into a future filled with hope as we let the past peacefully rest.

I'd talked with my friends on the phone after they had received the invitation to my wedding, but the rascals hadn't let on that they were planning to attend. They told me they needed to consult with their husbands and family. They promised to let me know a couple of days before the wedding. Now here they stood, with their husbands, letting us know that they were attending.

I couldn't be happier. The three of us had been friends for years, working at the same school, and kindred spirits in our devotion to our students. Our friendship and the opportunity to freely share our challenges and frustrations allowed us to survive as long as we did. They were a bit older than me and had retired a few years earlier. Those years without them had been hard, and I'd missed them terribly. After they retired, both moved away to be closer to their children and grandchildren. We'd only seen each other when we got together for our yearly tradition of lunch and afternoon tea, accompanied by tales of our lives. They were both just as practical as I had been, and neither ever gave into any type of excess or activity out of the ordinary. Traveling to an unknown part of the country to be with me at my wedding would be considered excess. I never expected them to show up. Imagine my surprise.

"We've booked a couple of rooms at that little quaint bed and breakfast in town," Iris told us.

"It's so charming, we feel like we're in a storybook," Sonia added.

Harold and George were already deep in conversation with Conrad about how the house had been built. Our home had already captivated them.

"Both Harold and George were ready to come the moment we mentioned you lived in the middle of nowhere in the Cascades," Iris went on.

"They heard there's great fishing here and are looking forward to spending time getting to know these parts," Sonia added.

Hearing them talk one after the other with such ease brought me back to how much the three of us would just go on and on chatting about anything and everything.

"I don't know how you could think we wouldn't be here for your wedding," Iris said. "Sarah, you must be crazy to think we wouldn't want to join you."

"After you spoke with us, and we heard about the wonderful things you were experiencing, we were jealous. We wanted a little bit of that magic," Sonia added.

And magic they got.

The days leading up to our wedding were filled with activities. Conrad and Tom had decided to open the store for only the first half of the day till after the New Year. As such, they would leave together shortly after breakfast and

Alyana would come over with the children. Along with Deidre and Sophia, we spent precious time connecting the past with the present and imagining the future.

Deidre recounted their early years, the fun times they had with their brothers, and how they played with their parents, Angela and Richard. Sophia's own tales of growing up with two mothers were delightful, and I learned much from her recollections of how her grandmother Angela had guided her in understanding her own extrasensory capacities.

Midmorning my friends Iris and Sonia would join us, and together we chatted, made decorations for the wedding, cooked, or baked our specialties for the wedding reception to be held in our home. Many of our guests had insisted on bringing a special dish for the reception, therefore we concentrated on preparing appetizers from Spain, Mexico, and France, as well as Alyana's Brie puff wheels and her special cranberry champagne cocktail.

The men would join us for lunch, and after that, the two visiting couples either went fishing or sightseeing while we stayed behind with the children and our wedding preparations.

With Deidre's approval, we placed the photographs from the tin can into the photo album Angela had put together of her twin daughters. Sophia wanted to keep the photo album so that she could share it with her husband and children. We all agreed that Angela had more than likely meant it for her. Deidre, however, took out several photographs and gave them to me to complete the leftover frames. She wished me to place them on the dresser along with the ones from Angela, her parents, and my family. One was a photo of Casey with Justin in her arms and another of the two of them with baby Sophia. She gave me a third photograph she kept in her wallet of Sophia and her husband on their wedding day, flanked by Casey and Deidre.

The next day, Sophia added to my collection several photographs of her children and their paternal grandparents that she'd asked her husband to mail to us.

"I'm glad none of my children have inherited the violent streak from my father," Sophia confided.

"I wouldn't think so. From what I saw, it appeared to be more of a learned trait than genetic," I told her, surprised with my own comfort in sharing my extrasensory perceptions.

"Thanks, Sarah. I appreciate your openness with me. I'll treasure it for all my days." She opened her arms and embraced me, a simple act of gratitude, yet life transforming for me, and a bond between us that would endure without end.

Conrad couldn't stop praising my cooking, so one day Sophia begged me to make paella for dinner. She'd seen the photos of the paellas my mother and grandmother had made and how ecstatic we all looked around the table as we enjoyed every morsel. Conrad had already ordered a paella pan from *The Spanish Table*, a specialy store in Seattle, and had been waiting for me to make it, so along with Deidre, he joined in the chorus.

"Imagine the reaction when you prepare this spectacular Spanish dish. Your friends won't believe it's the same Sarah." Conrad said.

"Well it isn't. Is it?" I laughed.

"C'mon, Sarah, let's do it. I'll help. The whole family will be so impressed to see you put the paella together. We'll do what you and your folks used to do. We'll all gather in the kitchen, sip a glass of wine, and watch as you add each ingredient. It'll be fun."

"You'll chop and make sure I get all the ingredients ready?"

"Sure."

"Boy, it's a tall order to make a paella without rehearsal, and it's not the typical paella. It's my mother's own adaptation."

"That's even better. C'mon, we can do it."

And with that assurance, we shopped for all the ingredients: meat, chicken, sausage, clams, shrimp, mussels, onion, garlic, peas, artichoke hearts, asparagus, and of course rice. Conrad and Sophia grew more excited with anticipation of the variety of flavors that made this dish so deliciously unique.

No one was disappointed. Conrad and I worked in perfect tandem as we prepared and added each ingredient, culminating with a beautiful paella, perfectly cooked. Everyone enjoyed each bite, including the children, who had a great time learning the Spanish names for each of the ingredients as they helped us assemble it. As Deidre savored the food, she reflected on the togetherness a paella creates as it is being prepared.

The day before our wedding, Conrad and Tom closed the store. Tom and Alyana wanted to work on the final touches for the wedding and preferred we weren't around. Sonia and Iris went shopping for the perfect wedding gift, and Conrad took a morning off to go fishing with their husbands. Sophia spent the day with Deidre visiting their friends in the area, and I was charged with caring for the children, as long as we stayed away from the first floor.

So we went to my attic. I'd not been in the attic for a long time and missed it. This morning the sun shone through and through, and I knew we would be welcomed to enjoy our visit there.

"I like this room," Elan announced when we stepped in.

"It's pretty," Nina added.

"I also like it a lot," I told them. "I heard great stories in this room when I first moved here."

Nina took my hand and led me toward the armchair. "Tell me the stories." She pushed me down and crawled onto my lap.

"Well, the first story I heard was about the people who built this house and your new home. They are twins, you know."

"Like the babies in Mommy's belly," Elan offered.

I nodded. "Did she tell you what it means to be twins?"

"They'll come home at the same time. Not like first I came and then Nina came. That's why I'm older."

"Your new home—"

"It's not new, Mama," Elan interrupted. "It's old like this one."

"You're right. What I meant was that it's new to you and your parents because you just moved in." He nodded. "So your home and this one were born at the same time. They have the same birthday; they're twins."

I don't remember how long we stayed in the attic; time just didn't seem to matter to us. I told them the stories I'd heard, crafting them for their young ears, and they were fully engaged. Elan explored the attic, listening to me while quietly looking into every trunk, searching every corner, opening every box. Nina was happy to sit on my lap for a long while and then joined her brother in the examination of the room and its contents while listening to my tales.

They didn't disturb any item. They simply explored and became acquainted with the attic and its contents.

"You should write the stories, Mama. I'd like to hear them again. That way Papa can read them to me," Elan said.

"Yeah," Nina agreed. "I want Mommy to read them to me."

"Well, I hadn't thought about writing them down, but now that you've suggested it, I'll give it a try."

"Mommy will draw the pictures," Elan said. "She's good at drawing pictures. We'll make a little book like the book my great-aunties made of the stories for aunt Sophia."

"Sounds like a great idea. I'll get started as soon as Papa and I come back from our honeymoon."

"How do you put honey on the moon?" Nina asked.

I chuckled and held her tightly against me. "Oh, darling, the word *honeymoon* was put together in the old times to describe how two newlyweds feel. Let's see. Imagine the full moon bright and shiny in the sky, and if you could taste it right after the wedding, it would be like tasting a delicious lollipop covered in sweet honey. It's a way of saying that the newlyweds are filled with love and happiness. So the honeymoon is like a holiday, a time to enjoy the feelings of delight and sweetness, just as if you were tasting the moon covered in honey."

"Oh," she said. "Let's go tell Mommy about our book. I'm hungry."

Careful to avoid taking a peek at the livingroom, we made our way down to the kitchen for lunch and found Alyana ready for us. As we ate, we planned how to put our book of stories together.

After we put the little ones down for their naps, I hankered to go back to my attic. Alyana must have sensed I wanted time to myself, and she ordered me to get some rest. She wanted me relaxed and beautiful for the wedding the next morning.

"Alyana, you're the one that should be resting," I protested.

"I will. I'll sit down on the sofa, put my feet up, and Tom and I will finish tying the bows. OK?"

"All right, it'll be nice to spend time in my attic before Conrad comes back."

"That reminds me," Alyana added, "Papa should spend the night with us tonight. He shouldn't see you until the ceremony tomorrow when Tom walks you down the aisle to present you to him."

I hadn't imagined not being close to Conrad the night before the wedding, but it made sense. He had not seen my wedding dress, and the idea of surprising him exhilarated me—although I would miss him.

Alyana had propelled me into the reverie of my own wedding. With all of the activity of the previous days, I'd not spent time thinking about it and had missed out on the enjoyment of anticipating the event.

Conrad and I agreed we would each write our own wedding vows, so I took mine with me to the attic and sat on Angela's grandmother's armchair to read them once more. For many days now, I'd not heard any more stories, and as I sat in the silence of the early afternoon, I wondered if I'd neglected the attic. But nothing cried out to be heard.

I'd used all of Angela's frames with the exception of two, and I felt pretty sure I knew what photographs she had in mind for those frames. One was reserved for the photograph that would be taken tomorrow of the wedding couple and the other for the photograph of Deidre and her daughter, Sophia, standing in front of our Christmas tree that Conrad had snapped a couple of days earlier.

"Angela," I whispered, "I hope you are content with the turn of events. I certainly can't sense any discomfort from you." I waited for a reaction, but feeling only the comfort and embrace of my attic, I settled in.

I reread my vows, whispering to Angela, enjoying the peace and quiet, the warm embrace of the afternoon sun, and the imaginings of the future to come.

"Your great-grandchildren crafted the path of what I should do with the memories you've left behind. I'll share the journey I've traveled through. I know there will be a book that will immortalize the lives of those you've loved and those whose pain and sorrow crafted the heritage you wish unveiled."

When I paused, I thought I heard a sigh. It could've been a bit of wind seeping in, but I chose to believe it was the sound of Angela's approval.

After the children woke from their naps, we were busy with the million final details in preparation for the ceremony and reception, as well as fixing dinner for all. The men had caught some delicious fish, and Conrad taught me how to clean and grill them. We ate a tasty "catch of the day" drizzled with olive oil and rosemary, accompanied by fresh vegetables, garlic mashed potatoes, and homemade bread, and enjoyed a delicious bottle of wine.

Tom and Alyana wished to decorate the house by themselves in order to surprise us the next morning. Conrad took his grandchildren home to put them to bed, and I put myself to bed and promised not leave my bedroom until the ceremony. Sophia and Deidre were to make sure I didn't peek.

Letting go of Conrad for the night proved difficult. Neither one of us wanted to be apart, but we both understood the significance of the moment, and in spite of ourselves, we said good-night. Before Conrad left, he gave me Angela's letter.

"Here it is for you to open tomorrow."

I held the letter in my hands as if its contents were made of delicate crystal. "I thought we would read it together," I whispered.

"It's addressed to you. She meant it for you." He smiled, caressed my face, and gently kissed me. It felt as if a warm feather floated between our lips. The exquisiteness of that kiss lingered with me for the remainder of the night.

I had a peaceful sleep, comforted by the knowledge that it was the last night I would spend away from Conrad.

CHAPTER 31

Angela

THE MINUTE I woke up the next morning, I sat up in bed and opened Angela's letter.

Dear Sarah,

As I write this letter I can see you in my mind's eye, eagerly waiting to understand why it is that I am writing to you.

It is quite simple, really. I dreamed of you. I have known for many years that you would arrive and would fall in love with my house and my grandson. I have known that you would bring joy and love to him and would join the twin houses in perfect harmony for generations to come.

I have dreamed of you reading to four little children, two boys and two girls, my great-grandchildren, the stories of their history, their heritage, the birth of our twin homes, and much more.

By now you already know that somehow I was born with the gift of communion with nature and with other beings. I did not understand this until I was in my teens. As you witnessed, I ran away from home at fourteen. I knew I had to leave home to search for clarity and spiritual calm. I did not know exactly how that would come about, but I felt certain that it was the path I needed to follow.

I found out when White Cloud came into my life and taught me how to clear the visions in my mind. She was an elder of one of our local First Nation tribes and took me under her wing shortly after I left home.

Please do not misunderstand why I do not name her tribe. It is only to protect their privacy from the curiosity of those who will want to retrace the ancestors mentioned in your book about us.

The Gift of the Twin Houses

Through White Cloud's teachings, I came in contact with my gift and understood what came before me, what awaited me, and what the future asked of me.

Upon my return I no longer had any doubts about marrying Richard. My need for clarity had been fulfilled. Unfortunately my quest left behind excruciating grief for those I loved, a heavy burden to bear but one that was essential if I were to marry Richard and give him children. I could not share with my parents the images of incest that overpowered my mind. I couldn't explain the reason for my departure. The images were uncertain and unclear, and if untrue, I did not wish to give them life by speaking of them out loud. So I left in search of the truth.

Even at a distance, I felt the tear in my parent's hearts and grieved for the sorrow I had caused them. It was through this anguish that I found you.

Unbeknownst to you, many years ago when you first were teaching, you helped a little boy named Christian come out of his reverie and rejoin his family. Christian was White Cloud's great-grandson.

I first saw you in a dream the day I met Christian. White Cloud had guided me through my grief, and the images of what you would bring back began to fill my heart with hope. Just as you had helped a little boy come out of his cocoon, you helped me by showing me how you uncovered the past and what the future held.

You would be pleased to know that Christian turned out to be a great man of honor and strength, successful in life, and well admired by his tribe.

My dreams showed me that with my help you would open up to your own gift and receive the stories left behind in my attic. So I knew you would come into our lives and bring with you the healing love to those I cared for, not only for Conrad and his family but also for my twin daughters and Sophia. My family will rejoice in the tales of our past and the clarity of our lineage.

That is why I never spoke of this with my children or grandchildren. You needed to be present to weave the tapestry of the past along with the fabric of the future.

By now you should have two frames left, and you know that one is reserved for your wedding photograph and the other is to capture the happiness of Deidre and her daughter, Sophia, once the truth is known. I have seen their photograph in my dreams, next to Casey's with her son, Justin, along with the others you have placed on the dresser in my old room.

The wedding rings you have agreed to wear were a gift from our beloved friends Heather and James Lewis. They not only designed them and had them crafted just for us, but Heather's jeweler delivered them in person to make sure they fit just right. It was hard for Richard and me to accept such precious gifts, but Heather and James wrote to us beseeching that we accept them as a token of their appreciation. They said that the individual pieces of gold represented the foliage of the Cascades we all loved so, and the fusion of each individual piece that resulted in the perfect wedding band signified the sanctuary of love. We wish you and Conrad to enjoy the love and bliss Richard and I experienced during our marriage, and we hope you will accept these rings as our wedding gift.

There are many more stories to be told in the photographs that remain and those that capture the future, but you will uncover them together with Conrad. I have not dreamed of them; I just know they will evolve as time goes by.

In closing, I would like to thank you for welcoming your unique abilities, for opening yourself to me and the history of the twin houses, for allowing the spirit of love to catch your heart, and for the joy you will bring to all whom I care for.
With loving thoughts and peaceful dreams,
Angela.

I held her letter close to my heart and wept for a long time. I wept for Angela and her resolve to seek the truth of her heritage in spite of the pain she caused her parents. I wept for her courage to rebuild the past and confront the future, for her fortitude, sensitivity, and conviction, and for the gift that had brought me here.

The Gift of the Twin Houses

I also wept for me. In an uncomplicated, candid letter, Angela had restored my honor. My splintered personality had been reunited. I no longer denied and feared the gift that resided within me. Now, I enjoyed its presence and realized it had been with me all along. Even though I tried to bury it and keep it under wraps, it had cohabited with me. Angela's letter helped me see that.

I'd left a lifelong career in teaching with deep regrets because of my inability to create what I thought to be meaningful change. In my attempts to modernize the establishment, I'd forgotten the most important focal point, the teaching itself, and the joy experienced in the give-and-take between teacher and student.

Angela's letter brought back the memories of little Christian, his sudden deafness as a result of a head injury sustained by a freak fall down a set of stairs, the concern of his parents, their love for their child, and their need for hope. My encounter with Christian had been early in my teaching career, and I remembered how his parents helped me understand their traditions, their spirituality, and their fears that their little boy might be irreparably broken. Yet, they never gave up hope, and I didn't either. Unaware of it, I had used my so-called gift all of my life as I helped my students. I had accepted it as part of my devotion to teaching and hadn't connected it to those frightening supernatural images of my youth.

Clearly, I had used it time and again. I remembered noticing, deep inside Christian's eyes, the sparkle of recognition after I had stepped out of the middle of the road and the traditional teaching methods and allowed my intuition to reach him. I had trusted my inner thoughts and persisted in my beliefs on how to reach him. Regardless of what the establishment dictated, I'd used my gift, even though at the time I had no conscious knowledge of doing so. I remembered the joy we all felt when, as Angela described, Christian came out of his reverie at the sound of the tones of a cowbell.

The images of those moments rushed into my mind. Christian had gone into shock when he became aware that he'd lost his hearing, and for some unknown reason, he had automatically shut his eyes as well. Although nothing was physically wrong with his eyes, he acted as if he were totally blind and deaf. As Angela described, he lived in a cocoon, a shelter of his own creation.

I'd sensed that the key to awaken his eyes was in reaching a part of him that gave him a sense of security, of confidence. In my attempts to elicit a reaction from him, I tried all kinds of ways to engage his sight but to no avail. I gathered items and musical instruments from his home and his tribe, hoping to reach a part of him that would awaken his self-reliance and free up his eyes. One morning, as we sat on the carpet in the activity room while I taught him tactile sign language, I grabbed the cowbell.

His parents had told me he'd enjoyed working, the summer before his tumble, on his uncle's farm in Washington State, so I'd gathered a series of items found on a farm, among them a cowbell. The minute I rang it, he lifted his head, and I knew I'd found the key that would open his cocoon.

I rang it again, and he turned toward me, not seeing me, still blind, but somehow hearing the cowbell. Interesting, that with nothing medically wrong whatsoever with his eyes, he couldn't see, yet although legally deaf, I had reached him through his ears. In the depths of his deafness, he found his soul.

I remember his process of recovery as I rang the cowbell again, and he reached for it. I pulled away from him, rang the cowbell once more, and he groped in my direction. I stood up and moved a few feet away from him and rang the cowbell. Again he reached for it, only this time, he actually moved toward it without relying on my touch to guide him. By the end of that morning, he'd walked on his own all around the room—me ringing the cowbell and him following it.

Eventually Christian's eyes regained their natural ability. Given that he could hear the tones emitted by the cowbell, they fit him with a hearing aid that helped him capture sound by adjusting it to that frequency. Not complete and perfect hearing but hearing nonetheless.

Christian's story, one among many others I had forgotten, were now playing in my mind, a series of snapshots reminding me of what I'd been a part of. Creating change in the teaching establishment had nothing to do with the success or failure of my career. Changing the lives of my students and offering them a hopeful future had been at the forefront, even if I had not recognized the inner vibrations that had made it all possible.

As I sat on the bed that once had belonged to Angela, my guardian angel, I thanked her for all that she'd given me, for the houses, for Conrad, for sharing her gift with me, and, most important, for dreaming about me.

Alyana arrived to help me dress by the time I finished drying my hair. Immediately, she sensed that I'd been crying but said nothing.

"My eyes too puffy still?"

"No, they're OK. Don't worry."

I handed her Angela's letter. "Please read it; it's from Angela. Once you're done, I'd appreciate it if you could take it to Conrad and Tom so they can read it. Angela should be present in our hearts today."

She read the letter and, as expected, lost control of her own tears.

"Now you'll have puffy eyes too." I chuckled.

"Well, didn't expect not to today, but thought I could wait until the ceremony."

"Before you go, let me share with you the other effect this letter had on me."

I told her all about Christian, about my shattered personality that had emerged as whole, about my career, and about my newfound appreciation for the teacher I had been.

"May I tell Papa and Tom about it as well?"

"Sure. Conrad knows much of it already."

"I'll come back as soon as I can to help you with your dress and hair."

"Don't rush. I can handle it."

We hugged and kissed, overflowing with the joy.

After she left, I fixed my hair and put on a bit of makeup. Conrad liked my hair loose, so I curled it and pinned it behind my ears with some lovely hairpins adorned with little faux pearls and white diamonds. I finished dressing in no time, everything coming together perfectly.

My dress looked beautiful. Alyana and I had gone shopping in Seattle and found the perfect dress off the rack. Not what you would call a wedding dress, since it looked more like an elegant two-piece cocktail dress, with the skirt tailored to highlight my figure but loose enough to be subtle. It came down to my ankles, made of white silk with a faint floral print that looked like roses sprinkled here and there. The blouse was made of the same material, with a V neck, and came down below my hips, accentuating my bosom and waist. Both the skirt and the blouse were adorned with exquisite crochet lace in white with creamy, soft blue and gray flowers embroidered throughout and with a few faux pearls and diamonds scattered about. I felt radiant, brimming with confidence and joy.

I went downstairs to take one last look at the house before all the guests arrived, when I would have to hide upstairs until the ceremony started. The house looked spectacular, dressed as a bride with white bows and garlands adorning the stairs and the fireplace, beautiful flower arrangements scattered throughout, and the Christmas tree a sparkling centerpiece. Conrad and I decided that the ceremony should take place before our Christmas tree, and seeing the chairs lined up facing the tree, their bows and white flowers adorning each one, tugged at my heart. I could feel the tears ready to burst.

Luckily, Alyana stopped my tears by running into the house at that very moment.

"Sarah! What are you doing here? C'mon! They're right behind me!" And she whisked me up the stairs.

We ran to my room, both out of breath and laughing like a pair of schoolgirls.

"We must've looked so funny coming up the stairs like scared rabbits." she said.

"Your effusive entrance helped me not shed more tears. You and Tom did a marvelous job decorating the house. She looks radiant."

"Thanks. We had fun. It's been a treat to put it all together, and Sophia and Deidre have been a great help." Having caught her breath, she twirled me around to assess if she needed to do more to get me ready.

"You look beautiful, the perfect bride. You've left me with nothing to do."

"Thanks. Tell me about Angela's letter and their reaction."

"Papa put the letter in his breast pocket, close to his heart, to keep it nearby as you asked. In fact, he did that before I told him you thought Grandma

Angela should be with us today. As you can well imagine, they both cried even more when I told them about Christian and your coming to terms with your gift and your career."

"I'm glad we are all sharing these moments."

"Tom was pretty taken that his grandma had seen his twins well and alive. He's been really worried about the birth of the twins, their health, and mine."

"I didn't know that. He hides it well. How about you, are you worried?"

"No, not at all. I know we'll all be fine, but this is one of those times when Tom doesn't trust my intuition and just worries. The neat thing that happened is that when Tom said how relieved he was, Papa remembered the old double wooden crib you'd seen in the attic. They rushed up there and brought it down. It's lovely. Papa thinks it may have been made in the latter part of the nineteenth century, maybe for Annie's twins. We're going to clean it up, restore it a bit, and have it in our bedroom for our twins."

"I'm glad."

"Enough of that now. You need to get ready and go over your vows. Papa's been memorizing them, and he's gotten pretty good. I'll go downstairs to welcome the guests and all that, and then Tom will come up when we're ready and escort you down."

I did as told, quietly pacing up and down my room whispering my vows.

Before I knew it, Tom arrived. "You look beautiful. Papa will be blown away."

I know I blushed, because he laughed.

"Ready?" He offered me his arm.

"Ready. Thanks for the compliment," I managed to say as we left the bedroom.

We made our way down the stairs, and I heard music...guitar music. I hadn't even considered music as we prepared for the wedding. How thoughtful of Alyana and Tom. Then I recognized Tom's voice...and Conrad's.

I turned to look at Tom, and he smiled and nodded.

"Yep. Papa wrote the lyrics and music, and we played it together. It's recorded. Surprised?"

"Boy, am I! Hope I can control the tears until I reach Conrad."

"Concentrate on the lyrics and the melody. That might help," Tom advised as he placed his free hand on top of my hand resting on his arm.

I liked the sense of reassurance his hand offered. I took a deep breath and focused on the lyrics and the melody of the two guitars.

Conrad had written the music to best express the sentiment of each phrase with the guitars in perfect harmony, yet each instrument contributed its own character, its own comment on the music as the melody developed. With each step we took, we were accompanied by a lyrical moment, the strings of each guitar emanating independent yet simultaneous resonance, adding their individual expression to the imagery of the lyrics.

I was transported into the music, its rhythm providing a soft embrace, a cushion welcoming each step, a wave of bliss.

Come and join me by the sea,
And we'll build castles in the sand.
Or just come and talk to me,
And the world is in our hands.

I don't want to be alone,
And I like to feel you need me.
If you help me sing my song,
I will have your voice to lead me.

If my hand you want to hold,
All you have to do is take it.
Although winters may be cold,
If we're together, we can make it.

If I ever see you cry,
I won't turn the other way,
'Cause there's more to love than sighs,
And there's more to life than days.

The Gift of the Twin Houses

We can do it all together,
You and I.
We can watch the sunset glowing,
You and I.
We can always have each other,
We can share the joy of growing,
We can do it all together,
You and I.

By the time we reached the bottom of the stairs, you couldn't find a dry eye in the house.

Elan and Nina waited for us to reach the first step so that they could escort us toward their grandfather. Elan looked quite the young man, dressed up in a beautiful suit and tie, and Nina wore a gorgeous white dress sprinkled with flowers. Elan began the march. He must have thought he needed to march because his steps were those of a soldier, in perfect rhythm with the beats of the song, but a soldier nonetheless, officially making his way toward his grandfather and the minister. His arms were stretched out, clutching the little box that held one of our wedding rings. Nina followed behind her brother, gliding along the floor like a ballerina, twirling here and there so she could see her dress fan out, loosely holding but never dropping her box with the other wedding ring.

When we reached the minister, Tom took my hand and eased it onto Conrad's. Conrad looked magnificent, immaculately dressed in a dark-blue suit with a light-blue shirt and a beautiful silk tie multihued in blue.

We looked into each other's eyes and smiled as the ceremony began.

The minister welcomed all, proceeded with the invocation, and followed with the traditional reading of scriptures that culminated in a passage from Corinthians 13:1–8, which Conrad and I had chosen.

"Love is patient, love is kind, and envies no one," the minister read. "Love is not boastful, nor conceited, nor rude, nor selfish, nor quick to take offense. Love keeps no score of wrongs, does not gloat over the errors of others, but delights in the truth. There is no limit to its faith, its hope, and its endurance. Love will never come to an end."

He then introduced the vows, explaining that Conrad and I had chosen to write our own vows separate from each other and were about to share them in the presence of our friends and family. He nodded toward Conrad.

"Sarah," Conrad said as his eyes brightened and his face radiated with love, "this is my hand; take it. Grasp it when the going gets too rough. Hold it when the moon begins to rise. Use it when your own begins to shake and you need a little help to dust the clouds out of the sky. This is my heart; take it. Hear it when the storm covers the moon. Touch it when the morning gets too cold. Feel it when the fear becomes too strong, when everything seems wrong, when the night is dark, and when nothing seems worthwhile, or simply when you are sad. This is my life; take it. Enjoy it, for you're the one who's made it. Fulfill it because you gave it reason for existing. Take it in your hands and hold it. Press it to your heart and keep it warm. Love it until the end of time. Take this hand, this heart, this life, and lock it in your love and never let it go."

"Conrad," I said, "if there is such a thing as destiny, mine is with you. I will do all that I can to bring joy, understanding, and passion into your life. I promise to honor and respect you, to be your friend, lover, and ally. I will hold you when you are sad. I will celebrate the wonders and challenges of life with you. And above all, I will love you. I promise to bring joy to your heart, to nurture and to love you, to support you in being true to yourself, to encourage you through times of change, to listen with an open heart so that you can share yourself with honesty, to solace you when you are downhearted, and to join you in joy and laughter. Together, we will hear the sounds of roses growing and walk along the mountain paths, riding with the sun and moving through the clouds. We will live the breeze of autumn days and run our fingers through golden flower fields. We will kiss the water of the rushing streams, embrace the snow of a winter storm, and hold the moon when it's over the valley of our love. I pledge to share all that I am with you and to celebrate all that you are. I promise this with my heart and my soul for all the days of my life and beyond."

The Gift of the Twin Houses

The wedding did more than just unite Conrad and me—it also reunited the twin houses. Only, this time the prospect of a blissful future lay ahead, and all of the ancestors were now at peace.

Our wedding kiss was delicate, soft, and tender as we bequeathed our souls to each other for all eternity.

The house sighed with joy.

"Did you hear that?" Conrad whispered.

"I sure did."

V. & D. Povall

Completed Family Tree of the Residents of the Twin Houses

First Generation

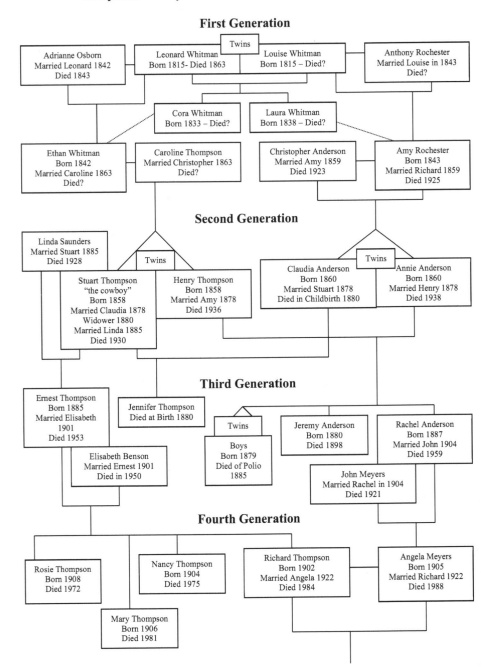

Twins

| Adrianne Osborn
Married Leonard 1842
Died 1843 | Leonard Whitman
Born 1815- Died 1863 | Louise Whitman
Born 1815 – Died? | Anthony Rochester
Married Louise in 1843
Died? |

Cora Whitman
Born 1833 – Died?

Laura Whitman
Born 1838 – Died?

Ethan Whitman
Born 1842
Married Caroline 1863
Died?

Caroline Thompson
Married Christopher 1863
Died?

Christopher Anderson
Married Amy 1859
Died 1923

Amy Rochester
Born 1843
Married Richard 1859
Died 1925

Second Generation

Linda Saunders
Married Stuart 1885
Died 1928

Twins

Twins

Stuart Thompson
"the cowboy"
Born 1858
Married Claudia 1878
Widower 1880
Married Linda 1885
Died 1930

Henry Thompson
Born 1858
Married Amy 1878
Died 1936

Claudia Anderson
Born 1860
Married Stuart 1878
Died in Childbirth 1880

Annie Anderson
Born 1860
Married Henry 1878
Died 1938

Third Generation

Ernest Thompson
Born 1885
Married Elisabeth
1901
Died 1953

Jennifer Thompson
Died at Birth 1880

Twins

Jeremy Anderson
Born 1880
Died 1898

Rachel Anderson
Born 1887
Married John 1904
Died 1959

Elisabeth Benson
Married Ernest 1901
Died in 1950

Boys
Born 1879
Died of Polio
1885

John Meyers
Married Rachel in 1904
Died 1921

Fourth Generation

Rosie Thompson
Born 1908
Died 1972

Nancy Thompson
Born 1904
Died 1975

Richard Thompson
Born 1902
Married Angela 1922
Died 1984

Angela Meyers
Born 1905
Married Richard 1922
Died 1988

Mary Thompson
Born 1906
Died 1981

250

The Gift of the Twin Houses

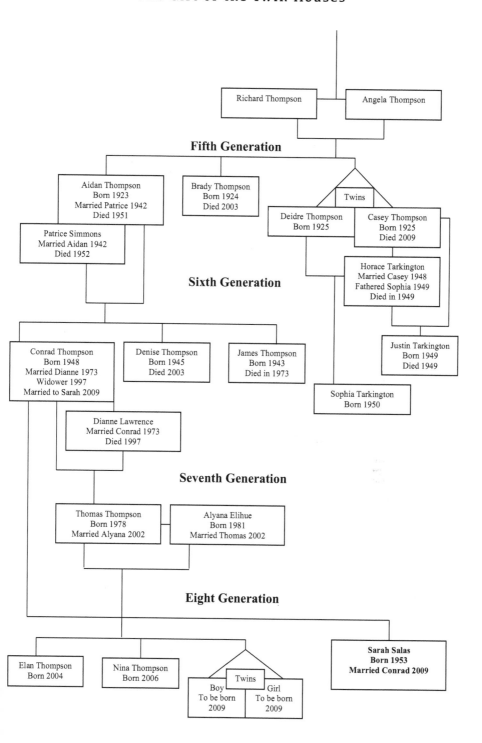

Richard Thompson — Angela Thompson

Fifth Generation

Aidan Thompson
Born 1923
Married Patrice 1942
Died 1951

Brady Thompson
Born 1924
Died 2003

Twins

Deidre Thompson
Born 1925

Casey Thompson
Born 1925
Died 2009

Patrice Simmons
Married Aidan 1942
Died 1952

Horace Tarkington
Married Casey 1948
Fathered Sophia 1949
Died in 1949

Sixth Generation

Conrad Thompson
Born 1948
Married Dianne 1973
Widower 1997
Married to Sarah 2009

Denise Thompson
Born 1945
Died 2003

James Thompson
Born 1943
Died in 1973

Justin Tarkington
Born 1949
Died 1949

Sophia Tarkington
Born 1950

Dianne Lawrence
Married Conrad 1973
Died 1997

Seventh Generation

Thomas Thompson
Born 1978
Married Alyana 2002

Alyana Elihue
Born 1981
Married Thomas 2002

Eight Generation

Elan Thompson
Born 2004

Nina Thompson
Born 2006

Twins

Boy
To be born
2009

Girl
To be born
2009

**Sarah Salas
Born 1953
Married Conrad 2009**

251

Bonus
Sarah's Recipes

SARAH UNCOVERED HER mother's cookbook, a small three-ring binder that contained all of the recipes she'd collected over the years, a devoted collection of recipes she'd learned from Sarah's nana—those they had advanced together, as well as the many they had invented. Over the years, they had improved upon them, and as a result, most recipes had little notes here and there as to what they had eliminated, added, or altered.

Each handwritten note revived the memories of the two of them and the feeling that somehow they were alongside Sarah as she created each meal, baked each loaf, or crafted delicious desserts.

Now this precious homemade compilation has Sarah's own notes and alterations and has become a three-generation cookbook.

Alyana, her children, and all those who follow, will most certainly incorporate their own contributions and continue the tradition.

To view Sarah's recipes, please visit our website: www.2authors.com.

V. &. D. Povall

A HUSBAND AND wife writing team who have authored and published non-fiction manuals and articles as well as written four short screenplays, six full-length screenplays, two women's fiction novels, the first installment of a murder mystery series, and a science fiction epic.

Between them they possess a doctorate and years of practical experience in film, theater, and television. Thanks to their rich international family backgrounds, they bring to the page a wealth of experiences and points of view. They have lived in different cultures, are multilingual, and bring to their writing a broad understanding of human nature.

The *Gift of the Twin Houses* is their first novel in the *Perils of a Reluctant Psychic* series.

Made in the USA
San Bernardino, CA
24 April 2020